NORWICH BOOKF
McMahon, Richard.
A web of evil /

FEB 0 2 2016

GUERNSEY MEMORIAL LIBRARY

W9-DFQ-582

A WEB OF EVIL

RICHARD MCMAHON

Guernsey Memorial Library
Court Street
Norwich, NY 13815
www.guernseymemoriallibrary.org

A WEB OF EVIL by Richard McMahon

First Edition, April 2015

Published by Ironwoods Press

Copyright © 2015 Richard McMahon

Author Services by Pedernales Publishing, LLC.
www.pedernalespublishing.com

Cover by Pedernales Publishing, LLC.

This is a work of fiction. Names, places, characters and incidents are either
the product of the author's imagination or are used fictitiously, and any
resemblance to actual persons, living or dead, business establishments,
events, or locales is entirely coincidental.

All rights reserved, including the right to reproduce this book or portions
thereof in any form whatsoever. For information address Ironwoods Press,
richard27@hawaii.rr.com.

Library of Congress Control Number: 2015935393

ISBN: 978-0-9961568-7-5 Paperback Edition
         978-0-9961568-8-2 Hardcover Edition
         978-0-9961568-9-9 Digital Edition

Printed in the United States of America

There is no evil from which some good does not result, and consequently men should do evil as much as it suits them, since it is merely one more way of doing good.

— Voltaire, *Zadig*, Chapter 18,
quoted at the beginning of *Justine*.

Once my grave has been filled in, it will be seeded with acorns, so that the dirt of said grave will eventually hold vegetation, and once the thicket has grown back to its original state, the traces of my grave will disappear from the face of the earth, just as I hope that my memory will be erased from the minds of men....

— Last will and testament,
Donatien Alphonse Francois,
Marquis de Sade

1

URL: http://www.darkchateau.com/bb

FROM: MichelleIverson@lava.net

Hello Members of the Dark Chateau,

My name is Michelle. I am 21 years old, blond, with blue eyes. I am 5 ft 6 inches tall, weigh 118 pounds, and my measurements are 36-22-34. I am shaved everywhere and pierced everywhere. I need a harsh, cruel master to put me through intense humiliation, degradation and pain. You can do anything to me: hurt me, beat me, humiliate me, treat me like a dog—I mean <u>ANYTHING</u>. Send me email describing what you will do to me. Make me be your slave!

Mason Grant handed the computer printout back to Frederick Iverson. "How long has your daughter been missing?"

"It's been two days." Iverson's bloodshot eyes stared vacantly out the large picture window of his home high on Tantalus. The view encompassed almost the whole of Honolulu, from the mountains to the sea, but Iverson didn't appear to notice.

The note had been posted two weeks ago, Grant noted. Enough time for the weirdos and kooks to respond, and perhaps do more. "I think this is a matter for the police," he said.

Iverson exhaled deeply and walked away from the window, his slippered feet making no sound on the highly polished koa planks. Grant's own shoes had been left at the door, Japanese style, a custom that most people followed in Hawaii. When Iverson finally spoke, his voice sounded despondent but emphatic.

"You read that damn thing. I could not possibly let something like this become public. It would ruin my business."

"Your daughter's life may be in danger," Grant replied. "Don't you think that's more important than a threat to your business? Besides, I think you may be exaggerating the consequences of this becoming public. In today's social environment—"

"Mr. Grant, I am the financial manager of some of the largest fortunes here in Hawaii and on the West Coast. This is old money. I am sure you know what that means."

Grant did. Old families, rich for generations, living on inherited wealth, shying from publicity of any kind, conservative to a fault.

"I am entrusted with virtually complete authority over these funds," Iverson continued. "Mine is a business where trust and reputation are paramount." He paused for a moment, running his fingers nervously through his uncombed hair. Grant sensed that Iverson was trying to find a convincing argument, for himself as well as his listener. "To my clients," Iverson went on, "trust and conservative behavior are synonymous. Their morals tend to be old-fashioned, and they look closely at the family as well as the firm. If it became known that one of my daughters was dabbling in…" He struggled to find the words, "kinky sex…well, I could lose everything. This entire matter must be handled in the strictest confidence, investigated privately."

"I'm not a private investigator," Grant reminded him.

"I know that, but General Talbot recommended you very highly. I am confident that you will be discreet. You're one of us."

Grant wasn't, but he let it pass. The wealthy always assumed that because he was financially independent he was a member of their society. He wondered what some of them might think if they knew that he had grown up in one of the poorest sections of New York City, with a widowed mother struggling to raise three children on a combination of welfare, and support from the men who came and went in her life.

Grant walked over to the place at the large window that Iverson had vacated, mulling over what he had heard. It seemed clear to him that further attempts to persuade Iverson to turn this matter over to the authorities would prove fruitless. Although he seemed obviously worried about Michelle, Iverson's concern for his business appeared to override that worry. Grant also thought he detected a certain anger, a resentment on the father's part toward his daughter for putting him in this predicament. If that were indeed the case, such resentment might be reinforcing Iverson's decision not to call in the authorities. Grant turned back toward his host.

"Is there anyone beside yourself who knows about this?"

"My other daughter, Tracy. It was she who found—that." Iverson grimaced toward the printout, which he had replaced on his desk.

"Did Tracy find anything else? How about Michelle's email, have you checked that?"

Iverson shook his head. "We cannot get into Michelle's account. It is password protected. And there is nothing else in writing. Tracy has been through all her things."

"Have you tried to find the password, things like birthdays, significant dates, familiar names?"

"Tracy is trying all of that. So far nothing has worked. Can you help with that?"

Grant was no computer geek, but he had friends who were. "I may know someone who can help," he said.

Iverson nodded, his eyes returning once more to the printout, and he picked it up again. "Pierced everywhere! What the hell does that mean?"

Grant did not answer. He didn't think it was really a question. Instead, he posed one of his own, deciding to be direct rather than delicate with his approach. "Mr. Iverson, did you have any reason to suspect earlier that Michelle had masochistic fantasies?"

Iverson winced, but did not hesitate in his reply. "Absolutely not. And I'm not sure that she does have them. Tracy pointed out that lots of people post that sort of thing on computer bulletin boards just to…well, for titillation. And she thinks Michelle may have done the same thing. She has always been rather impish. But she is not like that. I cannot believe that she wanted…really meant those things. I'm sure it was a lark, some new way to be far out, to push the limits. Maybe she enjoys doing that."

"Mr. Iverson, unless we can get into Michelle's email, we may never know what happened to her."

Iverson sighed. "I am aware of that."

Grant decided to try one more time. "And you still don't want to go to the police? HPD is a good police department. They might find her quickly."

"There is no assurance that she is in the city, or even in the state, for that matter."

"Missing Persons Bureaus cooperate with each other, exchange information, and have access to federal government files."

Iverson dismissed Grant's remarks with a wave. "Missing persons are the lowest priority of police departments everywhere." Grant felt that all depended on who the missing person was, but he didn't interrupt. "Besides," Iverson continued, "it's just not possible. I cannot risk this… this obscenity becoming known."

"Informing the police doesn't necessarily mean publicity. The case might be handled in confidence."

Iverson grunted. "Do you really believe that? Well, I do not. There are just too many opportunities for a leak, for the media to find out. Can you imagine what the press would do with a story like this?"

Grant tried one last tack. "How does your wife feel about keeping this away from the police?" Grant asked.

"My wife died years ago."

Grant was now convinced it was useless to pursue the matter. Above all, Iverson seemed determined to conceal what he obviously considered would be a fatal embarrassment to his business and his social standing. Grant watched him turn to the printout again. He seemed unable to let it go.

"The Dark Chateau," Iverson read aloud. "What has that got to do with what she…what is described here—humiliation, beating, piercing…?"

From the heading of the printout, Grant surmised that *darkchateau.com* was a web site for those interested in unusual sexual practices, a place where they could communicate with each other by bulletin board postings, and perhaps obtain other services. Again, Iverson was not really asking a question, so Grant said nothing. Finally, Iverson dropped the printout back on the coffee table and turned toward him.

"Well, where are we then? Are you willing to help me and keep the police out of it?"

Grant knew that Frederick Iverson had pretty much said all he wanted to say. "I'm willing to try, although I don't know how much help I can be."

In spite of the weakness of Grant's answer, Iverson seemed satisfied. They spent some time settling financial and other details, and Grant prepared to leave.

"Is there a time when I can talk to Tracy?"

"Right now, if you wish," Iverson replied. "She's out by the pool. She's waiting for you."

2

THE POOL WAS surrounded on three sides by the house and open on the fourth to the same view of the distant city that Grant had just seen inside the house. A young woman was sitting in a white lounge chair, her attention focused on a book. An apricot bikini bottom stood out like a neon patch against her sun-bronzed body, its minuscule size accentuating the fact that she was not wearing a top. She was not so far away that Grant was prevented from seeing that her breasts were lovely and perfectly formed. When she saw him, she reached down without haste, retrieved the upper part of her suit, and fastened it in place. She then removed her sunglasses, tossed her long, blond hair away from her eyes, and watched him approach.

"Miss Iverson, I'm Mason Grant. I think your father has told you about me."

She smiled. "You're going to find my sister." Her voice was low, with a slight husky quality.

"Well, I'm going to try." Although he would not describe her as center-fold beautiful, there was an arresting allure about Tracy Iverson, some attraction that operated below the surface, that made Grant's pulse quicken. "May I sit down?"

She nodded and raised her chair back to the upright position. Grant sat on one of the chairs at a small table.

"Would you like iced tea?"

"Thanks." Mason rarely drank iced tea, but he felt it would give him a point of focus other than her nearly nude body. As she poured, he forced his eyes away from her and took in the surroundings. Instead of paving of some kind, the ground was covered with thick, lush grass. Areca palms ringed the pool at irregular intervals, each tree a clump of thin, bamboo-like trunks circling an inner core. Wide, sliding doors opened on to the pool from all three sides of the house, and the way the pool furniture was arranged made for a relaxed, unpretentious atmosphere.

"It already has lemon in it," Tracy Iverson said, handing Grant the glass. "Would you like sugar?"

"It's fine the way it is, thanks," he said, accepting the glass. "Miss Iverson—"

"Call me Tracy, Mason. I'm certainly not going to call you Mr. Grant."

He smiled at her directness. "Your father told me you're trying to find the password that will access your sister's email."

She frowned. "I'm trying, but I'm not getting anywhere."

"What operating system does she use, Mac or Windows?"

"Windows 7."

"Can you get into her computer at all?"

"Everything but her email program. It won't let me in without a password."

"You've tried all the usual possibilities?"

She nodded. "And all the variations I could think of."

Mason realized there was nothing he could do at the moment to help Tracy with her password search. Knowing her sister gave her a better chance than anyone to find it, unless Michelle was one of those few people who selected a completely random password. In that case it might never be found. He wondered if the devices used in crime novels which could keep trying infinite combinations of words and numbers until the right one was found actually existed. He'd have to find out.

"Tracy, how well do you know your sister?"

She thought about that for a moment. "Probably not as well as most sisters know each other. Actually, she's my stepsister." Seeing Grant's eyebrows raise slightly, she asked, "Didn't my father tell you that?"

"No, he didn't mention it. He probably didn't think it was important."

"My father was married twice. Michelle is his second wife's daughter by her previous marriage. As for our relationship, we're friends, but we're not real pals. We have different interests, travel in different circles. That's probably because of our age difference."

"Michelle is twenty-four—"

"And I'm twenty-seven. And those three years put us worlds apart."

"How do you mean?"

"Well, Michelle is sort of…she seems so much younger than I was at her age. She's very naive, and she's very trusting. Michelle would believe almost anything anyone told her. That's probably why…well, why this happened. But it's not like her to just walk off like this, without telling anyone. That's why we're so worried."

"But not worried enough to go to the police." He was sorry as soon as he said it. He saw her expression harden as her eyes narrowed.

"I wanted my father to go to the police. I still do. It would be far better than having some amateur meddling in our affairs."

"I agree completely."

That surprised her. She had expected to offend him. She hadn't. "Then why are you here?"

"I couldn't convince him. And even an amateur might be better than no help at all."

She nodded. "I couldn't convince him either. I think he doesn't quite believe it has happened, or doesn't want to believe it."

"Why don't you go to the police on your own?" He expected another frigid response, but this time it didn't come. Her voice was so low he could hardly hear her.

"I want to, I want to. I wish I could." Her face mirrored her inner struggle. "But I can't. If it turned out that I was responsible for ruining my father's business…." She shook her head. "It's a miserable situation, having to choose between my father and my sister. I hate myself no matter what I do."

Mason knew he could do nothing to help solve her dilemma. It was time to change the subject. "Have you talked to any of her friends, to see if they have any idea where she might be?"

"I've talked to everyone I know, both here and on the mainland, and some of them have contacted other friends. Nobody knows anything, or has any idea where she is."

"How about a boy friend? Is she seeing anyone on a regular basis?"

Tracy's face betrayed just the hint of a frown. "She sees someone on a fairly regular basis. Kevin Medeiros. She met him on the cruise ship that sails between the islands."

"He was a fellow passenger?"

"A porter. He cleaned up the rooms."

"You don't like him much. Is it because of his job? You think Michelle is too good for him?"

"I don't like him at all, it has nothing to do with his job, and

I *know* Michelle is too good for him. Anyway, he lost his job because he was caught smoking pot with a teenage passenger. She shook her head. "I don't know what she sees in him, except his 'island beach boy' image. He calls her his 'cute *haole* chick.'"

"Is he Hawaiian?" Mason had been in the Islands long enough to know that surnames were not always a clue to ethnic background.

"As Hawaiian as you can be if your parents were born in Manila. But to listen to him, you'd think he was descended from Kamehameha the Great." She shook her head again, remembering. "And as far as his feelings for Michelle are concerned, you know what he said when I told him Michelle was missing?" She began mimicking the sing-song tone of local pidgin speakers. "*Auwe*, too bad, eh? I going town for shopping. You tell her call me wen' she come back."

Despite the seriousness of the situation, Mason had to suppress a grin. "How can I find this wonderful South Seas lover?"

Tracy wrote a phone number down and handed it to him. "This is his mother's place. He's there when he's not sleeping somewhere else, which is most of the time. If you find him, it won't take you long to like him as much as I do," she said. "You can count on it."

With his next question, Mason decided to be as direct as he had been with her father.

"Tracy, are you close enough to your sister to know if she has masochistic tendencies, overtly or otherwise?"

Her eyes returned to the book she had been reading before answering. "Other than that bulletin board posting, you mean?" He nodded. She pointed to two soft-cover books lying on the table. "I found those, and this one," she held up her book, "as I was going through her things."

Mason picked up the top book and looked at the cover. It was titled *The Claiming of Sleeping Beauty* by A. N. Roquelaure, and the other was called *Beauty's Release*, by the same author. He thumbed through the first few pages.

"A retelling of the Sleeping Beauty legend?" He didn't understand why she thought the books were significant.

"A lot more than that." Tracy leaned forward, handing him her open book. "Start reading from the top of the left-hand page."

Mason held her place, but turned to the cover. This one was titled *Beauty's Punishment*, again by the same author. As he began to read, he felt the color rising in his face. The passage described a naked woman tied down to a platform on her back, her arms and legs spread far apart. Another woman was standing over her, whipping her with a leather strap. The story was told from the viewpoint of the victim, who was apparently the heroine, Sleeping Beauty. As she screamed in pain, it was made abundantly clear that she was experiencing another sensation as well, a powerful sexual arousal.

Mason considered himself far from being a prude, but he felt decidedly uncomfortable reading the passage while a nearly nude young woman he hardly knew looked on. He began to wonder just how far he would have to read, when she came to his rescue.

"All three books contain scenes like that," she told him, "and both men and women are involved. A little something for everyone." A slight smile showed that she was amused by his discomfort, which apparently was showing. Angry at his embarrassment in the face of her perfect composure, he searched for something to say that would regain his poise.

"You've apparently read all three books."

Her eyes narrowed slightly. "Only to try to understand what's happened. If you're wondering if it runs in the family—it doesn't."

"Pretty strong stuff," Mason said, regretting his previous tone and now trying to be conciliatory. "Do you know anything about the author?"

"Yes, and so do you. A. N. Roquelaure is a pen name. The author is Anne Rice."

He looked up, surprised. "Anne Rice? The lady who writes about vampires?"

"One and the same." Again, she seemed to enjoy surprising him.

Mason turned to the front matter of the book, and found that Anne Rice was indeed writing under a pseudonym.

"So, to get back to your question," Tracy said, as he put the book down, "There's something else. When we were children, Michelle received a lot of spankings from my stepmother, more, I think, than she deserved."

"How do you mean?"

"I think my stepmother enjoyed spanking Michelle. She seemed to *look* for reasons to punish her. She was always threatening her with 'You just wait until your father comes home.'"

"Did your father do the spanking then?"

Tracy shook her head. "He never laid a hand on either of us. And my stepmother never touched me. But he would always be there to watch. Maybe he wanted to be sure my stepmother didn't go too far with the punishment. Anyway, I read somewhere that sometimes children who had been spanked often when they are young can begin to find a perverse pleasure from it, which can develop into masochism as they grow older. I'm not saying this was the case with Michelle, but it could be. I just don't know."

Mason decided to move on. "Where did you find the printout of your sister's bulletin board posting, the one that you gave your father?"

"It was folded in half in here." She held up *Beauty's Punishment*.

"And that's all there was? No answers, no other postings or email replies?"

She shook her head. "I've been through all her things, not just the computer stuff. If there is anything else, it must be in her email folders."

"Have you tried to log on to Dark Chateau?"

She nodded. "I couldn't find anything relating to Michelle's posting, just a lot of weird SM stuff. I guess it's too late now for anything about Michelle to still be there."

Mason felt reasonably sure that, once logged on to the site, there would be a way to call up previous messages, but he preferred to do that later, when he was alone.

"How about the Recycle Bin on Michelle's desk top?"

"I looked. There's nothing in it." She sighed in frustration. "Isn't there anything we can do in the meantime? I feel so... helpless. She's already been missing two days, and we've done nothing."

Mason held back saying they could have called the police. "You're trying to find the password—"

"But I'm not accomplishing anything. Couldn't we post something on the Dark Chateau site, offering a reward for information about her?"

Mason shook his head. "I think if we did that, we'd be swamped with phony messages from people trying to turn a dishonest buck. We could spend weeks trying to sort them out, and we don't have weeks."

"Well, then, how about just a message saying she's missing and asking if anyone knows anything about her?"

He thought about that. "I don't know...I'm not sure it's the right medium for something like that. Besides, if someone who read her message is responsible for her disappearance, he's not likely to tell us about it."

"But it couldn't hurt, could it?" she persisted. "Any number of people might have sent her email replies. And she could have replied to them. That could tell us something."

"No, I guess it wouldn't hurt," he said after a pause. And he had to agree that at least they would be taking the initiative. "I'll post a message when I get back to my computer."

"Let me do it," she said. "It will sound better coming from a member of the family."

Mason could see a problem there. He didn't want the situation to get out of his control, and he did not want Tracy involved, but he couldn't see any justification for turning down her suggestion.

"Well, go ahead. But promise me you won't act on any responses until you check with me." She agreed. "And don't post anything else on that board—anything at all. We don't know what we're dealing with yet, and an inadvertent mistake might ruin our chances of finding Michelle." She agreed to that, too. He could think of nothing else to cover with Tracy, and he was anxious to get to his computer. He gave her his phone number and she said she would call if she learned anything. As he turned to leave, he thought of one more thing.

"You told your father that you thought Michelle posted that notice as a lark, to get some titillating feedback, but that she had no intention of actually following through on anything."

For the first time since he had joined her, Tracy's expression fell. She looked down at her hands and it was a moment before she spoke. "I told him that mainly to set his mind at ease. Whether she intended to follow through or not, I really have no way of knowing." She looked up at him then.

"But she's missing, isn't she?"

3

LEAVING THE IVERSON mansion, Mason Grant put his Ford Escape in second gear for the long roll down Round Top Drive. He was not a car buff, and he found this small, inexpensive SUV suited all his needs. Rounding the Punchbowl, he turned onto H1 and eased into the freeway traffic. Fifteen minutes later he was on H2, crossing the plain between the two volcanic mountain ranges that formed the island, the Waianae on the west and the Koolau to the east. When the freeway ended, he began the descent to the North Shore, passing the forlorn, abandoned remnants of the last sugar crop on Oahu. Where miles of stately cane had waved in the northeast trades, young coffee trees now grew, protected from those same breezes by tall Cook pine trees and walls of panax hedge. Sugar had dominated Hawaii for so much of its modern history that it was hard for Mason to adjust to the new look. He bore right just before Haleiwa, and with the ocean on his left, continued along the coast until shortly past Sunset Beach. He turned off at a house on the water, almost hidden from the road by a grove of ironwood trees. He was home.

Building this house had represented the end of a long, turbulent period in his life which began with a personal tragedy that he had finally learned to live with, mostly by keeping his mind occupied with other things. He fixed a bowl of instant saimin for supper, adding slices of carrot, celery, green onion, lots of garlic, and topping it off with a large dollop of *kimchee*. He then went to his study and turned on his computer.

He logged on to the Internet and typed the URL, *www.darkchateau.com.* Within a few seconds his screen filled with the image of a large, gray, fortress-like structure, with a heading in red capital letters across the top of the page,

WELCOME TO THE DARK CHATEAU.

Mason took a few moments to familiarize himself with the screen. The building did indeed present a dark, foreboding appearance, something Dracula would be comfortable in. The windows of the "chateau" were actually buttons, which when clicked would take the viewer to the area indicated in the window. There were six topics, About the Dark Chateau, Membership, Chat Rooms, Bulletin Board, Events, and Store.

Seeking the shortest route to information about Michelle, Mason clicked on Bulletin Board, and was immediately asked for his password. He returned to the home page, and clicked Membership. An application appeared, which he completed, and then checked a box agreeing to follow site rules, and finally selected a password. A message appeared:

"Thank you and welcome to membership in The Dark Chateau! You may now use all the facilities shown on our home page. We suggest you begin by clicking on About The Dark Chateau to learn about the benefits and obligations of membership."

Ignoring the suggestion, Mason returned to the home page, clicked again on Bulletin Board, entered his password, and the board appeared. After briefly examining the introductory screen, he saw that, as he expected, he would be able to change the current date box back as far as six months, in order to call up messages that were no longer displayed. He changed the date to the day after Michelle had posted her message, and a topic list appeared of all the messages that had been posted on the board since that date.

Scrolling down quickly, he soon found Michelle's entry and he clicked on it. Michelle's message appeared on the screen. A box above her message informed him there had been eighteen public replies on the board, even though she had requested replies by email. He could not get into her email, but at least he could read these messages. He clicked on "Read Replies." The first message was short.

Daaammm! Sounds like lotsa fun! Keep talkin!

It was posted by a male, as was the case with the next two postings, which were equally meaningless. The fourth was sent from *laura.evans@att.net*, who apparently had the same interests as Michelle. Rather than actually replying to Michelle's message, she used the opportunity to voice a similar request.

I am also seeking a special person who can punish me severely and make it very painful. I possess strong masochistic desires and would like to talk to you if you are sincere. Tell me how you would plan to make me suffer, and I will respond. Remember, make it painful!

Laura had prompted four replies to *her* message, and reading them took Mason on a detour. Laura had appended her message to Michelle's, and Mason wanted to see if Michelle had answered publicly. She hadn't, and the replies to Laura had nothing to do with her. He returned to the replies to Michelle.

The next two, both from men, were silly and irrelevant. One of them took Michelle at her word, and pretended to treat her like a dog, demanding that she sit up, bark, roll over, and do other doggy things. The other was simply the phrase "WAY TO GO!" repeated five times. There were two more from women, like Laura, who wanted to join the party.

He continued to scroll through the remaining postings, which had less to do with Michelle as the dates advanced and threads diverged to different spanking topics. Other women had joined in, claiming to be "bad little girls," and "daddies" had responded, offering to chastise them. A continuing discussion of OTK spankings (over-the-knee, Mason soon figured out) compared the merits of using the bare hand, hairbrush, or paddle, and one spirited lady proclaimed that while OTK was all right, she liked it best "bent over the back of a high-backed chair, stripped naked, and flogged with a belt." One of the last messages, near the end of the postings, caught his eye. It was a simple comment.

What a bunch of sickos................

Mason agreed, tired of the unrelenting weirdness. Suddenly he wanted to be far away from Michelle and her strange playmates. He printed out all the messages for future reference and turned off the computer. The sun had long set and a nearly full moon had risen, silhouetting the shoreline palms against a silver sea. Turning his eyes away from the darkened computer, he leaned back and stared out at the waves breaking gently on the reef in front of his property.

She would have loved this house. She would have loved

Hawaii, too, and the life he had made here. But then, he realized that made no sense. Had she lived, he would not have this house, he would not be in Hawaii. He had married late, his Army career filling most of his time and needs before then. And he just hadn't come across any woman he wanted to marry. Until he met Kathryn. Even now, more than three years after her death, he couldn't forget how special she was.

They were stationed in Germany, with their 4-year old daughter, Merrie, when Desert Storm began, and his unit was sent to the Middle East. Kathryn took Merrie and went home to live with her parents and wait out the war. Mason was somewhere out in the Saudi desert, training his tank battalion for the coming battle, when the American Red Cross representative informed him that his wife and daughter had been killed in an automobile accident.

He was still deep in shock when he arrived in the small midwestern town, where he was met by Kathryn's grieving parents. He drifted through the next days in a haze of grief and mounting rage. Kathryn's car had been hit head-on by a large truck, whose driver had been drinking. The local community had seen a rash of alcohol-related accidents during the past year, and emotions were high. An investigative reporter for the local newspaper discovered that the driver of the truck had two previous DUI convictions—both while he was working—and that Star Transport, his employer, had been aware of them.

The senselessness of his family's death fueled an obsession for revenge. Mason wanted the driver to hang and he wanted the company to pay. The punishment of the driver was out of his hands, but he could go after the company. One afternoon, he drove downtown from his in-law's house and stopped at the first law office he found. A lone, white-haired man with a florid complexion occupied the only desk in the office. Mason was too obsessed and distraught to realize what this might mean; the man agreed to take the case, and Mason hired him. Later, friends of the family suggested gently that he should have selected his attorney more carefully. J. Enright Coddington, they said, was well past his prime, and had other problems as well. But Mason was still too distraught to want to change anything.

Whatever his lawyer's limitations were, they did not show in court. If his powers were waning, J. Enright Coddington mustered every ounce of them for Mason's cause, and presented a masterful case. He drew tears from the spectators and jurors, and Mason had to leave the court room for some of it. The verdict was the largest ever awarded in the county—twenty-eight million dollars, which stunned even J. Enright Coddington. Star Transport announced it would appeal, which meant there would be no money for a year or more. That was apparently a longer dry spell than the lawyer could afford. He closeted himself with Star's legal representatives for two days of intensive negotiations and came out with a settlement. Star's insurers, shaken by the jury's award, offered Mason an even ten million dollars. He never knew what his lawyer received, but as soon as the checks were issued, J. Enright closed his office and retired to Puerto Vallarta.

For a time Mason tried to resume his Army career. Although he put in long hours and immersed himself in his work, he knew he was not giving his men the care and attention they deserved. The spark was gone, and he realized he was just going through the motions. Over the objections of Major General Roger Talbot, whom he worked for early in his service, and who had taken a personal interest in his career, Mason opted for the early retirement being offered as a result of the downsizing of the Army following Desert Storm. He then embarked on a program to break out of his melancholy and redirect his life.

To keep his mind from dwelling on what had been, he sought new interests. He had always liked to travel, and that is what he did. He trekked in Nepal, attended a mountain climbing school in the Alps, went on safari in Kenya, and learned to scuba dive on Australia's Great Barrier Reef. He hiked most of the Pacific Crest Trail. He fished for salmon on the Russian River in Alaska, and watched the bears do a better job of it at Katmai. Finally, he bought an RV and began a tour of all the national parks, starting from west to east.

But at Zion, in Utah, it all gave out. Standing atop Angel's Landing after a rugged climb, something happened. Gazing at the valley winding below him to the base of the Three Patriarchs, he finally realized that he was trying to run away from something that would always be part of him, just as those three soaring buttresses would always be part of this valley. For the first time since the accident, he felt something reasonably close to peace.

He sold the RV and flew to Honolulu, where General Talbot had retired. If anyone could set his life back on course, his old mentor could. He, like Mason, was now alone. He had lost his only son in Vietnam, his daughter was married to a Foreign Service officer in the American Embassy in New Delhi, and his wife had died two years ago.

They did a lot of fishing, a lot of talking, and drank a lot of vintage wine from the general's well-stocked cellar. And the general put Mason's financial affairs in order. For almost two years Mason had ignored the settlement, letting it sit in his bank account, drawing funds as he needed them. The interest rate was miniscule.

"That bank must love you," the general chuckled.

Through his financial contacts, Talbot arranged for most of the money to be invested in tax-free municipal bonds, with an average return of five percent. Mason set aside five million dollars to establish a charitable trust in memory of Kathryn and Merrie, which would provide college scholarships to financially underprivileged young women. Despite his world-wide extravagance for nearly two years, that still left him with over four million dollars. His annual income would be far more than he could visualize spending, and he would not have to touch the principal. It finally dawned on him that he was a reasonably wealthy man.

Gradually, General Talbot got Mason involved in what he called his "projects." The general had established himself firmly in the upper level of Honolulu society and served on the boards of about a dozen organizations, most of them nonprofit or devoted to worthy causes. He did all of this without pay. He liked to take on difficult, out-of-the-ordinary problems, particularly those that others had been unable to solve. He was pleased when Mason was able to resolve several particularly sticky ones, including finding the son of a trustee of one of Hawaii's largest landed estates, who had vanished while hiking on the island of Molokai. The general seemed to be grooming Mason to take his place, and Mason did not object. It gave him the opportunity to meet people, go places, and stop dwelling on the past. He enjoyed living in Hawaii, and was beginning to come out of his shell.

When he told General Talbot that he had decided to settle in the islands, the old man embraced him, and then sat him down over an unopened bottle of champagne. Talbot left the room for a moment and returned with a pistol in a highly polished leather holster.

"I carried this during the wars," he told Mason. "When I

retired, it was presented to me as my personal property." Removing it from the holster, he showed Mason a .32 caliber Colt automatic, a small, carbon copy of the Army's hefty .45, which was now no longer in service. "I had intended to give this to my son," the general said. "But since...since that didn't work out, I would like you to have it." It was an emotional moment for both of them.

"Of course," Talbot said, before the silence got too deep, "Clint Eastwood would laugh if you pointed it at him." They opened the champagne and toasted the future.

"Everyone should live in a house," the general announced, "even a bachelor. But not someone else's house. Go find yourself some land and build a house that is yours." With that he gave Mason the name of a builder, a good friend, he said.

Despite the scarcity of vacant land on Oahu, Mason found a narrow stretch of oceanfront property on the North Shore, shaded by mature ironwood, sea grape, and milo trees, with a ground cover of naupaka and beach morning glory. It was fenced, overgrown, and unused. It turned out the land belonged to one of the large estates, which owned all the surrounding agriculture-zoned property, and the estate had no interest in selling any of it. Discouraged, Mason half-heartedly started looking for something else. But he had not reckoned with the general. A few well-placed phone calls, and it seemed that the land might be available after all.

It was hard at first for Mason to accept Aaron Laau as a builder. He was a huge Hawaiian, well over six feet tall and weighed nearly 300 pounds. He rarely spoke. He accepted the job in a matter of fact way that did not inspire confidence. But when Mason's frustration mounted after three architects in a row tried to convince him to build the house that *they* wanted, rather than the one that *he* wanted, Aaron made one of his few utterances.

"Why we need those guys?" he asked. "Let's go build 'em ourselves." And that is what they did.

Aaron brought his crew to the site, and with Mason participating, they built by the seat of their pants, planning as they went. It was inefficient, and they made mistakes, but there was no one with more feel for the land and how to put things on it than Aaron Laau. When it was finished, the house blended so perfectly into the setting that Mason felt it looked as though it had always been there. It was all he could have asked for.

Mason sighed and brought his mind back to the current problem. Even during his reverie, a part of his brain had been working on it. It was late and he was tired, but a young woman was missing, her life might be in danger, and he had agreed to help. He called the president of a computer club he belonged to, but rarely visited, and explained the problem with Michelle's password. The man could offer no immediate ideas, but agreed to look for a solution on a priority basis.

He then turned to the printouts he had made, and re-read the posting from Laura Evans, the writer of the "copycat" message, who had answered Michelle's posting. He rebooted his computer, went to the internet once more, and called up his favorite email address search program. It was a long shot, but worth a chance. When the program loaded, he typed in "Evans, Laura," and clicked on "Nationwide." After about four seconds, the computer responded with,

Your search has found 8,613 entries with the match "Laura" and "Evans." Do you wish to proceed? Yes. No.

Dismayed, Mason clicked "No." His only recourse now was to send her an email. But would she bother to respond, and respond quickly? He composed a short letter, referring to Michelle's posting, explaining that she was missing, and asking Ms. Evans if she had received any messages from her. He then asked her to also let him know if she, Laura, had received any messages from anyone she might consider dangerous or threatening, or from someone seeking a meeting. Finally, he pointed out that time was critical and requesting that she reply as quickly as possible.

Before turning in for the night, he sent it off, knowing that the chances were good that he would not receive any reply at all, let alone something of value. But it was his only lead, unless they could get into Michelle's computer.

4

THE NEXT MORNING, as soon as he got out of bed, Mason Grant turned on his computer. He was only mildly disappointed when he found no email waiting for him. He had not really expected an answer so quickly. He fished through his wallet, and dialed the number Tracy had given him for Kevin Medeiros. It was a 638 prefix, so Mason knew the location was nearby. A woman answered the phone.

"He sleeping," she said, in answer to his request to speak to Kevin. "You call back, maybe two hour."

Mason returned to his bedroom, changed into his trunks, grabbed his mask and snorkel, and left the house through the bedroom's sliding glass doors. Instead of a sandy beach, a flat reef fronted the house. A thin strip of sand separated the reef and the house, and that gave Mason privacy from the beach crowd, which preferred the abundant sands of Sunset Beach, just a short distance away. Only an occasional fisherman bothered to come by, as entry into the water was difficult over the sharp, jagged rock. But Mason knew where the passages were, and he was soon swimming with powerful overhand strokes toward the surf breaking on the outer reef, about 500 feet offshore.

The tide was low, and when he reached the reef, he was able

to pull himself up on its flat surface, cushioned by soft, low-growing seaweed. The summer surf washed gently over his legs as he sat and gazed back at shore. In a few months his perch would be impossible, as winter swells bearing waves of ten feet and higher would come crashing down on the reef. His house, half hidden by trees and lush vegetation, seemed totally isolated. A lone net-thrower stood motionless on the shoreline, waiting to cast his web over any quarry that came within range. It was hard to believe he was looking at a shoreline on populous Oahu.

On his return, he took it more slowly, gliding over green and purple coral heads. Moorish idols, yellow tangs, and brightly colored wrasses darted in and out of crevices, nipping at the coral. A small octopus swam by, attaching itself to an underwater ledge, where it became completely invisible thanks to its remarkable ability to blend its coloring with its background. Only because he had seen it land was Mason able to dive down and grab it. The animal promptly wrapped itself around his arm and shoulder, its suction cups adhering tightly to his skin. After unsuccessfully trying to tease the creature into releasing a cloud of ink, Mason let go. Sensing it was free, the octopus released its death-grip on his arm, and dove to another ledge, once more taking refuge in virtual invisibility.

Returning to his house, Mason reactivated his computer screen. This time he found his mail indicator flashing. He clicked to his mailbox, and his sagging spirits rose when he found a message from Laura Evans.

Hi – I'm writing this quickly because I know you need help. I hope you will keep what I say here in strict confidence. As you will see, it would cause me a lot of embarrassment if you didn't. I have no information about Michelle Iverson. She did not answer my posting and I did not expect her to, since we both were looking for the same thing. My posting did bring other responses, but nothing that involved Michelle. As far as whether or not I have met other people in the kink, well, I'm a guy, see? I mask as a lady because I enjoy reading about what the doms want to do to a woman who lets down all the barriers. Obviously, I don't respond to meeting requests. I've been honest with you, so once again I'm asking you to keep this to yourself, okay? Sorry about your friend.

Barry, aka "Laura"

Mason's spirits fell again. He wondered how many more role-players there were out there in cyberspace. Was Michelle herself playing a role? Did she have some hidden agenda of her own? He might never know. Hoping breakfast would lift his mood, Mason whipped up a batch of buckwheat pancake batter, mixed in a mashed, slightly overripe banana, and added a shot of dark Trinidad rum. He heated up the old, well-seasoned black iron skillet that he never used for anything else. The mixture made three large hotcakes, which he took out to eat on the lanai.

At a time when every postage-stamp-size balcony on every apartment house in Honolulu was called a lanai, Mason took satisfaction from the fact that his was what it was supposed to be, an extension of the inside living area of a home that blended so subtly with the outdoors, that it was difficult to tell where one left off and the other began.

Like all the main rooms of the house, the lanai faced the ocean, but it was the only part of the house that did not command a sweeping view of the water. Taking advantage of a low spot in the land, and surrounded by thick naupaka, the lanai provided privacy and seclusion, while allowing a view of the ocean to the immediate front. It was Mason's favorite place, and he often spent time here when he wanted solitude or needed to think.

This morning, however, the lanai was not having its usual, soothing effect. He had agreed to help Frederick Iverson, but he found himself frustrated as to how to proceed. Other than what might be in Michelle's computer, there were no clues, nothing at all to go on. And he could not gain access to her computer.

He was half-way finished eating when the phone rang. It was Tracy Iverson.

"I have an email message," she told him.

"About Michelle?"

"Yes."

"That was fast. What does it say?"

"It's very short. I'll read it to you. It says,

Tracy,

Michelle is with me. We need to talk. Email me.

John

"The email address is bigbadjohn@lava.net," she added.

"He sounds lovely."

"Doesn't he? But he's lava.net, which means he's here in Hawaii. And he knows I am, too. I use lava.net."

"In the words of your new correspondent, we need to talk."

"Can you come over now?"

"I'm on the way."

Mason pulled into the Iverson driveway an hour and a half after his call to Tracy. Opening the swinging wooden gate, he crossed the short bridge leading to the entrance. The house had been built on a small, rock plateau in the center of a gulch, giving it the appearance of a castle surrounded by a moat. It was a site that most builders would have shunned, but Iverson had evidently seen its possibilities. The house had the feel of being on its own island, floating high above the city. The impression of isolation was enhanced by the absence of any other houses nearby.

Tracy met him at the door in halter and jeans, her long hair twisted in a bun on top of her head. She was every bit as seductively attractive as she had been at the pool, where she had worn far less clothing.

"My computer is in my bedroom," Tracy said, leading the way through the wide entry hall. She turned away from the large room where Mason had talked to her father, and led him to another wing of the house. Her room was one of those which opened out on the pool, and was brightened by the light entering from the sliding glass doors. A beige couch stretched along one wall, a low, Japanese-style dining table serving as its coffee table, and a matching chair completed the "L" of the grouping.

Across the room, one corner held a large color TV, and the other a computer desk, the screen glowing. A wall-to-wall window above a line of bookshelves occupied the entire fourth side of the room. The shelves were overflowing with books and knick-knacks, and magazines and newspapers were piled high on the coffee table. It was not what Mason expected, and he saw no bed.

"You're wondering if I sleep here," Tracy said, grinning. She gestured toward the couch. "It makes into a bed. When school's out, I do a lot of work and reading here. I don't want it to feel like a bedroom."

"You teach?" It would have been another surprise for Mason, but she shook her head.

"I'm doing post grad work at the university."

Although that aroused his curiosity, he was more interested in "bigbadjohn" right now, and he could sense she was also. She opened the sliding door, and led Mason out onto a small patio, where a table and two chairs were shaded by a large royal palm. The pool glistened about thirty feet away. A pitcher of iced tea stood on the table, and as she sat down, Tracy poured two glasses. Sitting down in the other chair, Mason wondered if he was going to become a fan of iced tea.

"Well, what do you think?" Tracy sipped her drink, watching him closely over the rim of her glass.

Mason took a few moments before he replied. "It's kind of hard to say. He hasn't given us much to go on. The main thing we have to decide is whether he's for real, or is he playing games." He told her about "Laura."

"But what kind of game could he be playing?" Tracy asked. "Either Michelle is with him, or she isn't, right?"

"It may not be that clear cut. Reading the stuff on that board yesterday and this morning has been an education. All kinds of people are posting there—serious ones, playful ones, role players, and possibly even a few psychotics who could be downright dangerous. Our problem is, which category does 'bigbadjohn' belong to?"

She thought about that for a moment. "Well, if we're going to do anything, don't we have to assume that he's telling the truth?"

Mason noticed the "we" she kept using in her conversation. One thing he did not want to encourage was Tracy's participation in his investigation. True, by agreeing to her posting the message seeking information about Michelle, he was responsible for her involvement up to this point. But he couldn't afford to have her go any further into it with him. The last thing he needed was a member of the family looking over his shoulder. He would have to find a way to gently, but firmly, deflect her interest.

"I wouldn't assume anything with these people," he said, "especially that they're being truthful. Not after 'Laura.' But you're right. We have to answer as if we believe she's with him. It's all we've got." Now *he* was using "we," he realized.

"So how do we answer him?" Tracy asked.

"In a way that gets him to open up. Even if Michelle is with him, he wants something. Otherwise his message would have been more forthcoming."

Tracy's expression grew somber. "You're not thinking something like ransom, are you?"

"Whatever it is, we're not going to know until we answer him."

They spent the next half hour going over what to say in the message. They agreed they should try to get as much information possible from him. Where was Michelle, was she all right? Most important of all, they would make an appeal to have Michelle contact Tracy by phone. Tracy suggested that they ignore the brusque, demanding tone of the message, and reply as if it had been friendly and helpful. It was not something Mason would have thought of, but he could see its value. More time was consumed in drafting the reply, but they soon had a message they were satisfied with.

Dear John,

Thank you so very much for your quick reply to my posting. I can't tell you how relieved my father and I are to hear some word about Michelle. Can you tell us where she is? And can you please ask her

to call us right away so that we know that everything is all right?
We have been so worried.

You said that we need to talk, and I am anxious to do so. If you
will give me your phone number, I will be happy to call you. Or
you can call me at any time. Please contact me again as soon as
you get this. We are so worried about her.

> *Sincerely,*
> *Tracy*

Mason had wanted to leave out Tracy's phone number. "It's one way we would know if Michelle is really with him," he said. "If she is, she certainly knows the number, and our friend can get the number from her to talk to you."

But Tracy insisted. "I don't want to play games with Michelle's welfare," she told him. "Just in case she is injured or ill, and she isn't able to give him the number, or whatever. I want him to have it." So the phone number was added to the message.

Mason watched as Tracy typed the email letter on the computer. After sending it, she leaned back in her chair, staring at the screen.

"What's the matter?" Mason asked.

Tracy sighed and shook her head. "I just wish I felt better about this. I've probably said it a dozen times, but it's just not like Michelle to simply disappear. Maybe none of this is voluntary. Maybe she was abducted or something. Couldn't he be holding her against her will?"

"If that were the case, why did he answer you? Wouldn't he want to remain hidden?"

"Maybe. Unless, like you said, he wants something."

It was only a couple of hours after Mason returned home, and he was just getting ready to make supper, when his phone rang. It was Tracy.

"I have a reply from 'bigbadjohn.' He wants me to meet him,"

"That's probably the worst thing you could do," he replied.

"What choice do we have? How else are we going to find out if he really knows anything about Michelle?"

"By keeping him talking on the computer and getting him to give us as much information as we can."

"Without knowing what's happening to Michelle in the meantime? What he may be doing to her?"

That stopped him. "Better read me the message."

She did.

Tracy,

I received your E. I'm not going to give you my phone number or call you because things are too complicated to discuss over the phone. Michelle is okay, but you'll have to take my word. She is not going to call either. The best thing is for us to meet in person, and I will make everything clear. Be at Moose Maguire's on University Avenue tonight at 7PM. Sit at one of the small tables on the raised platform that surrounds the bar. I will find you. Make sure you are alone.

John

"He's certainly sure of himself," Mason said. "Telling you to *be* there."

"I *will* be there." Sensing how negatively her remark affected him, she continued. "How else are we possibly going to find out anything about Michelle?"

"Tracy, I'm not sure this guy knows anything about Michelle. He sounds like a complete phony to me. What kind of information could he possibly have that he couldn't tell you over the phone, or by email?"

"I don't know, but I'm not going to find out unless I meet him. And I am going to meet him. You can count on it."

He saw it was useless to argue with her. "And I'm going to be with you. You can count on *that*."

"Mason, no. You saw what he said about coming alone."

"You'll be alone. I'll get there early, be just one of the boys drinking beer and watching the game on the big TV." She started to object, but he stopped her. "Tracy, you can't go off to meet someone who might be a total creep without protection. If you're going to be there, I am. That's settled."

It was her turn to see that further argument was useless. "Promise me you won't interfere."

"Not unless it looks like you're in trouble."

5

MASON KNEW IT was going to be a long day. Tracy's meeting with "bigbadjohn" was more than twelve hours away, and he was already on edge. As he was deciding what to do with the time, he remembered that, in the excitement of the previous day, he had forgotten to call back Kevin Medeiros.

When he placed the call, the same woman came on the line. "He no here now. Maybe you call back aftah lunch."

Mason sighed. That still left the morning to fill in. Unable to think of anything more productive, he logged on to the Dark Chateau bulletin board. He began clicking through the new messages, but soon saw that they no longer had anything to do with Michelle. Leaving the bulletin board, he clicked on *About The Dark Chateau*. Here, he learned that the website was devoted to providing a forum and a meeting place for those whose sexual interests inclined toward sadism, masochism, and bondage. It professed to take a "scientific" approach toward such preferences, stating that they were no more of an aberration than homosexuality and Lesbianism, which were now widely accepted in society. With that in mind, members were encouraged to explore the netherworlds of their feelings, and write about, discuss, and engage in whatever activity was mutually agreed upon.

There was a lot of wordage concerning the philosophy of the Marquis de Sade, who seemed to be the posthumous guru of the website, and to a lesser extent, that of Count Leopold von Sacher-Masoch, the two writers who defined the opposite poles of sadomasochism. Mason skipped the philosophy and next clicked the *Membership* button, skimming through the rules he had ignored yesterday. He found that he had agreed, among other things, not to use pornographic language, either on the bulletin board or in the chat rooms. He would not post or discuss anything scatological or relating to pedophilia, would not engage in "flame wars," and would not insult or violate the privacy of another member.

In the Store he found virtually every book written by de Sade, as well as books about his life and philosophy. Even Sacher-Masoch's relatively rare "Venus in Furs" was on hand, as were many more modern sado-masochistic works. Mason noted that the three "Sleeping Beauty" volumes which Tracy had introduced him to were also available. Many of the books could be downloaded for a fee, or purchased in the Store, which also offered a variety of whips, restraints, and T-shirts with motifs Mason had never seen anywhere else. The only area of the website he had not explored were the Chat Rooms, but he could see no reason to do so, and shut off the computer.

He decided against going out for lunch. He still had half a loaf of sourdough rye he had made two days ago. Cutting two large slices, he layered them with Braunschweiger, raw onions, and Dijon mustard. He opened a bottle of Kona Long Board and sat down in the kitchen alcove.

Mason was no baker, but he did make bread. Years ago, in the Arabian Desert, an Arab cook in his mess hall had shown him how to make bread without the laborious kneading process.

After mixing the ingredients, he would allow the dough to rise for about two hours, then flattened it into a pizza shape. He then folded in the sides, making an oval he let rise for another hour, before baking in a pre-heated oven. The result was a round, peasant-style bread, with a crunchy crust. Checking his watch, he dialed Kevin Medeiros again. Once more the same woman answered the phone.

"Kevin!" The shout was so loud Mason recoiled from the phone. After a long wait, a surly male voice came on the line.

"Yeah?"

"Mr. Medeiros, my name is Mason Grant. I've been asked by Frederick Iverson to help find his daughter, Michelle." Mason thought he could detect something like a stifled laugh at the other end of the line.

"Wha', she still not come back?"

"No, and I was wondering if I could see you for a few minutes to talk about it."

"Hey, man, I don' know nothin' about it. Crazy chick wen' disappear, not my problem, you know?"

Mason tried to keep the irritation from his voice. "If I could talk to you for just a few minutes it might help. I'm close by, and could come over now, if it's convenient."

"Hey, I dunno, man. Surf's comin' up, you know? Not so many waves in summer. Gotta go catch 'em."

Mason gritted his teeth. "Mr. Medeiros, I know you want to do all you can to help find Michelle. If you can't see me now, how about later today?"

"Nah, no can later. Going Kaena, night fishing." There was a pause, and then Medeiros continued. "I live Sunset, where you at?"

"Less than ten minutes away."

"Okay, you be here in ten minutes, I give you ten minutes more, then I'm outta here." He gave Mason an address and the line went dead.

Mason hung up the phone. Tracy was right. Kevin Medeiros was easy to dislike.

Turning off Kamehameha Highway near Sunset Beach, Mason drove slowly down the narrow, dusty road lined on both sides by small, wooden houses, crowded closely together. He eased into a mere postage stamp of a yard, stopping beside two rusted car hulks. A young man holding a surfboard sat on the steps, obviously waiting for him. Behind him, on the dilapidated porch, a corroded washer and dryer, and a useless refrigerator completed the outside decor. As Mason got out of the car, the young man came to meet him, still carrying the surfboard.

"Kevin?"

"Howzit?" The young man extended his right arm upward for a hand clench. It reminded Mason of the typical arm-wrestling position, and he had never quite gotten used to it. Grasping the outstretched hand, Mason reluctantly admitted that Kevin Medeiros was strikingly handsome. He seemed to be in his late twenties, and his bronze body rippled with the subdued, but powerful muscles of a regular surfer. Dark curls ringed his forehead, and perfect white teeth graced his smile. He seemed friendlier than he had on the phone, and Mason couldn't help wondering why he had decided to turn on the charm.

"So, you a private eye, or what?" Medeiros remained standing in the driveway as he asked the question, as if to remind Mason that he didn't have much time.

"A friend of the family. I'm just trying to help out."

Medeiros seemed disappointed at the news, and shrugged his shoulders slightly. "So, what you wan' from me?" To Mason's ear, Medeiros' Hawaiian pidgin did not ring true. While the sing-song accent was there, the sentence structure, even on the phone, wasn't right. This was a guy *trying to* be a member of the local pidgin-speaking crowd, without being completely successful. And he was relatively certain that Medeiros could speak conventional English any time he wanted to.

"Can you tell me the last time you saw Michelle?"

"Hey, I dunno sure. Maybe four, five days ago. Why, you think I hiding her?" He said it with a grin, signaling he was not particularly concerned or angered by the question. Mason also smiled, as if both men had shared a small joke.

"Do you know anyone who might be hiding her, or have any idea where she might be?"

Medeiros shook his head. "Nah, I'm her only guy. No reason for hide."

"You didn't have an argument, a fight?"

"Fight? That chick crazy about me, man. Hot for my body. No reason for fight." His smile became a self-satisfied smirk.

Mason knew Medeiros was enjoying showing him how much power he held over Michelle. He might brag some more, but Mason was convinced he knew nothing of Michelle's disappearance. He was ready to leave when Medeiros spoke.

"Hey, her ol' man, he pretty rich, yeah?" Mason said nothing, but Medieros continued. "He make reward for find her?"

Mason shook his head. "No reward."

Medeiros shrugged and lifted his board to his shoulder. The interview was over. "Too bad," he said as he turned away. "He should make reward. Maybe then somebody find out something."

6

TRACY ARRIVED AT Moose McGuire's ten minutes early. The place was crowded with young university students, mainly male. Four large television sets were spaced strategically, all tuned to the same basketball game. The noise level was oppressive.

Although she had promised herself not to, she glanced quickly around, looking for Mason. She did not see him and her heart lurched. She suddenly realized that she wanted him there. Making her way to the bar platform, she found a free table for two and sat down. When the waitress came over, she ordered a glass of chardonnay, which she did not touch. Glancing around the room, she tried to pick out "John", but had no success. No one seemed to be paying any attention to her. Most eyes were riveted on the TV screens. She still did not see Mason.

By ten past seven no one had approached her, and her nervousness increased. She decided to give it another ten minutes. Damn it, where was Mason? Just as she made up her mind to leave, a man eased into the chair opposite her.

"Hi Tracy."

He was overweight, with sparse blond hair, and a small, sharp nose. Searching green eyes peered out from behind round, steel-rimmed glasses, which seemed lost in his pudgy face. He was older than she had expected, somewhere around fifty. He exuded an arrogant confidence, including the smile on his face, which was more like a leer.

"Sorry to keep you waiting, but I had to be sure you were alone. I'm John Bridges."

She decided to say nothing, waiting for him to go on. The leer grew wider, revealing irregular, yellow teeth.

"You're a looker, Tracy, you know that?"

She suppressed her anger. "This is supposed to be about my sister."

The toothy smile did not waiver. "Oh, sure, Michelle. She's fine."

"Where is she?"

"At my place."

"And where is that?"

"Not far."

Tracy could tell he was enjoying this. She was convinced that this man knew nothing about Michelle and that he was putting her on for some weird reason of his own, but she would have to play his game.

"When can I see her?"

Bridges shifted in his chair and brought out a pack of Marlboros. As he lit one, she noticed his yellow-stained fingers. "In a little bit," he said, exhaling a plume of smoke in her direction. "We need to talk some, first."

She waited, but he seemed in no hurry to go on, enjoying the silence as much as he had enjoyed the previous conversation.

"That Michelle," he said finally, staring squarely into her eyes. "A real hot number, she is. You anything like her?"

Shaking with fury, Tracy rose to leave. As she passed him, he reached out and grabbed her arm. "Hey, wait a minute now."

She wrenched her arm free and once more started to go.

"You gonna just walk out on Michelle?"

That stopped her. Slowly, she walked back to the table and stood over him. "Look, if Michelle is really with you, either take me to her right now, or I'm calling the police."

"Okay, okay." He stubbed out his cigarette. "It's just that…well, Michelle turned out to be a lot to handle. I wanted to be sure that—"

"Just take me to her."

Bridges pushed his chair back and rose from the table. He was taller than she had realized, and heavier. He led the way from the bar to the parking lot and a red Ford pickup. "You wanna ride with me?"

"Then how would Michelle and I get home?"

"Oh, yeah, that's right. Well, follow me then."

He headed toward the University and then turned right on Date Street. As Tracy made the turn after him, she watched her rear view mirror. Several pairs of headlights made the turn behind her, but the darkness prevented her from telling anything about the vehicles or their occupants.

True to his word, Bridges soon pulled into a parking lot in front of an apartment, and Tracy swung in beside him. The building was one of those awful concrete-block walk-ups that she hated, and she remained inside her car, wondering whether to get out. There was a tap on her window.

"You comin' or not?"

Reluctantly, she removed her keys from the ignition and opened the door. He took her arm and she allowed him to lead her toward the darkened entrance. Nearing the building, her heart began to pound. As he reached to open the door, she stopped and pulled back. He turned and looked at her, a scowl forming.

"I have to go back to the car for a minute. I forgot something."

He stared at her without releasing her arm. "It's medicine for that infected cut on Michelle's hand. It was really nasty before she disappeared. Has it gotten any better?"

"Oh, yeah, we been watching it. It's much better."

Tracy jerked her arm from his grasp, eyes blazing. "You lying bastard! There was nothing wrong with Michelle's hand. I'm calling the police." As she turned to go, she felt both her arms pinned tightly to her sides. Bridges' body pressed against hers, his breath reeking of tobacco.

"Now hold on, little girl. We need to talk this over."

"Let her go."

Bridges looked up at the figure that had materialized behind Tracy. "Who the hell are you?"

"Let her go," Mason repeated.

For a long moment, Bridges did nothing, staring belligerently at this new arrival. Then, with a sneer, he released Tracy, shoving her in Mason's direction. "So it was a goddam setup." He turned to enter the building.

"Just a minute," Tracy shouted. "What do you know about my sister?"

"Not a goddam thing," Bridges said, without turning or breaking stride.

Moving quickly, Mason positioned himself between Bridges and the doorway, bringing the other man to a halt. Tracy, too, came around to face him.

"How do we know she isn't up in your apartment, like you told me she was?"

"You take my word."

"That isn't good enough," Mason said.

"Tough shit." Bridges started toward the doorway again. Mason did not move.

"Since you brought us all this way, why don't we just see for ourselves."

"Like hell."

"We're going upstairs, one way or the other," Mason said.

Bridges clenched his fists and the muscles of his arms tensed. He took a step forward. Mason still did not move. As Bridges approached, something in Mason's eyes made him stop. After a long moment, he decided not to push the issue further. In a final gesture of defiance, he spat on the walkway, wiping his mouth with the back of his hand. "Come on, then, let's get it over with."

The room they entered was intended as a dining-living combination, but John Bridges evidently had other ideas for its use. A large overstuffed couch and chair, a coffee table, and a TV were the only major items of furniture. A leather whip was displayed prominently on one wall. Manacles suspended from a hook occupied another. A riding crop lay on a coffee table, beside a pile of glossy bondage magazines, where a DVD of *The Story of O* stood ready to be popped into the player.

Mason made a quick inspection of the single bedroom and its only closet. There was no sign that anyone else occupied the apartment. Bridges glared at him when he returned to the main room.

"Now that you're satisfied that she ain't here, you can get the hell out."

Tracy was not about to leave without some explanation. "Why did you answer my posting, if you knew nothing about Michelle?"

"Why not?" A suggestion of the leer returned to Bridges' face. "How'd I know your sister was really missing at all? Maybe you wanted to play, too. Like they say, two peas in a pod."

Tracy surveyed the room. "And just what were you planning to do when you got me up here?"

The leer grew wider. "I thought that maybe after I showed you a few of my things that we'd get it on."

Her eyes narrowed as she stared at him. "You pathetic creep." She turned away. "Let's get out of here, Mason. Leave him with his sick toys."

As Mason drove her home, Tracy sat beside him without speaking. It was only when he turned into the Iverson driveway that she spoke.

"I feel stupid and… used," she said. "You were right."

"It doesn't do any good to be right if it doesn't get us anywhere."

She sighed. "What do we do now?"

He eased the car to a stop. "It's late. There's nothing we can do tonight. Let's sleep on it, and I'll call you in the morning."

She opened the door and got out. Before closing it, she leaned back into the car. "Mason?" As he turned, she offered a weak smile. "Thanks."

He smiled back. "Any time."

7

MASON'S PHONE WOKE him the next morning. Light was barely beginning to appear over the ocean outside his bedroom. It was Tracy Iverson.

"I just got a note offering information about Michelle."

"You got it just now?" Mason looked at his watch. "It's not even five o'clock. How did it arrive?"

"The doorbell rang and kept ringing. Someone had stuck a pin in it. When I got to the door, an envelope was taped to it. The note offers the information in exchange for ten thousand dollars."

There was a moment of silence on Mason's end of the line, then he told her about his visit with Kevin Medeiros. "He didn't seem at all concerned about Michelle's disappearance, except whether or not your father had offered a reward for information about her."

"I'm not at all surprised," Tracy said. "That guy is pure slime." As Mason paused, Tracy asked, "Are you thinking what I'm thinking?"

"Right after talking about a reward? I can't believe he's that stupid."

"Trust me," she said, "he's that stupid. What are we going to do?"

"I'd better come down again."

Both Frederick Iverson and Tracy met Mason when he arrived. Tracy handed him the note. It was printed in block letters on a sheet of standard typewriter paper. The lettering appeared to be deliberately crude, in an attempt to disguise the hand.

IF YOU WANT TO KNOW WHERE MICHELLE IS BRING $10 THOUSAND DOLLARS IN USED TENS AND TWENTYS TO SACRED FALLS PARK TONIGHT AT 9PM ONLY ONE PERSON NO FLASHLIGHT WALK UP THE DIRT ROAD TO THE FALLS AND YOU WILL BE CONTACTED YOU ONLY HAVE THIS ONE CHANCE I WILL NOT BE THERE AGAIN

"I feel like I'm part of a bad detective novel," Tracy said, nodding toward the note. "What do you think we should do?"

"If it's from Kevin, we can ignore it," Mason replied.

"We do not know that it is from Kevin," Frederick Iverson said. "I do not share the confidence that both of you have about it being from him. And if it is *not* from Kevin, I cannot afford to ignore it." He paused only a moment before continuing. "I am going to do as the note requires."

Mason raised his eyebrows. "In spite of the fact that this could be just a scam to get the money?"

"I will have to take that risk."

Mason sighed, knowing there was no chance of changing Iverson's mind. "You told me on Tuesday that you and Tracy were the only ones who knew about Michelle's posting," he said. "Are you certain of that?"

"Absolutely."

"Well, then, if the note is not from Kevin, it can only be from someone who is involved in Michelle's disappearance."

"Which is precisely why I intend to follow the note's instructions."

"That person could be extremely dangerous."

"I do not see much risk involved. He wants money, I want my daughter. It is a simple business transaction."

"Assuming that he's a businessman and not a psychotic pervert," Mason warned. "Again, if the note is not from Kevin, there's a strong suggestion of kidnapping about it, which is a federal crime. I suppose I'm wasting time suggesting you notify the FBI."

"You are," Iverson confirmed. "And for the same reason I advanced previously."

Mason shrugged. "How do you plan to go about it?"

"Straight-forwardly. I will get the money from the bank and take it up the road."

"Why not let me do that?" Mason said. "After all, you've given me responsibility for finding her. And remember, Sacred Falls Park has been closed since the Mothers Day landslide. The gate is locked, but I can get over it. Besides, I still think there's a certain amount of danger involved."

Iverson smiled as if amused. "If you can get over the gate, I am certain I can also, and why should you be more capable of dealing with danger than I am? I do not want to play games, Mr. Grant. In spite of what you may think, I love my daughter and want her safe return. I am willing to pay for that. I do not want her return jeopardized by cowboy tactics against whoever sent that note."

"There won't be any. I'll do it exactly the way you want."

The mirthless smile appeared again. "Then there is no reason for me not to do it myself."

"At least let me drive out there with you. I'll stay in the car. That way, I'll be there to look for you if you don't come out."

"Thank you, but no. The instructions said to come alone. I intend to follow them to the letter." Iverson glanced at his watch. "I have to get ready. I have an appointment at eight o'clock." As he was leaving the room, he turned to Mason. "Mr. Grant, I want your promise that you will not follow me tonight, and that you will stay away from the Sacred Falls Trail."

Following a moment's pause, Mason nodded. "You have it."

After Frederick Iverson had left, Tracy suggested they have a cup of coffee. As he took his first sip, Mason saw Tracy staring at him. "You're planning something, aren't you?" she said.

"I intend to keep my promise to your father."

"That doesn't mean you're not planning something."

Mason smiled ruefully. "Is mind reading one of your talents?"

"When the mind is as easy to read as yours is right now, no talent is involved. What are you going to do?"

"You won't say anything to your father?" She shook her head. "I'm going to see if I can intercept our note writer."

"But you promised to stay away from the Sacred Falls Trail."

"I will. I don't think he'll come back that way. He's not going to take the chance that your father won't have somebody waiting there for him."

"I don't think there's any other way out of Sacred Falls. I've been up there several times."

"I have too, and I agree that there doesn't seem to be. But I can't see the guy boxing himself in like that. He must have a way out without going back along the entry road." Mason finished his coffee and stood up. "I've got to get going."

Tracy walked him to the door. "Are you going to scout things out."

"No, I don't think so. Punaluu is a pretty local neighborhood. A *haole* snooping around there will draw attention. I have a file cabinet full of maps at home. I'll start there."

"Will you let me know what you find out?"

He took a moment to think about it, then nodded. "Sure. I'll call you."

Once he was back home, Mason went to his map cabinet and pulled out the US Geological Survey index for Oahu. Ever since he was a child, he had loved maps, and he had collected them the way other kids collected stamps. One of his childhood ambitions had been to be a surveyor, like George Washington. Over the years, he had collected hundreds of maps, including all those that came with his National Geographic magazine over the last fifteen years. One of his first purchases after deciding to settle in Hawaii was a complete set of the USGS Topographic 1:24,000 sheets for the Hawaiian Islands. He now selected the Hauula sheet, which contained the Sacred Falls Trail.

Access to Sacred Falls was first by a dirt road leading from the parking lot over a relatively open area. The route followed Kaluanui Stream for about a mile until it reached a forest, where the road ended and a foot trail took over. Mason traced the dirt road on the topo map, and found what appeared to be an old plantation road crossing it, running from the town of Hauula, south to Punaluu Valley. Mason could not recall seeing such a road on any of his trips to the falls.

Cross-checking with the latest road map of the area, he found no sign of the northern portion of the road, the one from Hauula, but the map did show the southern part of the road. It ended in less than half a mile, at a street named Puhuli, which connected to Kamehameha Highway, the main coastal road.

Mason could recall no road leading off the falls access, and wished now that he had not promised Frederick Iverson he would stay away from the area. Of course, he could reconnoiter from the end of Puhuli Street, back toward the falls, seeking the connection, but that would involve an element of risk. He knew nothing about that particular street, but the entire area from Hauula to Punaluu was heavily local, and, as he had indicated to Tracy, he would stand out as a stranger, someone who did not belong. And, for all he knew, the sender of the note might live nearby, which could be the reason for choosing this particular place for the meeting. But, after thinking long and hard on the matter, he decided he had to accept the risk. It was either that or stand by and do nothing.

He changed into his hiking boots and shorts, selected one of his oldest T shirts, and put on a floppy hat with a wide, drooping brim. He stuffed a bottle of water in his day pack, along with two apples. Remembering his promise to Tracy, he reached for the phone. He did not want Tracy involved, but he could not justify telling her anything but the truth. As he feared, she suggested going with him, but quickly accepted his reasoning that two people, especially a couple, would be more conspicuous than a lone hiker.

It took about twenty minutes for him to drive to Sacred Falls, and Puhuli Street was half a mile farther south. To his surprise, a large wrought-iron gate barred entry to the street from the highway. A "No Trespassing: Private Property" sign was posted conspicuously on the gate. Mason drove past the street and parked a short distance down the highway, in the midst of a group of fishermen's cars.

Taking his pack, and with the hat drawn tightly down on his forehead, he walked back to Puhuli Street. In spite of the standard county street identification sign, the gate was firmly locked with a heavy chain and a rust-coated lock that looked as if it had not been opened for a long time. Peering through the gate's bars, Mason saw that the street on the other side was paved, but beginning to deteriorate, and both sides of the pavement were heavily overgrown with brush and high grass. He could see no sign of houses.

To the left side of the gate, a single section of concrete water pipe, with a diameter of about three feet, penetrated the fence. It was clearly there to allow access to the property by foot, despite the no trespassing sign. Crouching low, Mason crawled through the pipe, and made his way down the road. The street was less than half a mile long, and he saw no buildings or structures of any kind along the way.

At the end of the road, he found himself in a rough cul-de-sac. There was no connecting road in either direction. Poking around at the edge of the pavement, he almost missed a faint trail that led into the underbrush. Following it brought him to a heavily overgrown trace that had once obviously been a road. Two parallel tracks headed north. Waist-high grass grew between them, and both sides of the track were lined with dense brush, guava trees, and passion fruit vines.

Mason began following the old road, his nostrils filled with the pungent smell of rotting fruit, which littered the ground. In less than half an hour the road ended at a stream bank, where a collapsed concrete abutment was all that remained of a bridge. Mason recognized the stream as Kaluanui, the one draining from Sacred Falls. He knew that the road and trail leading to the falls was on the other side. He checked his watch; it was 3 pm. In six hours Frederick Iverson would make his rendezvous on Sacred Falls road. Satisfied, Mason retraced his route, and drove home.

8

FREDERICK IVERSON HAD been walking up the road for about twenty-five minutes, a briefcase clutched in his right hand. The gate to the park had been closed, forcing him to climb the fence. A half-moon provided sufficient light to see the surface of the gravel road, and he was able to walk at almost normal speed. But he was beginning to worry. He judged that he was close to the point where the road ended at the forest line, and he knew that there would not be enough light penetrating the heavy tree cover to follow the trail. Five minutes later, he thought he could detect the outline of the trees ahead, and his uneasiness increased. He looked at his watch.

"Don't turn around."

The voice came from about twenty feet behind him. It was rasping and unnatural, an obvious attempt at disguise. Iverson stopped walking and stood perfectly still. A flashlight played over his body.

"Put the case down, and walk forward 'til I say stop."

Iverson held his ground and the briefcase. "What about the information concerning my daughter?"

"You get that after I'm sure what's in the case."

Iverson put down the briefcase and began walking forward.

After he had gone about twenty steps, the voice told him to stop, and once more, not to turn around. He heard the snaps of the briefcase open. There was a brief pause, and then the voice came again.

"Okay, keep walking to where the road ends at the trees. On the right side is the flash flood warning siren. At the base is a large envelope. There's a rock on top, so you can see it. Wait five minutes before you start back, or maybe you won't get back."

Iverson began walking again. He soon found himself at the end of the road, and he was able to make out the pole holding the warning siren. At its base he found the promised envelope. He waited the demanded five minutes, and then returned to his car as fast as the darkness would allow. Turning on his dashboard light, he tore open the envelope. Inside were three sheets of blank paper.

Mason had been waiting in the brush alongside the old road for over half an hour, and the mosquitoes had found him. He had decided against applying repellent, afraid its scent might give him away. Now, he regretted that decision, as he tried futilely to wave them off. From where he stood, he could see only about thirty feet, but it was enough to give him warning of someone approaching. And that someone would not be able to see him.

Mason's plan was simple. There would be no one coming down this abandoned road at this time of night except the writer of the note—if anyone came at all. His Army training had taught him the value of surprise, and the danger and stupidity of "fighting fair." He intended to disable whoever it was, and find out his identity. He had thought about bringing his pistol, but decided against it. Although it was registered, he had no permit to carry it, and if he was forced to use it, he could find himself in big trouble.

He heard the man approaching before he saw him. He was moving quickly, almost trotting down the path. He reached his position faster than Mason had expected, forcing him to act in haste. Impressions of a stocking mask and a briefcase flashed in his peripheral vision as he lunged toward the passing figure, his right arm raised to deliver a rabbit punch to the back of the man's neck. Some sixth sense or a crackling branch caused the man to increase speed and hunch over so that the blow fell on his left shoulder. Although missing its target area, the power of the strike staggered him, almost bringing him down.

As Mason closed in, the figure suddenly turned, swinging the briefcase in a deadly arc. Mason was barely able to deflect it from his head by taking the blow on his upper right arm, sending an almost paralyzing pain coursing all the way to his shoulder. The man brought the briefcase swinging back in a reverse path, once more aiming for Mason's head. This time Mason intercepted the blow by striking hard with the knife-edge of his left hand, hitting the man's lower arm. The blow caused a cry of pain and the release of the man's hold on the briefcase, which missed Mason's head by less than an inch as it sailed into the brush.

Before Mason could react, his assailant kicked out with his right leg, aiming for Mason's groin. Only a frantic turn sideways prevented a heavy boot from connecting dead center, but even so, the blow landed heavily on his hip, knocking Mason to his knees. He was able to deflect a hard punch to his head by taking it on his right shoulder, and he responded by slamming his right fist into his assailant's gut, just below the waist. Although the man staggered and fell back, the impact on Mason's already injured arm brought stars dancing in front of his eyes, as intense pain lanced toward his shoulder. As he struggled to his feet, he saw his assailant turn and run back in the direction he had come, bent over, and clutching his right arm close to his side.

Mason took off in pursuit. He had covered about 50 yards before he realized what he was doing. He stopped, stood perfectly still, and listened. There was no sound of running, or of any movement at all. He had little doubt that his assailant was waiting for him somewhere up ahead, concealed by the darkness and the brush, and possibly armed with a rock, or fallen tree limb. Having sprung such an ambush himself, Mason had no desire to risk being the victim of another one, especially with an almost useless right arm. Turning, he made his way back down the path.

He retrieved the briefcase, and returned to his car. He thought of staking out the area, waiting for the man to come out, but realized that the man could escape via the Sacred Falls Trail, and he could not monitor both locations. Besides, his arm was killing him, and he didn't know how much damage had been done. Before driving off, he wrote down the license numbers of all the cars parked in the vicinity.

Once home, Mason dialed the Iverson home. Frederick Iverson answered, and in a dispirited voice, related the events of the evening.

"You were right," he admitted. "It was just a scam."

"Well, at least it didn't cost you anything." Mason could sense Iverson's confusion in the silence that followed.

"What do you mean?" Iverson finally asked. "It cost me ten thousand dollars."

"No, it didn't. I have the money." Mason summarized the incident on the old road, but cut short Iverson's questions. He was tired, his arm still throbbed, and he wanted to get off the phone.

He offered to bring the briefcase by in the morning, and they would then discuss what to do next.

Mason stepped into the shower and for a long time let a steady stream of hot water massage his arm and shoulder. When he emerged, his phone was ringing. He looked at his watch. It was almost 1 A.M. When he picked up the phone, it was Tracy Iverson.

"I've got it," she said.

Despite the excitement in her voice, it took him a moment to realize what she was saying. "The password?" He could feel his own excitement rising.

"Yes."

"Terrific! How did you find it?"

"It was right in front of me."

"What was?"

"Sleeping Beauty."

9

FREDERICK IVERSON OPENED the briefcase and stared at its contents. The morning had dawned clear and beautiful, and sunshine streamed into the Iverson living room.

"You know," he said, his voice subdued, "I would rather have received some useful information about Michelle than have this money back." He looked up then, an apologetic expression on his face. "Oh, I'm grateful that you retrieved it, Mr. Grant, but somehow, I wish it would have worked out." He sighed and turned toward the window. "But you were right. It was a mistake to go along with it."

Mason cleared his throat. "Well, then," he said gently, "how about letting me handle things from now on? After all, that's why you called me in."

Iverson agreed. "I assume, now that Tracy has found Michelle's password, you will want to get busy looking at her files. Should we put last night's fiasco aside for the time being?"

"We may have to put it aside for good," Mason said. "Even if we find out who that guy is, which is not very likely, there's nothing much we can do about it as long as you want to keep the matter away from the police."

"I have business affairs in town most of the day," Iverson said, ignoring Mason's comment, "including a dinner engagement. I will be leaving in about an hour. Tracy can fill me in when I return, if you find anything significant."

"Why don't we go out to the lanai," Tracy suggested, after her father had left. "We can have coffee out there."

When she brought out the steaming silver pot, Mason thought Tracy more subdued than he would have expected under the circumstances. She seemed slightly nervous, and even apprehensive. Mason put it down to the events of the previous day.

"How do you like the coffee?" she asked, after Mason had taken his first sip.

"It's fine."

"It's from Kauai. I also have some from Molokai."

He nodded, puzzled by this small talk in light of her discovery. Until recently, coffee had only been grown on the Kona coast of the island of Hawaii. As sugar declined, coffee was taking over some of its former acreage on Oahu, Kauai, Maui, and Molokai. But Mason had no interest in a discussion about coffee right now.

"Have you read any of Michelle's files?" he asked, trying not to let his impatience show.

"No." She saw his surprise. "I thought I'd wait for you."

After they finished the coffee, Mason expected her to take him to Michelle's computer, but instead, she just sat there, staring out over the city. She seemed to be mulling something over in her mind. Mystified, Mason decided to wait her out, and poured another cup.

"I want to work with you," she said finally.

Mason slowly placed his coffee back down on the table. "What exactly does that mean?"

"I want to work with you," she repeated. "I want to be your partner, your assistant— anything. I want to help find my sister."

"Tracy..."

"I don't want to be left out in the cold on this." She leaned forward, her eyes fastened earnestly on his. "I'll go crazy just sitting here doing nothing while God-knows-what may be happening to Michelle." Seeing that he was unconvinced, she reached out and grasped his arm. He could feel the tension in her grip. "Look, Mason," she pleaded, "there's no reason why we can't work together. I can be a big help to you. I'm smart, hardworking—and I won't cost you anything." She smiled, probably hoping a little humor might sway him.

"Tracy, I understand how you feel, but that's just not a good idea. First of all, I work alone. I only get help in technical areas when I need it. More important, you're emotionally involved here. There are times when that might work against..."

"If you think I can't control my emotions, you're wrong. I can, you can count on it. And Michelle being my sister is a plus, not a minus. I know her, I'll work hard to help find her."

Saying no to her at that moment was one of the hardest things Mason had to do in a long time, but he just did not think it would work. He shook his head. "I'm sorry."

For a moment she just stood there, staring at him. Then her features hardened. "You won't be able to do anything without me."

Mason's own feelings began to harden in response. "I'll just go to your father. I'm sure he'll allow me access to Michelle's computer." He rose, and started toward the main house.

"It won't do you any good," she called after him. "I deleted her email program."

Mason stopped in his tracks and turned to face her. "You did what?"

"Oh, don't worry. I copied it to a flash drive. But it's no longer in her computer." Her self-satisfied expression made her next words almost unnecessary. "So, if you want the file, we'll have to work together."

"And if I refuse?"

"Then I'll work on it by myself, go my own way. And you'll never see the file."

"Your father will certainly make you give it to me."

"I won't do it. I'll tell him I'm convinced I can do as good a job as you. You're not the police. You're not even a private investigator. And she's my sister. I know one hell of a lot more about her than you do. And I have more interest in finding her than you could ever have."

Her words gave Mason reason to pause. She and her father were two strong-willed people, if in a strange, perplexing way. Her father would not risk his reputation to find his daughter. Would the sister withhold information from him unless she could participate in the search? He had no way of knowing, but he felt he couldn't take the chance. And, deep down, he had to admit to himself that seeing more of Tracy wouldn't really be all that bad.

He sighed and came back across the room. "Okay, but on one condition. We give it a try. If things don't work out, I go it alone. Agreed?"

Her smile was so radiant it almost blinded him. "Don't worry, we'll make a great team. You can count on it."

He was already beginning to believe her.

Michelle's room was surprisingly small, considering the size of the Iverson mansion.

"It was supposed to be a maid's room," Tracy explained, "but we've never had a live-in maid. Michelle wanted it because of the private garden."

Mason noticed the sliding glass door leading to a small, but attractive Japanese-style garden, surrounded by a wooden fence. It made an ideal place for a servant to spend quiet time, away from the family, yet be on the premises if needed. Mason noted that the computer was already on. He asked Tracy for the memory stick containing Michelle's email program.

"I have a confession to make," she said, with an impish grin. "The program is still on the computer. It's up and running now. I was looking at it just before you arrived. I didn't delete it, I was afraid I'd mess it up."

Taking in her "bad little girl" pose, Mason realized he was not as angry as he should have been. He was already finding it difficult to be angry with Tracy.

"It looks like I've been conned," he said, accepting the situation with good grace.

They sat down together at the computer, and Mason was glad to see that Michelle used Windows Live Mail, the same email provider he did, which would make his work that much easier. He glanced down the folders on the left side of the screen.

Inbox (2)
Drafts
Sent items
Junk email
Deleted items (6)

Clicking on the Inbox, he found both entries were chatty messages to friends, and contained nothing that related to Michelle's Dark Chateau posting. He then opened the Deleted items folder. The first four messages were similarly irrelevant, and Mason's disappointment increased, until the fifth, from a George Haupt appeared on the screen.

Insolent bitch! How dare you give orders? You can demand nothing, you can only beg and crawl like the worthless slut you are. If you want me to punish you, come to me on your knees, tell me exactly what you want me to do, and what you will do for me in return.

"I don't see how Michelle would have responded to something like that," Tracy said.

"She evidently did, though," Mason said, when he brought up the final message. "Look."

Slut! Your appeal to be my slave is not acceptable. Did I not say that you had to beg and crawl? If I am to be your master you must learn the meaning of true debasement. Strip yourself naked, get down on your knees, and then tell me how you will serve me. Remember, I want specifics. If I am to whip you, tell me on what part of your body and with what instrument. Do not anger me again with your generalities.

Tracy shook her head. "I can't believe Michelle is doing this."

"I wouldn't be too alarmed," Mason said. "At this point, it's no more than a game."

"Why aren't copies of her answers in her Sent items?"

"She must have deliberately deleted them," he replied. "They would have gone to her Deleted items folder, but it's empty, so she must have deleted them from there too."

It was a moment before Tracy spoke. "Is there any way we can find him?"

Mason right-clicked on the message and discovered it came from *georgehaupt45@hotmail.com*. "If he isn't using an assumed name, I might be able to. It's not too common a name." He had brought his laptop with him, and entered the name *Haupt, George* into his *PhoneSearch* program. To his dismay, it turned up 710 George Haupts nation-wide.

"There's no time to wade through all that. And I don't know any way to reverse search an email address."

Tracy broke the silence that followed. "Was his name on any of the postings you saw on the darkchateau bulletin board?"

"I don't think so, but I can go back and check."

"How far back can you go?"

"I don't know exactly. Pretty far, I think. At least six months, why?"

"I was thinking that a guy like that probably not only answers messages, but maybe posts some of his own. And if we can find some of them, we might find out more about him."

Mason looked at her with new respect. "Tracy, that is one good suggestion."

She grinned. "I told you I'd be useful."

Mason logged on to the darkchateau bulletin board. Before clicking on "Read Messages" he back-dated the date window by six months.

"One hell of a lot of messages," he noted.

"Well, what else do we have to do?" Tracy moved her chair closer to his, and although he knew it was so she could see better, it still had an unsettling effect. In order to see the screen, he now had to look directly over her cleavage. To call that a distraction was an understatement.

He began tabbing through the messages, from the oldest forward, Tracy watching the screen with him. They had gone through about a hundred messages, when Tracy jabbed her finger at the screen.

"That's him!" It was just a short message, but it was under the name George Haupt.

Are you a submissive female slave seeking a cruel, dominant master? Tell me what you want me to do to you and I will respond.

Scrolling further down the list, they found only one response. It was from a woman.

Hey George,

How about I tell you what I will do to YOU, if I ever get you kneeling at my feet? You sound like a closet masochist to me.

> *Donna*

There was no response from George Haupt, nor were there any more postings from him for the next month.

"Do you suppose Donna put him off?" Tracy asked.

"I don't think people like that are put off easily," Mason said. "He may have gotten some email answers, and is corresponding that way. Remember, that's how Michelle answered him."

They continued to tab through the messages.

"Here he is again." Mason found him this time. It was virtually the same message, and again there was only one response.

Come on, George,

Are you still trying to convince us you want to recruit female slaves? Why not admit that you are dying to feel my black boots on the back of your neck as I beat the shit out of you with my riding crop?

"Donna again, "Tracy remarked. "She's really after him."

"It's called a flame war," Mason replied. "A fight in cyberspace."

"A pretty one-sided fight. He's not hitting back."

"But she's embarrassing him in front of everyone who reads the board."

Again they ran down the message board, and again it was about a month before George Haupt reappeared. The message was the same, and once more it was followed by Donna's taunting.

George, George, George,

When are you going to admit to yourself that you don't want to OWN a slave, you want to BE one?

"It looks like our friend has finally had enough," Mason said, indicating the screen. George Haupt had finally responded.

You Pig! You are fortunate that you can hide behind the safety of your computer. I know what you are. You yearn for the yoke, but fear and hate those who would place it upon you. You are not worthy to be my slave. You are not worthy of my whip, or to lick my boots.

It was only a day before that drew an answer from Donna.

Well, Georgie, Porgie, what a nice response! Finally got under your skin, didn't I? Now, you know you're really not angry, and that I'm

not afraid of you, don't you? I know you want to grovel at my feet.
Why don't you come visit me, Georgie? I live in Tucson. Would
you like my phone number? Where do YOU live, Georgie?

When, after a week, that brought no response, Donna rang
in again.

Are you afraid to tell me where you live, Georgie? Afraid that I'll
come to see you and give you the whipping of your life, which is
what you've wanted all along?

The next day she had her answer.

BITCH! I ENCOURAGE YOUR VISIT. MY GARAGE IS FULL
OF IMPLEMENTS OF WELCOME THAT WILL MAKE YOU
SCREAM IN AGONY. I AM EAGER TO HEAR THAT. IT WILL
BE MUSIC TO MY EARS. I LIVE IN SEATTLE. IF YOU WANT
MY ADDRESS, YOU MUST BEG FOR IT, NAKED, ON YOUR
KNEES, IN FRONT OF EVERYONE ON THIS BOARD.

"We've got him!" Mason quickly logged on to PhoneSearch,
but his elation vanished when it found no phone number for a
George Haupt in Seattle.

"What does it mean?" Tracy asked.

"Either he lied, or he has an unlisted number, or he has a cell
phone and gave up his land line service."

Tracy rose. "I think we have a road atlas around somewhere."
She left the room and returned shortly with a Rand McNally Road
Atlas already opened to Washington State.

"Try Bellevue," she said, reading off one of the communities
that made up the Greater Seattle area. He did.

"Nothing," he said.

"How about Federal Way?"

"Nothing."

She took him through the towns along Interstates 5 and 405, all without result. When she moved a little east of 405, to Redmond, PhoneSearch showed a George P. Haupt, and gave his address.

"It's got to be him," Mason said, his spirits rising again. "It's the only George Haupt in the whole area."

"What now?" asked Tracy. She was as excited as he was.

"I think he has to be gotten to right away. If he has Michelle, there's no time to play games on the Internet. I'd better get a ticket on the first flight to Seattle."

"You mean two tickets."

"Tracy, I have to do this alone. It could be extremely dangerous. This man might have abducted your sister, or—"

"Or worse," she interrupted. "Why will it be safer if you go alone? It seems to me just the opposite is true. And two heads are better than one, we just proved that. I was the one who suggested we look for him in the old postings."

"I would have thought of it, eventually, if you hadn't."

"Sure you would."

His statement was lame, and he knew it. It was one of the reasons he gave in.

Mason booked two seats on Hawaiian Airlines 3 P.M. flight to Seattle, and then headed home to pack, promising to pick Tracy up on the way to the airport. Even though he only had a few hours, Mason swung off the highway at Sunset Beach, stopping at the house where he had spoken to Kevin Medeiros. He found

Medeiros lounging in a battered wicker chair on the porch. The young man stared as Mason came up the stairs, but made no move.

"How's it going, Kevin?" Mason said, clapping him solidly on the right arm, just above the elbow. Medeiros showed only the slightest grimace, which, Mason recognized, could have been caused, not from pain, but from dislike of the unexpected gesture of comraderie.

"What's up, man?" Medeiros' voice was anything but welcoming.

"I had a little run in last night with someone up near Sacred Falls. You wouldn't know anything about that, would you?

Medeiros spit on the floor of the porch, then ground the spittle into the wood with his thonged slipper. "Why would I? I was with my chick las' night."

"I thought Michelle was your chick."

A self-satisfied smirk appeared on the young man's face. "Hey, man, a dude like me got more than one chick. That's what it's all about, right?"

Mason ignored the remark. "Funny. I could have sworn it was you."

"No way, man." Medeiros leaned back in the chair, his eyes continuing to lock on to Mason's.

Mason reached into his pocket and withdrew a notebook and a ball point pen. "Do me a favor, Kevin. Write this for me," and he recited, "Bring ten thousand dollars in used tens and twenties to Sacred Falls Park tonight."

Medeiros made no attempt to take the proffered pen and pad. "What for?"

"Let's just say it would make me feel a lot better."

"Go fuck yourself."

"That would be hard to do, Kevin. But it wouldn't be hard for Frederick Iverson to convince the police to bring you in for questioning in regard to an attempt to extort money from him."

"I don't know nothin' about no attempt to extort money from nobody."

"Then you have nothing to worry about. Just write it out like I asked you to, and it's all over."

Medeiros continued to stare at Mason for a long moment before he spoke. "So, lemme see. Somebody wrote old man Iverson a note asking for money, and you want me to copy it to check my handwriting?"

"Something like that."

Medeiros sneered. "Sounds like bullshit to me." But he took the pen and pad. "Tell me again what I gotta write." Mason did. When he was finished, Medeiros handed the note book back. He had written, "Bring ten thousand dollars in used tens and twentys to Sacred Falls Park tonight." The flowing script bore no resemblance to the crude block letters of the actual note.

After reading it, Mason appeared to be putting the pad back in his pocket, when he suddenly lunged forward, seized Medeiros' right arm, and dragged him out of the chair. Medeiros screamed in pain. It was all the additional proof Mason needed. Twisting the arm behind his back, Mason slammed Medeiros into the wall.

Medeiros cried out again. "Goddammit, look, man— "

"No, *you* look, *man!* You try a stunt like this again and I'll see that you go to prison until you're sixty." He gave the arm a further wrench. "From now on, you stay away from the Iversons. *Far away.*" Giving the arm a final twist, which caused a final scream, he shoved Medeiros head first back toward the chair. Under his weight, the chair tipped over backwards, sending Medeiros sprawling to the floor. With a last glance at the hate-filled eyes looking up at him, Mason turned and left.

Later, as they were driving to the airport, Mason related the incident to Tracy.

"But, how did you know for sure it was him?" she asked.

"It seems Kevin has a small problem with spelling."

10

THE FLIGHT TO Seattle was uneventful, and they landed at Seatac Airport at 10:20 P.M. Mason had made reservations at the Red Lion Inn, just outside the airport, which would give them an early start the next day. While making the hotel reservations, Tracy overheard him asking for two single rooms.

"There's no reason why we can't share a room," she told him. "They all have two double beds, and we're not teenagers."

Not exactly sure what that meant, Mason shrugged. "You decide. It's your father's money."

"Let's share. I hate staying in a hotel room by myself."

By the time they picked up their rental car and drove to the Red Lion, it was close to midnight. As Tracy had predicted, the room had two large beds. Tracy dropped her bag on one, and Mason opened the mini bar.

"Want something?"

"Is there gin and tonic water?"

"There is. Or should that be, there are?"

"I don't know, I'm too tired to figure it out. Plane rides exhaust me, especially in steerage."

"Well, it's your—"

"I know, it's my father's money. On the way home we'll spend a little more of it and go first class. He won't mind." She removed a small toilet kit from her luggage and sat down on the edge of the bed. "I guess the evening's festivities are going to be a drink, shower, and bed."

The drinks went down quickly, and Mason nodded toward the bathroom.

"Ladies first."

While he waited, Mason caught the late news on CNN. When she came out of the bathroom, Tracy was wearing a flimsy shortie nightgown. It was all he could do to keep his eyes from following her as she crossed his line of vision in front of the TV screen. When he returned from his turn in the bathroom, she was already in bed, her back turned toward him, her long, blonde hair spilling out over the sheets. The TV was still on, as was the lamp between the beds. He watched the news a while longer, and then turned them both off.

They ate the next morning at the hotel restaurant, wanting to get an early start. But they were both hungry, and they ordered large breakfasts. Tracy was wearing a sweater, which she had put on as soon as she got up.

"I'm still cold," she told him. "It was freezing in that room last night. I really don't like air conditioning. How did *you* sleep?"

"About as well as could be expected with a beautiful woman in the next bed."

"Why didn't you come over?" He didn't meet her glance, but in his peripheral vision he could see the mischief in her eyes.

"And have you scream for help?"

"I wouldn't have. What I would have done was snuggle up to get warm."

Even though he was pretty sure she was teasing him, Mason was still left with the feeling that he might have missed an opportunity.

They drove north on Interstate 405, turning east on Washington State 520 until it ended. Asking directions at a service station, Mason then took Highway 202 east, turning at an Albertson's supermarket, and drove until he reached Fernland Estates. It was an upscale neighborhood of large, attractive homes, on nicely landscaped, acre-size lots.

"Not quite what I expected," Mason said, as they passed circular driveways, all with three-car garages.

"Me either," Tracy agreed.

The house they sought looked much like the rest, except for a slight run-down appearance. Mason drove past the house, pulling over about a block away.

"I think I should go alone," he said. "We don't know what to expect. If I'm not back in 30 minutes, you can go to the police."

"I have a better idea," she replied. "We both go up to the house. Whoever answer's the door will see two of us. If the situation seems threatening, I'll say I'll wait in the car. That way they'll *know* there's someone who can go for the police."

"Tracy, if it turns out bad, they can come after you in the car, if they know you're there."

"They won't know where the car is. I'll wait until you go inside before I leave. And we can park the car so that I can watch the house, to see who comes out."

"And what are you going to do it turns out to be some thug, run him down?"

"You can count on it."

Mason sighed, but did not argue further. He parked as Tracy has suggested, and they walked back to the house. Mason rang the bell.

A short, middle aged woman answered the door. Although pleasant featured, her eyes and her expression projected a permanent weariness.

"I'm sorry to bother you," Mason began, "but does George Haupt live here?"

"Yes." The woman volunteered nothing more and remained standing in the doorway, staring at them, her expression unchanged.

"Uh, may we see him?"

"What do you want to see him about?"

Mason decided to be direct. "I think he may be able to help us. We're looking for a young woman who has disappeared."

The woman sighed slightly. "I don't see how he could help you with something like that."

Tracy spoke up then, her voice containing just the right friendly, but pleading tone. "It's my sister who's missing. Could we talk to him anyway, just for a moment, please?"

"Well…yes, but…" Shaking her head slightly, the woman stepped back allowing him to enter. "He's down there, in his study." She pointed to a room at the end of a hallway. Tracy and Mason exchanged glances, in an unspoken understanding that she would remain with him.

They paused at the entry to the room, and Mason knocked lightly on the open door. It was a bright room with windows on three sides. A dark-haired man at a computer turned to face them. As he did so, they could see that he was in a wheelchair.

"Mr. Haupt?" Mason asked. The man stared at them through thick glasses without speaking.

"I'm sorry to disturb you. My name is Mason Grant, and this is Tracy Iverson. We're here because we thought—because we *had* thought—that you might have some information about a missing person." The man in the wheel chair still made no effort to say anything or gave any indication that he had heard him. Mason now saw that his head lolled slightly to one side. Embarrassed, he thought about apologizing and leaving, but this had to be the man who had corresponded with Michelle. He decided to press on.

"It has to do with some postings you made on the Dark Chateau bulletin board," he continued.

A slight, lopsided smile appeared on the man's face, and he raised his right hand, motioning them to come closer.

"I can't talk very loud," the man said when they reached him. His head nodded down toward the chair, as if inviting Mason to look. "I have MS."

"I'm sorry, we had no way of knowing."

Haupt waved his right hand. "Oh, it's okay. Actually, I'm lucky in some ways. I work for Microsoft, and they let me do everything from here. Without the job, things would really be much worse."

Mason pushed aside his growing doubt that the trip would produce anything useful. "Mr. Haupt, there is a chance that you can help us. Do you recall answering a posting from a Michelle Iverson about three weeks ago?"

Again, there was the slight, lopsided smile. "Oh, yes, Michelle. Very nice. A very erotic posting. She's missing, you say?"

"Yes, and we think it might have to do with her posting." Mason nodded toward Tracy. "Tracy is Michelle's sister, and we're trying to trace her. I believe Michelle emailed something to you."

Haupt turned his chair back to the computer. Mason saw that he was extremely quick with his right hand, faster than some typists would be with two. A message appeared on the screen.

Master,

I am sorry if I offended you. I am on my knees now and I humbly beg your forgiveness. Please punish me severely for angering you. Whip me without mercy until I crawl and beg to lick your boots. I am waiting for your judgement.

Your Slave, Michelle.

"That's a great reply," Haupt said. "Very erotic. She's very good."

Mason cleared his throat and avoided looking at Tracy. "You posted another note to her after that."

Haupt nodded. "But she never replied." Sadness had crept into his voice. "I even emailed her when I got no answer on the board. But…nothing."

"Do you have a copy of what you sent her?" Tracy asked. When Haupt nodded, she continued. "May we see it?"

Again Haupt's right hand raced over the keys and another message appeared.

ARROGANT SLAVE!

YOU DARE TO IGNORE MY DEMANDS? REPLY AT ONCE. THE MOST EXQUISITE TORTURES AWAIT YOU FOR YOUR INSOLENCE.

"I had to maintain the dominant pose, you know," Haupt explained, "even though I really wanted her to reply. But I couldn't come out and *ask* her to. It would have been a reversal of roles, which could have completely turned her off."

"Did you receive any other messages that might refer to her, even indirectly?" Mason asked.

"No. Laura Evans replied to her, though, and she and I got a nice exchange going, all on email. She is very good, too. Do you want to see that?"

Mason declined. "Mr. Haupt, have you ever seen or received anything from someone who suggested getting together, meeting somewhere?"

"Getting together?" Haupt glanced down at his legs. "I haven't been able to walk for three years. My left arm has been useless since March…"

"I'm sorry. I didn't mean to suggest—"

Haupt waved his hand. "It's all right. But how did you find me, anyway?"

Mason explained.

Haupt nodded. "Oh, yes, Donna." He smiled again. "We became great friends, you know. We write to each other often. I never gave her my address, though…obviously." He glanced down again at his legs, and then waved his hand dismissively.

Mason and Tracy sensed the interview was over, thanked him, and made their goodbyes.

"I hope you find your sister," Haupt said, as they were leaving. "I'd like to hear from her again. She has a real feel for this."

They were able to book a late flight that same afternoon on United, which, with a quick change in San Francisco, would bring them back to Honolulu at 9:30 that evening.

"It means steerage again, though," Mason said, as he held the phone open. "There's nothing in first class until tomorrow."

Tracy sighed. "Go ahead and take it. At least it will get us home."

Once they were settled on the plane, drinks in front of them, Tracy looked over at Mason. "What now, Mason?"

Mason stared at his drink. "I want to go back to Michelle's computer," he said finally. "I think I have an idea."

11

SHE WAS TIED spread-eagled to the bed, arms and legs stretched wide, face up. The whip lashed mercilessly at her naked body.

"Harder!" she cried.

He complied, striking the next blows with all his strength. She moaned, arching her back and forcing her taut breasts into the path of the whip. As it slashed repeatedly across her body she thrashed so desperately that it seemed she would be torn apart. Finally, he stopped and began to lay down the whip. But she continued to writhe, her face flushed and contorted, her eyes glazed with an insane passion.

"More! More!" she screamed.

Martin Sandler woke abruptly, his body bathed in sweat, his breath coming in gasps. A rock-hard erection pounded between his legs. He shook his head, but the woman from his dream still lingered in his consciousness. He groaned. The dreams were becoming more frequent, more vivid. He leaned back against the headboard and masturbated, but there was no pleasure in it, only release. He longed to go back to the dream world, and to *her*.

He looked at his watch. Four A.M. It was too early to get up, but he knew there would be no more sleep that night. He rose, and made his way to the kitchen. The clutter of dishes and pans in the sink and on the counters offended him. He was normally neat, and kept the house that way. But this current experience had depressed him. After all the erotic invitation in her message, she had refused to meet with him. Was she just another despicable teaser? The decision to take her involuntarily was based on the possibility that, once involved, she would fulfill the promise of her words. But it didn't seem to be working out that way, and he was having serious reservations about continuing.

He made a cup of tea, then walked through the living room to the open wooden porch, noting with distaste that this room was just as disorderly as the kitchen. He would correct all that today. Personal disappointment was no excuse for living like a pig.

It was not only this latest disappointment, it was the dreams. They were sapping his energy as if he was actually living them. At times they were so real that the line between dream and reality blurred. But so far, he was able to distinguish between the two. He hoped he would never reach the point where he could not do so. He knew what that would mean.

He turned his eyes toward the small cabin that stood at the far end of the property. Its outlines were just visible in the predawn light. He felt the stirrings of another erection coming on. Should he…? The urge grew stronger, but he turned his mind away and looked at his watch. He would have to wait a few more hours.

12

WHEN MASON ARRIVED at the Iverson home that morning, he was carrying a CD.

"I'm going to try something," he told Tracy. "There's a way to restore files even after they've been deleted, but I'll have to leave Windows and work from the C:/ prompt. Not all files can be restored, and I have no idea which can and which can't, or why. I've never done it, but I'm going to see what I can do with Michelle's files."

"There's fresh coffee in the kitchen," Tracy said. "Why don't you pour yourself a cup while I bring up Michelle's files?"

When Mason entered Michelle's room with his coffee, Tracy had her email program up and running. He once more went through all the messages they had seen previously. Satisfied that he had missed nothing, he closed the program, exited the Windows environment, and went to the C:/ prompt. He then placed his CD into the combined CD/DVD drive. Following instructions appearing on the screen, he navigated to Michelle's Windows Live Mail, then to her Deleted items folder. A message appeared almost immediately on the screen.

Delete Sentry Control has detected 31 files. Of these, 23 can be recovered. Do you wish to see a list of these files? [Yes/No].

When Mason clicked *Yes*, the list of 23 recoverable files appeared, each identified by a long number meaningless to him, and each showing the date it was deleted. Also, following each file number was the entry

This file can be 100% undeleted. Undelete? (Y/N)?

Noting that three of the messages were dated after Michelle had made her Dark Chateau posting, Mason decided to open only those, beginning with the earliest one sent. He clicked on Y, and a message appeared.

FROM: an06755@anon.penetr.fi.

SUBJECT: Stations of Pain.

Michelle - In my basement I have a soundproof room where I have established the Six Stations of Pain. They are designed to test the endurance of the most determined subjects. No one has yet been able to endure all six stations. Are you willing to try?

The Painmaster

"God," Tracy exclaimed, "I guess I really didn't know Michelle if she responded to something like that."

"This an anonymous posting," Mason said, not happy. He undeleted the next message. It was from the same originator.

*Michelle - I admire you for agreeing to try the Six Stations of Pain.
Your response was brave and spirited, but I shall break that spirit,
I assure you. I must be certain of your resolve. Tell me why you
think you can suffer what no one has been able to stand before.*

    The Painmaster

"There it is," Mason said. "She did answer."

Tracy shook her head, saying nothing, but staring intently at
the screen.

Mason undeleted the final message. It was much longer than
the other two, and it, too, was from "The Painmaster."

*Welcome, Michelle, to Station Number One – The Horse. What
you see in front of you appears to be a simple sawhorse, about
waist high. Above it a rope hangs from a beam, and there are two
short ropes resembling stirrups on each side, which are fastened to
the floor. You note that the top of the sawhorse comes to a rounded
point, much narrower than normal. You will not be permitted to
remain clothed during the ordeal, and I order you to strip. Then I
command you to straddle the horse. As soon as you do so, you can
feel the pain between your legs as the weight of your body bears
down on the horse. To alleviate it, you try to push yourself up
from the horse with your hands, but I immediately order you to
raise your arms over your head. When you do so, I tie your wrists
together in the rope suspended from the ceiling, and tie your feet
to the floor on each side of the horse. The pain in your groin grows
worse, and you are able to relieve it only by pulling yourself up
by the rope. But the strain of doing so soon causes your arms to
ache, and you must lower your body down onto the horse, where
THAT pain begins again. After it becomes too severe, you again*

pull yourself up by your aching arms, and you keep repeating the process. By now your body shines with sweat, and your breath is coming in labored gasps. Your cramped arms finally give out and you must surrender to the horse, which now sends waves of agony through your body. Despite your resolve to be brave, you begin to moan. I decide you are ready.

From the wall I remove the whip. It is a three-thonged martinet, each strand made of strong, supple leather. As the first lash rakes your back your body arches under this new torture. Your sudden movement causes unbelievable pain in your groin, and you cry out. Again the lash falls, and again you cry out. I now circle your body slowly, whipping you everywhere. No part of your body is safe. Your shoulders, back, loins, abdomen, and breasts all feel its vicious sting. You are screaming now, and rivers of perspiration pour down your body. You beg for mercy and plead with me to stop. Finally, I grant your request. I untie you and you collapse on the hard, cold floor, still moaning. I command you to lick my boots. You do so. I demand that you thank me, and you do. You will have a week to recuperate before we continue.

Are you strong enough for Station Number Two?

For a moment after they finished reading, neither of them spoke. The scene depicted was shocking and frightening in itself, but the imperious arrogance behind the words suggested a personality that was both deranged and dangerous. Tracy was the first to speak, her eyes still glued to the screen.

"My God, who *is* this guy?"

Mason said nothing.

"She's in terrible trouble, isn't she?"

"Maybe not," he said. "This is probably all fantasy. It's hard to believe that this guy has a sound proof torture chamber in his basement."

"And if he does?"

"They could be just acting out their fantasies, without anyone getting hurt."

"You don't really believe that."

"I don't rule it out."

"Well, if this is just a game, why is she missing? Why haven't we heard from her?"

Mason had no answer for that.

She turned her attention back to the computer. "And how are we going to find him if he posts anonymously?"

He had no answer for that, either.

Tracy finally broke away from the computer screen, and turned her eyes toward him. "What do we do now, Mason?"

He said the only thing he could.

"We need help."

13

"HOW MUCH ARE you charging my father?" Tracy asked, looking up from her plate. She had chosen *opakapaka,* grilled over *kiawe* wood, while Mason had opted for *opa* sautéed with capers, tarragon leaves, and Madeira.

"Nothing," Mason replied,

"Nothing?" That's rather hard to believe."

The Cannon Club, a former military officers club on the slopes of Diamond Head, had one of the best views in town. Their table, beside a large picture window, looked out over the lights of night-time Waikiki.

"Your father will pay all expenses, but I receive no money," Mason replied, pouring her another glass of chardonnay. "But he has agreed to make a donation to a charity of my choice in lieu of any payment to me."

She went back to her dinner. "I still don't see why you're making all this effort if you get nothing out of it for yourself."

"Would it sound insincere if I said that I don't need the money and I like to help people?"

She thought about that. "I'm not sure," she said finally. "I don't know you well enough."

"It also gives me something useful to do, and it keeps the black moods at bay."

"Now *that* I can relate to," she said with a smile.

They ate in silence for the next few minutes, enjoying the changing colors of the sky over the slowly darkening sea. Mason had invited a friend, Ray Hatcher, to join them at dinner. Hatcher, a professor at the University of Hawaii, held a doctorate in psychology, and had also become one of the university's leading experts on the Internet. Mason had met him when he was researching a disappearance case at the university library, where Hatcher had shown him how he could greatly expand his search and shorten his research time by using the resources of the Internet. Unable to join them for dinner due to a previous commitment, Hatcher was stopping by for a drink afterward. He had agreed to help in the search for Michelle.

"What charity?"

Mason looked up, his train of thought broken, momentarily not understanding her question. "Oh, it's a scholarship," he said, trying to avoid saying any more. But Tracy would not let it go.

"What kind of scholarship?"

As briefly as possible, relating only the basic details, he told her about the fund he had established in memory of Kathryn and Merrie. To turn the issue aside, he asked her about herself. He learned that she was in the final year of her doctorate in English, which surprised him.

"Why should that surprise you?" she asked, accurately sensing his reaction.

"Uh, I guess I just don't think of you as the doctorate type."

"Sounds like a sexist remark to me," she said, but her voice was playful, rather than irritated. "Are you referring to my body or my mind?"

"Your body, I guess," he ventured lamely. "I don't know much about your mind yet."

"So the body doesn't go with a doctorate, is that it?"

"I guess I haven't met many graduate students." He was becoming more flustered. "And you don't fit my picture of the typical doctoral candidate." He found his position awkward, and tried to deflect the conversation. "What are you going to do when you complete your studies?"

She grinned, and he knew she was aware of his tactic, but she went along. "The only thing English docs do is become professors—I know, I don't look like the professorial type either, right?"

She had read his mind again. "You certainly look like the type I'd like to have had in college," he said, unaware of the double *entendre* until she laughed.

The busboy began clearing their plates, and Mason felt it was a good time to change the subject. Now that they were working together, he felt comfortable asking a question that he might not have earlier.

"Tell me, was Michelle really pierced everywhere?"

"I really don't know what *everywhere* means, but I'm sure she wasn't. Her ears weren't even pierced. Her nose certainly wasn't, nor her lips or tongue, and her breasts weren't pierced anywhere— we both often sunbathe topless at the pool."

"I noticed."

"I would hope so," she said, staring directly into his eyes, then smiling broadly at his discomfort. She took a sip of her wine, then continued. "And that's one thing that makes me think she didn't really intend to follow through with anything. After all, it would come out right away that she hadn't been telling the truth—about being pierced, that is."

Before Mason could say anything more, he noticed Ray Hatcher making his way toward their table. He rose, and introduced him to Tracy. Hatcher was tall and thin, almost painfully so. His slouched shoulders, large nose, and gold-rimmed glasses made it seem as though he were constantly bending over to examine something. But behind this studious appearance, green eyes glinted mischievously.

"Well, Mason, I see the beauty of your dinner companions has improved significantly," Hatcher said, easing into one of the vacant chairs at the table.

"That's not quite the compliment he's making it out to be," Mason said to Tracy, smiling as he rose to shake Hatcher's hand. "My dinner companions for a long time have been other men."

"Nevertheless, I like a man who has imagination in complimenting a lady," Tracy said, rewarding Hatcher with one of her most dazzling smiles.

"And I like a lady who appreciates it," Hatcher replied, making a slight bow of the head in her direction.

"Would you two like me to leave?" Mason asked.

"No, better not," Hatcher replied. "I'm a happily married man. I need someone here to protect me from myself with the lovely Miss Iverson."

"Why is it that all the nicest men are married?" Tracy sighed.

"Thanks a lot," Mason said.

Tracy smiled and laid her hand over his. "But you *were* married, Mason, so that includes you, too." He was acutely aware of the sensation caused by her contact.

"This is very nice," Hatcher said, "and there's nothing I'd like better than exchanging nice things about each other all night. But, unfortunately, I have an early class tomorrow."

"On Saturday?" Mason asked.

"It's an Internet familiarization class for the Community Outreach Program. It's mostly folks who work during the week. It seems I do more teaching about the Internet these days than I do in my primary field."

Hatcher ordered a rusty nail, and Mason ordered a Louis Salignac cognac. Tracy opted to finish the wine. Mason spent the next half hour explaining the situation to Hatcher. He showed him printouts of the messages between Michelle and *The Painmaster*, which Hatcher read and passed back to Mason. He then turned to Tracy.

"I find it unusual that your sister would have used her real name on her darkchateau posting. Most people would use an alias or an email name, especially on a bulletin board like that."

Tracy shrugged. "As far as I know, Michelle is pretty naive. She probably never even thought of using an alias."

"Where do you plan to go from here?" Hatcher asked Mason.

"I'm really stumped," Mason admitted. "I'm hoping you can give us some ideas. One thing I really don't understand is why there isn't more of an exchange of messages between this *Painmaster* creep and Michelle after 'Station Number One.' There at least should be something from him proposing a meeting somewhere."

"I can think of two possibilities," Hatcher replied. "The first is that she probably deleted them and they are not undeletable." Hatcher stopped speaking suddenly, his face taking on an amused expression. "*Not undeletable*," he repeated, shaking his head. "Did I say that? Lord, what computerization is doing to the language! Anyway, for whatever reason, the undelete program can't recover them. I suggest you run Undelete for every appropriate directory in Michelle's computer. You may turn up something."

He stopped talking for a long moment, staring at his hands, which were clasped together at the fingertips, in a modified prayer position.

"You know, there are two sides to this problem, the technical side, and the psychological side."

Mason reached over and laid his hand on Hatcher's shoulder. "That's why I called you, Ray. You've got both bases covered."

Hatcher allowed himself a half smile. "Perhaps. Let's hope there isn't a third base to worry about. But for now, on the technical side, we have the problem of using Internet resources to find *The Painmaster*, and through him, Michelle. On the psychological side, we may have an even more difficult problem, understanding everything that's going on with Michelle and *The Painmaster*, both on the surface and below. And understanding that may be equally, or more important, if we are going to find her." Hatcher paused and took a sip of his rusty nail. "I'm going to have to bone up on my craft—my real one. I've been doing too much Internet stuff lately. But in the meantime, we've got to get moving. Are you both free to go to work on this starting tomorrow?"

Tracy and Mason nodded.

"I'm going to propose a two-fold program to try to find *The Painmaster*, Hatcher continued. "Obviously, time is critical. We must rescue Michelle as quickly as possible, assuming she needs rescuing." Hatcher glanced quickly at Tracy, but her expression didn't change. "Now, unfortunately, we are not going to be able to trace *The Painmaster* through his messages. I'm familiar with that particular anonymous code, and it goes through a double blind to a server in Finland."

"Finland?" Tracy exclaimed.

Hatcher nodded. "And without going into complicated technical details, I'll just say that this server will not respond to requests or demands to reveal the names of its users, and is immune to threats, penalties, and that sort of thing. So, the only thing we can do is study *The Painmaster's* three messages, especially 'Station Number One,' and try to find out if he has posted similar things on similar web sites."

"But that could take forever," Tracy said, "and meanwhile, God knows what's happening to Michelle."

"That's where the second part of our plan comes in," Hatcher said. "In the meantime, we bait him. We need to post one or more messages similar to Michelle's, hoping he'll respond."

"And what if he does?" Mason asked.

"I'm not sure yet. We might have to play it by ear. But once we establish contact, I'm thinking along the lines of seeing if we can lure him out into the open somehow."

Tracy saw where he was going. "You mean by offering a meeting with someone like Michelle."

Hatcher nodded. "Something like that."

"And who do you have in mind for that role?" Mason asked. "If it's Tracy, forget it." He was surprised at the conviction in his voice.

"Don't speak for me, Mason. If it will help find Michelle, I want to do it."

"Tracy, your father already has one daughter missing. Do you want to try for two?"

"I think we're getting ahead of ourselves," Hatcher interrupted, trying to smooth things over. "We haven't even found him yet, so let's concentrate on trying to do that. We need to compose a message."

Tracy's expression showed frustration. "It sure would help if we knew more about him. Jay, you're the psychologist, what makes this guy tick?"

"Well, abnormal psychology was not my main field of study, but from looking at Station Number One, I think it's safe to say that our man is a classic sadist, that is, someone who gets sexual pleasure from inflicting pain, or watching it being inflicted, on another person. Many people aren't aware of this sexual aspect, and think of any act of cruelty as sadistic. But without the sexual kick, there is no sadism. That's what makes sadists potentially dangerous, even though most of them repress or sublimate their desires, or act them out in relatively harmless fantasies."

"Do you think that's what happening in Michelle's case?" Tracy asked.

"At this point, there's no way to tell. Judging from Station Number One we're dealing with a seriously twisted individual."

"God, Jay, what warps a person like that?" Tracy asked. "What makes him get pleasure by inflicting pain?"

Hatcher shrugged. "We're not really sure. Some theories say it's genetic, some claim it's a learned trait, and some say it's a combination of both. We have the same problem trying to understand homosexuality, or even heterosexual conduct for that matter." He leaned back in his chair and studied his rusty nail without drinking from it. "The first person to report and discuss the aberration was Kraft-Ebing, a professor of psychiatry at the University of Vienna. I think he's also the one who coined the term sadism to describe it, named for, as you probably know, the Marquis de Sade, a French nobleman of the late 1700s who took sexual cruelty to extremes in his personal life and his writings.

"Kraft-Ebing wrote a book called *Psychopathia Sexualis* in the late 1800s, which discussed in detail cases of sadomasochism among his patients. He wrote the book for the medical profession, not the general public, and to avoid titillating non-professional readers, he wrote the "juiciest" parts in Latin. That made several generations of students wish we had paid more attention to Latin in high school," he added, smiling wryly at the memory.

"There are at least three types of sadists," Hatcher continued.

"The first gets sexual pleasure by inflicting pain on another individual and is not concerned with the desires of his victim. There is another type who gets his kicks from hurting someone who wants the pain inflicted. Then there is a third type who enjoys inflicting pain only on an unwilling subject. In all three cases, the victim is usually of the opposite sex, but not always."

"In other words, the second type wants a masochist for a partner, but the third type doesn't," Mason said.

"Exactly, and the first type doesn't care either way. Now, I think it's safe to assume that our friend *The Painmaster* wants a willing partner. It's evident by the fact that he responded to Michelle's masochistic posting, and even more so by his scenario in Station Number One. Look at the way he carefully outlines everything in minute detail, and then invites her to participate, asking her if she is strong enough and brave enough. Her willingness to subject herself to the ritual is a major turn-on for him. With that in mind, I think we can come up with something that may whet his appetite."

Hatcher paused to order another rusty nail, and Mason asked for another cognac. Tracy continued to sip the last of the wine.

"We'll need something on the style of Michelle's posting, Tracy said. "We know that got his attention."

"Not too much like her, though," Mason cautioned. "We don't want to make him suspicious."

Hatcher did most of the writing composing the false message, Mason and Tracy making a few suggestions. They decided to create a fictional female sender, Sara Miller, and to use Mason's email address. Mason then created an additional mail box in his email account under that name. When they finished, they looked the posting over one last time.

Are you a man looking for a woman who understands his need
to make her feel his power through pain and suffering? I am
blond, 126 pounds, and my friends say I have a beautiful face and
figure. Although I am only 26, all my life I have yearned to submit
myself to such a man and to endure whatever torments he desires
to inflict on me. Whips, clips, whatever you wish, I will gladly
endure, but only if you are the right person. No masqueraders,
pen pals, or gays, please. I am sincere, and if you are also, you
will possess a woman whose sole purpose in life will be to give
you pleasure by being your pain slave. Please send me email only,
I don't want our relationship displayed publicly on this board.
Sincerely, Sara

Mason nodded his head with satisfaction. "If I didn't know you, Ray, I'd be convinced you wrote these things all the time."

Hatcher smiled. "What makes you think you know me, and who says I don't?"

"I'm a little worried about the 'No masqueraders, pen pals, or gays, please' part," Tracy said. "It sounds too...like she's well acquainted with these bulletin boards."

"We want her to be," Hatcher replied. "We want to convince *The Painmaster* that she knows her way around, is serious, and is not playing games."

"Now that we've composed it, where are we going to post it?" Mason asked.

"The Dark Chateau site, first of all. We know he reads it. Then we'll post on the S&M, bondage, and similar bulletin boards in the Newsgroups. The "alternate life styles" boards. Things like "alt. sex.spanking," and "alt.sex.bondage." Also, we'll need to search out other sites similar to *darkchateau* and post there. Then the second phase of the job begins, looking for other messages that he may have posted. It will involve scanning hundreds of messages on dozens of sites, trying to identify his style."

Mason stirred uneasily. "It all sounds like a hell of a big job,"

"It is," Hatcher agreed, "but if we each take a piece of it, it will help. I'll take care of posting our bait message, and I'll also roam through the appropriate chat rooms to see if I can spot him there. Mason, why don't you take the Newsgroups? There is a lot of stuff to read and sort through, but it's well organized and relatively easy to find."

"Fine with me."

"To start off," Hatcher continued, "you'll be looking for topics beginning with 'alt,' like those I just mentioned. Pay particular attention to anything with the term "personals" in it. *Alt.sex. personals*, for example, is similar to newspaper classified ads, only here, people in the sexual underground are trying to get together. Our *Painmaster* might be one of them."

"Tracy, you have the more challenging assignment, using Google and the other search engines to ferret out other SM sites, similar to *darkchateau*, to see if he's out there somewhere."

"Thanks for the vote of confidence, Ray," Mason said, while Tracy grinned at him.

"Women are better at that sort of thing than we are, Mason. They are more curious, and they have more patience."

"We're smarter, too." Tracy added.

"You know what you're looking for, Tracy, sites with kinky sex bulletin boards. And don't forget to check *darkchateau* frequently, since that's where we found him. Search with key words, such as bondage, domination, S&M, B&D, and others you'll probably find as you go along. And keep your eye peeled for the same alternate lifestyle subjects Mason is looking for. As for my role, I'll search the appropriate chat rooms, looking for the same things you are. I have some experience with them, and can get in and out quickly, if they're not productive.

"Now, getting back to our baiting message," he continued, addressing them both, "when the answers start to come in, you're going to have to watch for *The Painmaster's* style. He won't necessarily use that title again. He may not even use the same scenario. But his signature should be all over the message. Study his three messages, especially Station Number One. Read it several times, until you have a feel for his style, his voice. Once you have that, you should be able to pick him out."

"I have a request," Tracy said, avoiding Mason's eyes. "I don't want my father to know about the "bait" message right now. I'll tell him when I think the time is right."

"He wouldn't approve of using you like this, would he?" Mason said, a statement more than a question.

"I don't know if he would or not, but we can't take the risk. This is the only chance we have of finding Michelle."

"Or losing another daughter."

"Mason—"

"Okay, okay, we'll keep him in the dark, for now." Mason turned to Hatcher, who nodded his acceptance. Tracy's relief was obvious.

"It's settled, then," Hatcher said, finishing his drink. "We'll get together on Sunday to see what we've got, although I don't think you'll find very much by then."

As Hatcher rose to leave, Tracy stopped him. "Jay, you said earlier that you could think of two reasons why we can't find any more messages on Michelle's computer, but you only gave us one. What is the other one?"

Hatcher looked from one of them to the other before he spoke. "The other possibility is that we can't find any messages because there are no messages to find. Michelle could have been repulsed by Station Number One and not responded at all." He let that sink in.

"That would mean that her posting on the bulletin board has nothing at all to do with her disappearance," Tracy said.

"And if that's the case," Mason added, "we have absolutely nothing to go on."

14

AT 10:40 THE next morning, Mason pushed back from the computer, his eyes glazed and his brain numb. He found it hard to believe that he had been at it only three hours. He already felt that he knew more about the nether world of sadomasochism than he wanted to, and his new knowledge depressed him. To his disappointment, there had been no answer to their baiting message. Too early, he supposed.

He had spent the first part of the morning collecting the names of "alt.lifetyles" Newsgroups, and had started reading through some of them, concentrating on the "alt.sex" category. There alone, almost two hundred separate bulletin boards confronted him, ranging across the alphabet from *alt.sex.aliens*, and *alt.sex.bestiality*, to *alt. sex.yoga*, and *alt.sex.zebras*. Zebras? Jesus!

He had soon found himself deep into revolting acts, described in disgusting language. Gratefully, he soon found that by concentrating on bulletin boards with SM themes, he was able to circumvent the bestiality and the sodomy, and focus on the merely cruel and unusual. But he had failed to find any sign of *The Painmaster* and his senses were close to overload. Idly, he wondered how Tracy was coming along. He thought about calling her, but decided against it. What would he say? He certainly didn't want to talk about what they were doing or compare notes. He had more than enough of his own garbage to process, and besides, they would be discussing this stuff with Hatcher tomorrow. That would be soon enough. He logged off the Internet, but left his computer on. He needed a break. He changed to his jogging shorts and headed for the door.

His normal route took him westward from his house, along the water, toward Sunset Beach. As usual, he ran close to the water line, where the sand was relatively hard packed, and the tracks of his bare feet were quickly obliterated by the waves which ran up on the beach as he passed. As he rounded a small point of land, two pit bulls suddenly charged down from a sand dune, heading straight toward him. Leaping up at his running figure, they licked his extended hand, and assumed their accustomed place, trotting along at his side.

When he reached Velzyland, there were no surfers in the water, and no windsurfers at Backyards. The winter swells were still at least two months away, and the winds were down. As he neared Sunset Beach, he saw large numbers of sunbathers lounging in the sand. He turned around, rather than jog through the crowd. The dogs turned with him, following along until they peeled off at the ramshackle beach shack where their owner exercised squatter's rights, unmolested by the city or the state.

Once more in front of his house, Mason plunged into the ocean, lolling in the gentle surf, rather than swimming, allowing the water to cool him down. For lunch, he made himself a Greek salad, going heavy on the feta cheese and kalamata olives. He splurged by complementing it with half a bottle of ice cold retsina. He washed the dishes, put things away, and admitted to himself that he was stalling. Resignedly, he returned to his study and the computer.

It was going to be a lousy afternoon.

15

MARTIN SANDLER CHECKED his watch, impatient for the hours to move by. The new approach was a major improvement, but it had its disadvantages. Like now, being forced to wait when his loins ached to begin. For years he had satisfied himself with books and magazines, and his dreams of *her*. Then came the VCR, followed by CDs and DVDs, opening a new world of sensory experience. But none of it was real, of course. It was a substitute for reality. He knew he needed a real woman, someone to share his life, someone like *her*.

He selected the women he dated carefully, modeling them on *her* as much as possible. As soon as he felt the time was appropriate, he would bring up the issue of the relationship between pleasure and pain. He did so cautiously, feeling his way, always sensitive to the reaction of the woman concerned. Some women's reactions were immediately and strongly negative. These women he never dated again. Others expressed interest or curiosity, and he would lead these women into a more intimate discussion, and where they permitted, mild experimentation. Things would usually end there, except for a few who treated it as a game, a form of foreplay, tolerating moderate pain. He would try to lead these women into more serious avenues, but his success rate was disappointing.

Either the woman would cut off the relationship when it became too painful, or he would abandon the attempt. Not one of them ever approached *her*. And through all the years of loneliness and disappointment that was what kept him going, kept him believing that he would eventually find someone like *her*.

With the advent of on line services and the Internet, suddenly there was a quantum leap in his opportunity. The bulletin boards did the work he could never do, concentrating hundreds of likely prospects, and making them easy to contact. For the first time he was able to choose from dozens of women who advertised themselves on explicit S&M bulletin boards, virtually asking for his "services." At first it was a heady, overwhelming experience, seemingly the answer to his dreams. But, slowly, he found that it was not all that it seemed. Many of the women who posted messages were willing, even eager to accept pain and torture, as long as it was done in cyberspace, and they were protected by the anonymity and distance of the internet. It was a game they could play with impunity, fantasizing, and probably masturbating over the scenarios he devised and sent them, always playing the part of the submissive slave, and begging him for harsher treatment. But when he suggested they meet to turn their fantasies into reality, he lost them. Once again, he began to feel that he would never be able to turn his dreams into reality.

He checked his watch again. Time seemed to be almost standing still. With no other options open to him, Sandler went to his computer. He saw it almost at once. The new posting was provocative, erotic, and full of promise. An erection pounded against his thigh. Normally, he would have responded at once. But the situation was different now. Now he would have to wait. He read it again, feeling the thrill course through his groin, then, reluctantly, he passed the message by.

He left the computer and made himself a cup of tea, which he took out to the porch. He sipped slowly, and gazed out at the darkened city sprawled far below. He knew that he did not really want to hurt women, or rather, he did not want to do them harm. That was why the dream world was so seductive. In the dream world, he could whip them, burn them, use pincers on their breasts, and when it was over they would have no wounds, no marks on their bodies. His dream women could endure unlimited agony without fainting and without begging him to stop. And they were always willing to let him start again. So far, the real world had not been like that. Not since *her*.

Sighing, he turned his attention to the view, which had to be one of the most expansive anywhere. He could see at least twenty miles, and even in the dark he was able to pick out the airport, a good twelve miles away. And beyond the airport, perhaps another eight miles, against the lightening sky he could clearly make out the silhouette of Diamond Head.

16

WHEN MASON JOINED Tracy on the Iverson lanai the next morning, Hatcher had not yet arrived. This time there were bloody Marys instead of coffee.

"I thought since it was Sunday," she explained. "I hope you like them."

"My favorite drink," Mason announced.

"You said Friday night that cognac was your favorite drink."

"That too," he said.

"How many favorite drinks do you have?"

"About a dozen."

They both laughed. Mason was surprised at how being with her relieved the tension of the previous day. It felt good, and so did the drink. He'd better sip it slowly.

Tracy told him that running "Undelete" against Michelle's directories had failed to turn up anything useful. "How did your day go yesterday?" she then asked him.

"It was long, boring, and unproductive. In the afternoon, I got seven replies to 'Sara,' but none of them were from *The Painmaster*. And I must have read hundreds of Newsgroup postings, but I didn't find him."

"I didn't find him either, but I'm learning a lot."

Mason looked at her over his glass.

"I'm finding out lots of things," she went on. "I have invitations to join the Eulenspiegel Society in New York, and the Janus Society in San Francisco. They're both S&M social organizations. And there's a slave auction coming up in London, with a free demonstration of how to brand your slave."

"That's nice."

"And I learned how to make a whip from leather boot laces."

"Uh huh."

"You use either three or nine laces, depending on whether you want a martinet, or a cat o'nine tails, and you make a handle by taping them together at one end with duct tape."

"I see."

"It leaves thin, red welts which begin to fade in about three hours."

"Interesting."

"And if you want to be nasty, you can put in overhand knots every four inches."

"Well, I'm glad you're improving your education."

"And then there's a Shadow Lane convention coming up in Palm Springs," she continued, enjoying his discomfort. "Activities include a spanking social, a clearest handprint contest, a most attractive spanking outfit contest, an OTK endurance competition, and Spanking Dice, a game where the roll of the dice determines how many swats the players receive."

"Now there's something we don't want to miss," he said, deciding to play her game. "How about we sign up for the OTK endurance contest?"

"Okay by me," she said. "How do we decide who bends over?"

"Well…uh…."

She had seized the initiative again. "I found a lot of information about piercing, and, remembering your question the other night, I read some of it. It wasn't very helpful for our situation, but you wouldn't believe the places where people pierce themselves. They even talk about labia piercing. Can you imagine?"

"Uh, no, I can't."

He was saved from further discomfort by Hatcher's arrival. After Tracy made him a bloody Mary and refilled Mason's glass, Mason and Tracy summarized the negative results of their efforts the previous day, and Hatcher reported that he also had no luck.

Mason admitted that there were dozens of Newsgroups he hadn't even gotten to yet. "I have a problem just keeping up with what I've found so far," he said. "I logged on to *alt.sex.spanking* yesterday morning, read over a hundred messages, zapped them all, and by the afternoon there were almost fifty new ones."

"That's par for the course," Hatcher answered. "We just have to try to keep up with it."

Tracy said she felt that she had just scratched the surface of the Internet.

Hatcher told them he had not expected anything else. "We just have to continue to march," he said.

"I think we need to send another message to the guy who calls himself Laura Evans," Mason said. "When I emailed him before, we didn't have the message from *The Painmaster*. How about if I send him a copy of Station Number One, and ask him if he's ever seen or received anything like it?"

Hatcher and Tracy both thought it was a good idea.

"I don't know whether to believe that *The Painmaster* didn't answer him, though," Tracy qualified. "After all, 'Laura's' message was very similar to Michelle's."

"Except that Michelle's message was posted first," Mason said. "If *The Painmaster* actually got involved with Michelle, he probably wouldn't want to take on someone else at the same time."

They all had a hand in composing the message to "Laura" that would accompany Station Number One, and Mason sent it, using his own return address. Hatcher could see that Mason and Tracy were in a somber mood as a result of their failure to accomplish anything. In an attempt to cheer up Tracy, he suggested that they drive to the Hale Koa Hotel at Fort DeRussy for its elaborate Sunday champagne brunch.

"We mere civilians can't get into places like that, except as invited guests, so I thought I might as well take advantage of you," he told Mason.

Although an attractive, modern, hotel complex on the beach, Mason was not particularly fond of the Hale Koa. It was in Waikiki, a place he usually avoided, and its clientele included a high percentage of older retirees. Maybe he just didn't want to face his future, at least not yet. But he could think of no reason to decline the suggestion.

Mason had never seen anyone do true justice to a Sunday brunch at a good hotel, but Tracy came close. A heaping plate of sashimi, followed by croissants, crepes, sausage, a small cheese omelet with home fries, capped with a large bowl of fresh fruit—papaya, honeydew, pineapple, and lychee, all washed down with repeated refills of champagne. How did she do it and still keep that marvelous figure?

"The secret is allowing yourself to pig out once a week," she said, noting Mason's expression of awe. She was still reading his mind.

"Wouldn't it be better if we could continue to work together?" Tracy asked, as they were finishing the last of the champagne. "I mean all in the same place, so that we could compare notes and stuff, like we were doing this morning."

"It's a good idea," Hatcher agreed, "but I have to stay connected, and that doesn't mean just my computer. I need access to my printer and even my fax machine, as dated as that sounds. Unfortunately, my work area is too small for all of us, not to mention disturbance from the wife and two little kids in a three-bedroom house. You and Mason could probably team up, though. Tracy, do you have wi fi at home? I know Mason does."

Tracy nodded, and Mason said, "I could bring my laptop down to your place tomorrow morning," he told Tracy.

"That's not such a good idea tomorrow, though. My father is having a big conference at the house. Lots of bankers and businessmen, sitting around the pool with drinks and munchies. It will be pretty noisy and distracting. Why don't I come up to your place this afternoon?"

"You don't mind coming all the way up there?"

"What can it take, all of an hour and a half?"

"A little less, actually, but most town folks think it's the end of the world."

"It's settled then," Hatcher said. "I'll drive up tomorrow morning to compare notes and see where we are. I could use a trip up to the country. Meanwhile, back to the grind."

"I hope we're not going to get too horny reading all that stuff," Tracy said, smiling slyly at Mason.

"I doubt it," Mason replied. "There's no greater turnoff than wading through tons of porn."

"Unless it's good porn," she countered.

17

"MASON, THIS IS beautiful."

Mason felt a surge of pride as Tracy gazed seaward from his deck.

"The house, the setting, everything." She turned to him. "How on earth did you find such a perfect place?"

"I built it." He went on to explain how he had found the lot, and how he and Aaron Laau had worked together on the construction of the house. They went inside, where she insisted on a tour.

"I think it's wonderful the way every room opens up to the ocean," she said. "This bedroom is great, and the bed is so huge. You must do a lot of 'entertaining' there," she added with a sly smile.

"Very little, I'm afraid. At least not for a long time." He didn't tell her that the bed was one of the few items of furniture he had brought to Hawaii from his marriage household.

"And your study. How do get any work done with a view like that?"

"It's hard sometimes," he admitted with a grin. After a quick cup of coffee in the kitchen, they began the afternoon's work. Picking up Mason's laptop, Tracy opted for the lanai, where he would be able to see her whenever he looked up from his computer.

"Two distracting views now," he said. She gave him a playful nudge in the ribs, which he found to be yet another distraction. After about an hour, Tracy began to exhibit signs of attention deficit.

"You know, Mason," she said, turning away from her screen, "some people actually write complete stories using S&M themes, and one guy wrote a whole novel, posting a chapter at a time, calling himself 'The Flogmaster.' Can you believe it? What prompts someone to do something like that? There's no money in it. And look at all the time consumed!" A short time later, she interrupted him again. "Listen to this. The U. S. Senate has banned 'crush videos' from interstate commerce. These are videos in which small animals are tortured and crushed to death by women for the sexual gratification of viewers. Now that is *really* sick."

Finally she moaned and pushed the computer aside. "I 'm completely drained. I can't look at that screen another minute. Does the host have anything liquid that might renew a flagging spirit?"

"The host has just about anything liquid you can think of," Mason replied. "What would you like?"

"A gin and tonic would be wonderful."

He brought the drinks out onto the lanai, where Tracy had collapsed in a lounge chair. They watched the small waves breaking on the reef. Before she finished her drink, Tracy rose and stretched her arms upward, causing her breasts to strain at her dress.

"I need to do something to get the cobwebs out," she said. "A walk, a swim?"

"Whichever you like," he said.

She gazed right and left down the shoreline, and then out at the water. Then, impulsively, she reached out and took his hand. "Let's go skinny dipping," she said.

Mason cleared his throat. "I'm not sure that's a good idea. Fishermen come by, so do beach strollers…"

"We can see them coming in plenty of time to leave the water and get back up here. Let's do it. I love to swim in the nude." Seeing he was not persuaded, she began to pull him toward the shore. "Come on, Mason. Don't be such an old fud. This is such a great place I'm surprised you don't do it all the time."

Reluctantly, he allowed her to lead him toward the water, where he showed her the narrow passage through the reef. It only took her a few seconds to step out of her dress and panties, and plunge in. Mason removed his polo shirt and shorts and followed her. She was right, it felt good to swim nude. He was surprised that the absence of something as small as bathing trunks created such a feeling of freedom. As he started to swim toward Tracy, she began to head out to sea with strong, overhand strokes. It took him a long minute to overtake her. He considered taking her to the outer reef, but the tide was fairly high, and he decided against it. She had stopped anyway, and turned toward him, brushing the long, wet strands of her hair from in front of her eyes.

"Isn't this great?" she shouted, and he had to agree that it was. She dove underwater, and Mason watched her swim toward a small stand of brain coral, about eight feet down. Without a face mask to see through, her body was a soft blur, her hair streaming upward. She turned, waved up at him, and then swam back to the surface. They floated for a while, their bodies close, but not touching, bobbing gently on the incoming swells. He was surprised that he didn't find the situation uncontrollably erotic.

He was able to enjoy the beauty of her nakedness without the pressure of intense desire. He blinked the water from his eyes and wondered, is this how nudists feel?

When they saw several people coming their way on the beach, they made their way to shore. Tracy picked up her things, but made no effort to put them on. Mason got back into his shorts. At the house, he guided her to the outdoor shower, just off the lanai.

"Aaah, it's nice and warm," she said, as the water coursed over her. "How do you manage that?"

Mason pointed to a coiled black hose, connecting the shower to the water pipe. "A fifty foot long solar water heater." Although Tracy was still nude, he did not remove his shorts as he stood under the other shower head. A cool breeze wafted across the lanai, as Tracy finished, and she shivered slightly. "Do you have a robe or something?"

He brought her a towel and a heavy, white terrycloth robe from his bedroom. She smiled at him as she put it on, turning her head sideways and shaking her hair out as she toweled it.

"You're thinking that you never met any woman like me," she said.

"That's exactly what I was thinking. You have an uncanny ability to read my mind."

"Your mind is pretty easy to read right now."

"I'm sure it is," he said, guiding her toward the lanai. "I suppose we should get back to work."

Tracy stared at him for a long moment, and then sighed. "I suppose we should."

As the afternoon wore on, they found several replies to "Sara," but none which appeared to be from *The Painmaster*. Finally, at about six o'clock, Tracy closed the laptop cover.

"I've had it," she declared.

Mason shut down his computer also. "Would you like a drink?"

"I'd rather have something to eat. I'm starving. Are there any nice places up here?"

He took her to Ola, an open air restaurant on Bay View Beach, within the grounds of the Turtle Bay Resort, only a few miles from his house. They began by sharing Kalua pork and goat cheese nachos, with beer. Tracy followed that with a seared beef poke appetizer and a lomi salmon salad. Mason marveled at how she then attacked a large plate of chicken long rice, helped herself to a good part of his five-spiced braised beef short ribs, and then polished it all off with lilikoi cheese cake.

"What happened to pigging out only once a week?" he asked.

"This still counts as only once. It's all part of yesterday."

When he brought her back to the house, she made no move toward her car, but instead, went inside, and then to the lanai. Before joining her, he stopped for a bottle of chardonnay and two glasses. He found her lying in the lounge chair again, and, after taking a sip of her wine, she leaned back and closed her eyes. He poured his own glass and took the chair beside her, content to let her rest quietly. After a time he became aware of her eyes upon him. Glancing over, he met her gaze.

"Mason, are we going to sleep together?"

"I don't know, are we?"

"We probably will eventually, so why dance around about it?"

"I can't argue with such superb logic."

"Do you think I'm callous because I can think about sex with Michelle missing?" Before he could answer, she continued. "It probably doesn't show much, but I'm really kind of miserable. I need something to take my mind off things." Realizing how it sounded, she smiled ruefully. "Not very romantic, is it?"

"Well—"

"But I do feel romantic," she went on. It was the most voluble she had been in his company. "This place, the house, the wine…"

"How about the guy?" Mason said, pretending to be offended. "Does he enter into it at all?"

She smiled. "Of course. You found the place, you built the house. It's you."

"This is probably going to be the first time in history a woman was seduced by a house."

She smiled again and held up her empty glass, but when he went to take it from her, she put her arms around his neck, drawing him down. He had imagined her kiss would be fiery and demanding. Instead, it proved to be sweet and gentle. It was he who ignited the passion between them, responding to her warmth, the vision of her naked in the surf, and the provocative scent of oranges and cinnamon that surrounded her. By the time their lips parted, they were both breathing heavily.

"Where?" she asked, her voice low and throaty.

"Where? Well, I was thinking of some place crazy, like the bedroom."

She shook her head. "Here," she whispered.

"Here?" He glanced at the Spartan outdoor furniture and the tile and redwood flooring. "Wouldn't it be, uh, uncomfortable?"

She pulled his head down toward her lips again. "I bet we can work something out."

18

THEY WOKE WITH first light, and Mason went immediately to his computer.

"We have an answer from 'Laura,'" he announced to Tracy. She came into the den and leaned over his shoulder to read the screen. Despite his interest in the message, he was keenly aware of the closeness of her breasts, and the cinnamon orange scent.

Dear Mason: I received your note along with Station Number One, and I sincerely appreciate you sending this to me. It is really great stuff. Your friend was really lucky to get a response like this— except of course, you say she's missing. Unfortunately, I can't help you with that any more than I could before. I have never received a message as good as you sent, or anything that reads that well or in that style. And I never heard of The Painmaster. Sorry. If you ever get another message like Station Number One, I really would be grateful if you would share it with me. That guy is fantastic!

"And *that* guy is sick," Tracy said. "He doesn't care at all that Michelle is missing. He just wants you to send him more stuff to drool over."

"Maybe he doesn't believe anyone is missing," Mason said. "Maybe he thinks it's a story I made up to try to find *The Painmaster*."

"For the same reason he'd like to find him—to find stuff to add to his S&M library."

"Probably. Anyway, I think he's telling the truth, so that's one more dead end."

Tracy sighed. "Mason, I'm not ready to go back to the *Grand Guignol* just yet." This time Mason did not need coaxing when Tracy suggested skinny dipping again. They didn't swim long. The morning chill was still in the air as they ran to the outdoor shower, and Tracy shivered as the cold water hit her. The sun had not yet reached that side of the house or the coiled black hose.

"I could use your robe," she said, crossing her arms over her breasts.

His gaze drank in her body, glistening with scattered beads of water. "I'll get it, but you won't need it very long," he said.

Later, in the kitchen, she watched as he made a frothy, white concoction in the blender, and poured two glasses, dusting the surface of each with nutmeg.

"Here you are," he said, offering her one, "the best Brandy Alexander in Hawaii. Made with VSOP cognac."

"Is this your favorite drink?"

"Absolutely."

She sipped and continued to watch as he mixed eggs, potatoes, onions, garlic, salt, and pepper in a large frying pan. When it was ready, they helped themselves and moved with their plates to a picnic table on the grass, just below the lanai.

"This is delicious," Tracy raved. "What is it?"

"*Bauern Fruestuck*," Mason said. "I learned to make it in Germany. It translates, 'farmer's breakfast.'"

"I'm impressed," she said between bites. "Brandy Alexanders, bauern whatever—you're very accomplished.

"Why, because I can cook?"

"You also built this house."

"A guy named Aaron Laau had a lot to do with that."

"Even so…" She left the sentence unfinished as she scooped up the last morsel on her plate.

"Hello in there! Permission to come aboard?" Hatcher had arrived. Finding them at the picnic table, he kissed Tracy on the cheek, and headed straight to the coffee pot. The white terry cloth robe and the just-finished breakfast were strong indicators that Tracy had spent the night, but nothing in Hatcher's manner was any different than when they had been together on Sunday. It was one of the things Mason liked about him.

Hatcher refused an offer of food, and they adjourned to the den. Mason showed "Laura's" reply to Hatcher, informing him that he and Tracy had no luck finding *The Painmaster* so far.

"I've had no luck either," Hatcher told them, and smiled as he added, "but I am making a lot of new friends."

"We've gotten lots of replies for 'Sara,'" Tracy said, "including quite a few interesting offers, but nothing seems to be from our friend. There are a few questionable ones you might look at, just to be sure."

After reading them carefully, Hatcher concurred that they were not from *The Painmaster*. They then agreed that all the replies to 'Sara' they had received so far would be erased without reply. Hatcher had brought his laptop, and working together, each searched his own area of responsibility, pausing occasionally to confer about an entry.

They took a break for lunch, and, remembering her performance at last night's dinner, Mason decide to go easy, soup from his stock in the freezer, a small Greek salad, and a cold bottle of retsina. After thawing and heating the soup, he covered the bottoms of three large bowls with tortilla chips, and poured the hot soup over them, adding a dollop of yogurt and several sprigs of cilantro to each.

"This is delicious," Tracy said, savoring a spoonful of the soup, and receiving a confirmation from Hatcher. "What is it?"

"I call it Aztec Sun," Mason replied. "I make it with butternut squash, carrots, yellow onions, and jalapeno peppers, seasoned with lime juice and my special blend of spices."

"Delicious," she repeated, helping herself to a second bowl.

After the meal, they returned to their search. But their quarry continued to elude them. It was late afternoon before they agreed to stop for the day.

"He just doesn't seem to be out there," Tracy sighed.

"Oh, I think he's probably out there," Hatcher replied, "he's just lurking."

"Lurking?"

"It's a bulletin board term. It means he's hovering in the background—surfing, reading, but not posting."

"We should keep in mind that he may not be a he," Mason said. "Let's not forget 'Laura.'"

"I hope we didn't overdo it," Tracy said. "Posting all over the place like we did could make him suspicious, couldn't it?"

"It could," Hatcher agreed, "but it's not likely that he's reading all the sites that we posted to. And we don't really have much choice if we want to find Michelle as soon as possible." Pleading a heavy work schedule, Hatcher suggested they keep in contact by phone, leaving the time of their next meeting open and dependent upon any new results in their search.

After Hatcher left, Mason suggested drinks and an early

supper at Leonardo's, another of the restaurants at the Turtle Bay Resort. They both settled for the catch of the day, accompanied by a crisp soave. Afterward, they walked along the deserted beach, toward Kahuku Point, the surf pounding against the beach-rock along the shore. They made love in a grassy depression, sheltered from the wind by low-growing ironwood trees. As they were walking back, they came upon a pair of very large birds.

"Laysan albatross," said Mason. "They're pretty rare here on Oahu, except during nesting season at Kaena Point. I've never seen one here before." The birds watched as they made their way around them, but did not seem particularly disturbed.

"I had no idea they were so huge," Tracy said. As she took his hand, she turned to him.

"Would you mind if I stayed over again?"

He squeezed her hand. "I'd mind if you didn't."

19

PATROLMAN CHARLES AKANA was about at the end of his night shift when he saw the woman. He watched her wandering aimlessly along the beach, where the morning sun had just broken over the horizon. She was not dressed for jogging, and something about the way she walked told him she was not just another morning stroller. As he approached, she made no effort to look at him.

"Miss? Are you okay?"

She wasn't, he could see that right away. Her dress, which appeared to be fashionable and expensive, was dirty and disheveled. Her hair was unkempt, her face smudged and unclean. But it was her eyes that told him more than anything. Wide and staring, they seemed unable to focus. She reacted to his question as though he wasn't there.

Kahana shook his head. Another druggie. What a goddam shame, a beautiful girl like this, probably even a rich one, judging from the dress. Well, crystal meth didn't care who you were, it destroyed the minds of rich and poor alike.

"Can you tell me your name?" Again, there was no response. He could see that she had no ID. She had no purse, there were no pockets in her dress, and she wore no jewelry.

"Where do you live?" Nothing. Just the vacant stare. Gently, he took her hand and led her to a bench as he pulled out his cell phone and called for an ambulance.

20

THE NEXT MORNING responses to the "Sara" posting were dwindling. After an hour discovering nothing new, Tracy decided to go home.

"Two days in the same clothes is about all I can stand," she announced. "But you're not sending me home on an empty stomach. "What's in your breakfast repertoire?"

Within fifteen minutes they were eating an omelet he had prepared. Finishing it quickly, Tracy looked up from her plate.

"Delicious and different. I can't place the main ingredient."

"Kimchee," he told her.

"Kimchee? I hate kimchee. And with eggs? Yuk!"

"I notice how much you disliked it," he said, eyeing her empty plate.

She had to admit then, that she'd enjoyed it. "Is it a milder brand than most?"

"Not really. I make it myself. Cut up a sink full of Chinese cabbage, sprinkle it with Hawaiian salt and let it sit overnight, then pack it in jars with red pepper, ginger, sugar, green onion, MSG, and white wine. The wine is my own refinement."

Amusement sparkled in her eyes. "And then do you bury it in the ground for six months?"

He laughed. "They do that in Korea to keep it cool. The fridge works fine here. I usually start eating it after about two weeks, but the longer you keep it the better it gets."

"I bet. I can't get over how good you are in the kitchen," she said.

"I don't see why that's so surprising. After all, most of the world's best chefs are men."

"But most of the world's best cooks are women."

Mason was not quite sure what that meant, but he decided not to display his ignorance.

"Did you do the cooking when...before?" Tracy continued.

"No way. Kathryn did all the cooking." He was mildly surprised how easy it was to talk about that now. "I started when I began living alone."

"Do you enjoy it?"

He thought about it. "To some extent. But it's nothing I would mind giving up again."

"Is that a proposal, Mr. Grant?"

"How could it be? I don't know if you can cook."

As he walked her to her car, Mason voiced something that had been troubling him. "It's been over a week since your father asked for my help," he said, "and I don't feel like I've accomplished anything. I can't understand why he isn't more concerned. I'm no closer to finding Michelle than I was when I first walked in your door."

"You can't blame yourself. I don't see how anyone else could have been any more successful."

"The police might have been. I should have insisted he call them."

"He wouldn't have."

He knew she was right.

21

WHEN MARTIN SANDLER returned from work, he fixed a cold supper and then turned his attention to his computer. So Sara Miller had posted on several Newsgroup bulletin boards also. That renewed his interest. Curious, he looked in the phone book, but found no listing. That, of course meant nothing. Cell phones were making huge dents in land line service, plus many women who lived alone chose to have unlisted numbers. Nor could he find a Sara Miller in the city real estate tax records, which merely meant that she did not own real property. Even if Sara Miller was a false name, it didn't necessarily mean that the message behind it wasn't genuine. Many people chose to masquerade in cyberspace, for any number of reasons. Yet, a seed of suspicion sprouted. All these postings. Desperation—or design? A cry in the wilderness, or a cunning plan? He would find out later. And he was now free to respond.

After posting the message, he let his mind wander back to his first experience, his introduction to what had become his life's obsession. He had been a young Marine, just back from completing boot camp at Parris Island. He had taken his high school girl friend to the movies, and afterward he took her home. Her parents, she said, would not be back until late. They kissed, and while they were in a close embrace he felt her hands trying to unbuckle the heavy black belt that was part of his uniform. He was pleasantly surprised, because they had never gone beyond kissing before.

He leaned back so she could take it off. Instead of displaying any interest in removing the rest of his clothing, she concentrated her attention on the belt.

"This is real heavy, isn't it," she said, her eyes very wide. "I bet it would hurt like the dickens to be hit with it, wouldn't it?"

He nodded, puzzled at the direction of the conversation. He had other things on his mind. He hadn't even seen a girl in over two months.

"Do you think it would make me cry?"

"What?"

"If you hit me with it. Do you think it would make me cry?"

"I wouldn't do that."

"Would you do it if I asked you to?"

Now he was really baffled. How naive he had been then. "Why would you want me to do that?"

"To see if it would make me cry."

She finally coaxed him into using the belt on her, primarily because he saw it as a way to get her to take off her clothes. But she only agreed to go as far as her bra and panties. They had to stay on. At first, he hit her gently, not wanting to hurt her. But at her urging, he hit harder. Then, as something deep inside him took over, he struck really hard. When he finally stopped, his chest heaving and trousers bulging, her question had been answered.

It had made her cry.

22

MASON HAD JUST finished a late lunch and turned on his computer when his phone rang. It was Tracy.

"Michelle has been found," she said, her voice sounding strained. The phrase sounded ominous, and Mason braced himself for the worst.

"Is she okay?"

"No. She's at Queen's, in the Kekela Ward. That's where I'm calling from."

"I'll be right there."

Quickly, he exited his email program and shut off the computer. In his hurry to leave, he did not see the message from *The Initiator*.

When Mason arrived at the hospital, he was told that Tracy and her father were with Michelle, but only family members were permitted to see her. He waited over an hour before the two Iversons finally appeared. They were both pale and drawn. Frederick Iverson excused himself, explaining that he had to make a report at the police station.

"The police found her wandering in a daze at Kahe Point Beach Park," Tracy told Mason.

Mason frowned. "How did she get out there?"

"We don't know. It was only a few hours ago that she was able to tell them who she was, and that whoever had abducted her had driven her to the park and released her. She's been going through periods of depression and hysteria. Sometimes she's lucid, sometimes catatonic. She's sedated now."

Tracy's eyes were wider than he had ever seen them. "She's been hurt, Mason. She's been hurt badly."

"Is she going to be all right?"

"I don't know. Her physical injuries are painful, but they'll heal. The doctors are more concerned with her mental state. I'm coming back later this afternoon. Meanwhile, I'm going home to get some of her things together to bring here." She promised to call him that evening.

Mason called Hatcher to let him know the latest development, and also talked to General Talbot, whom he had been keeping informed of their activities. He spent the rest of the day with personal business that he needed to do in town, returning home after seven. There was no message on his answering machine from Tracy. When he called her, there was no answer, and her machine was off. He decided against calling her again. She had probably turned her machine off to avoid all the calls from relatives, friends, and perhaps even the media.

With everything that was going on, he didn't even think of turning on his computer.

23

MASON WAS AWAKENED the next morning by a call from Tracy. She asked if he could meet with her father at the Iverson home as soon as possible. He agreed. He was pretty sure what that meant. Now that Michelle was back, there was no longer any need for his services. Father and daughter were waiting for him in the large living room where he had his first discussion with Frederick Iverson.

"How is Michelle?" Mason asked, as soon as he was seated.

"There hasn't been much change," Tracy told him. "When we try to ask her what happened, she gets hysterical. Thinking about it seems to bring it on. The doctors say we're just going to have to wait."

"Tracy has told me what you have been doing," Frederick Iverson said. Mason detected what seemed to be more anger at Tracy's failure to keep him informed about their activities than grief or concern about Michelle's condition. "Have you heard anything since yesterday?"

Mason said no, but admitted he hadn't checked his email in over twenty-four hours.

"Well, check on it, Mason," Tracy interjected, "and keep checking." It was Tracy who had spoken, before her father had a chance.

"I'm not sure I understand," Mason said. "You want to go on looking for this guy?"

Iverson appeared uncertain. "Well—"

"You're damned right we do," Tracy said, interrupting her father. "We want you to find him."

"Your father hired me to find Michelle. She's been found."

"Now we want you to find whoever did this to her."

Iverson appeared uncomfortable. "Tracy, don't you think—"

Tracy whirled on her father. "Dad, we've been all through this. He can't be allowed to get away with this. We've got to find him."

"Tracy," Mason said quietly, "that's a job for the police."

Iverson reacted immediately. "No! Absolutely not," he almost shouted. "I will not have the police involved in this." Seeing that Mason was about to argue, he went on. "What do you think the police would do about it?"

"Your daughter was abducted, she's been injured—"

"And she posted a letter to the world inviting someone do that to her. There has been no crime. And even if the Prosecutor's Office agreed to bring it to trial, there would never be a conviction. A good lawyer would convince a jury it was consensual. Rough sex, or whatever it is called."

Mason had to agree, but he was uncomfortable with what he was hearing. "Mr. Iverson, what is it you propose to do?"

"I told you, Mason," Tracy interrupted again, "I...we want you to find him."

"And if I do?"

Iverson turned his eyes away, staring across the room.

"We'll take it from there," Tracy said.

Mason was having trouble believing what he heard. "That's vigilanteism," he said finally. "I can't be part of that."

"Mason, you don't know what he's done," Tracy pleaded. "I want you to look at her."

"There's no need for that."

"Yes there is. I want you to see what he did to her. Maybe then you'll understand."

"Tracy, I don't want to see it."

"Well then I'll describe it to you. Remember when I told you that she wasn't pierced anywhere? Well, she is now—through her nipples. Her body is covered with—"

"I don't want to hear about it, either," he interrupted. To prevent Tracy from continuing, he turned to Iverson. "What did they say when you went to the police station?"

Iverson seemed distracted. It was a moment before he answered. "They wanted to know if I knew what happened. Why Michelle was found where she was. Did she have a history of drug abuse, alcohol addition, disappearances, things like that. They are not aware of her injuries. They did not perform a physical examination. They brought her right to the hospital."

"Surely the hospital will report the injuries."

"Not necessarily."

Mason let the implications of the statement pass. He did not want to be diverted by a discussion of another Iverson scheme. "Mr. Iverson, I can only advise you again to tell everything to the police. They are equipped to handle this, to find someone—"

"For God's sake Mason, do you live on the moon?" It was Tracy again, her voice rising. "Don't you read the newspapers? Just the other day a man shot a gas station attendant. He had just been released from prison after serving five years—for murder! Last week a burglar almost beat an old woman do death in her own apartment. He had twelve previous arrests—"

"What does that mean, that we're all supposed to take justice into our own hands? Justice belongs to the courts."

"But that's the problem. They don't provide it."

"Tracy, it's not justice you and your father want, it's vengeance."

"I don't care what you call it. I want him to pay for what he's done to Michelle. Doesn't it bother you that he is still out there, free to do something like this again?"

"Yes," he admitted, "it bothers me."

"Then help us. Please, Mason."

It was a long, painful moment before he spoke. "I can't Tracy. I'm sorry." He hated seeing the hurt in her eyes.

"I'm sorry, too," she said. But then her expression hardened. "We'll find him, though, with or without your help. You can count on it."

Returning home was something that always lifted Mason's spirits, but not this evening. He could still see Tracy's face, as she watched him leave her house. He didn't feel like eating or drinking. He made himself a cup of cappuccino, but it tasted like mud.

He was surprised how quickly Tracy had become so important to him. The house didn't seem the same without her, and the days ahead loomed bleak and without promise. He went for a swim, hoping to wash away the mood. Returning from the water, he felt better, until he started gathering laundry and picked up his white terry cloth robe. It still had a faint aroma of cinnamon and orange. He almost didn't put it in the washing machine.

Sitting in the study, deciding how to organize the rest of his evening, he thought about his email. Pointless now, but he decided to look at it anyway. As soon as he opened his Inbox, he saw it.

FROM: an47881@anon.penet.fi.(The Initiator)

TO: Sara Miller

I am the one you seek, but are you the one who will fulfill my needs, or will you fail the ultimate test? See a portion of what awaits you, and then tell me if you are worthy.

I take you down to my specially constructed basement, where two others, Marla and Carl, are present. They are to witness your initiation into my household. I lead you to a long wooden table with rollers on each end. Attached to the rollers are thick ropes with loops at the ends. I demand that you remove your clothing, and order you to lie on your back on the table, your arms over your head, and I attach the loops to your arms and legs. I move to the head of the table and Carl moves to the foot. You can see now that the rollers have long handles. We begin turning the handles, the ropes tighten, and your body stretches. You can feel the pain start in your arms and legs. When your body is taught and arched on the table, we stop. Marla comes over and stares at you. She has never seen a female form stretched as taut as yours, and she is fascinated. She glides her hands slowly across your body. She then reaches into a bag and removes what looks like a large clothespin, but you can see that it is much stronger. She attaches it to the soft flesh of your waist, just above the hip. The pain is immediate. Slowly, she attaches others, each sending a new pain coursing through your body. You close your eyes and bite your lip. You do not want to cry out before this woman. You do not want to beg her for mercy. But when she puts one on the nipple of each breast, you cannot stifle a moan. She has no more clamps, but she stands there, watching you in your torment. Your body now shines with sweat, and you toss your head from side to side in silent agony. Now I am ready for you.

I approach you with an instrument in my hand. It resembles a pliers, except that the jaws are blunt and the handles are longer. Your eyes widen and you tremble as you see it. I reassure you, telling you that although it will cause intense pain, it will not draw blood or leave permanent marks. You are to be my slave, my property. I do not wish to damage you. With a sweep of my arm I knock off all the clamps on your body. You cry out as they tear away from your flesh. I then place the pincers against your waist and squeeze the handles. Your body arches against the pain, and despite your resolve, you moan. I continue, moving to new places as you writhe desperately on the table. You have vowed to be brave, but this is too much to endure. When I apply the pincers to the tender flesh on the inside of your thighs, you scream for the first time. Soon you are begging me to stop. Marla comes forward and strokes your drenched forehead. "She can stand a few more minutes," she says. But you scream that you can't stand another second, that you are going mad with pain, and that you will do anything if I will only stop. I ignore Marla and grant your wish. I release you from your bonds and help you from the table. You cannot stand, and collapse on the floor, panting and gasping. I remind you of your statement that you would do anything to stop the torture, and I tell you what you must do for me while the others watch. When you are finished, I help you to your feet. You have passed your initiation. It is but the beginning.

Are you the one?

Mason leaned back in his chair, staring at the screen. It was him. There wasn't the slightest doubt.

Now what?

24

"AFRAID...SO AFRAID..."

Tracy leaned over her sister's bed, listening carefully to her words. Michelle tossed her head fitfully on the pillow, her forehead sweaty, eyes rolling. Her soft moans were broken by disconnected words. "...find me...can...he knows." Her head rose suddenly from the pillow, her eyes wide with panic. "He knows how to find me." Her voice was nearly a scream.

Tracy gently pushed her back toward the pillow. "No one will find you. You're going away for a while to a place where you'll be safe."

The words seemed to calm Michelle slightly, and because she had uttered a complete sentence for the first time, Tracy decided to try to question her. She took her hand, hoping that the contact would reassure her.

"Michelle, can you remember what happened? Can you remember anything at all?"

At first it seemed as if Michelle had not heard, but then she began to speak, her eyes closed, her words coming in fragmented phrases. "In the garage... got out of my car... awful-smelling rag over my mouth..." Her eyes opened, and her breath began to come in short gasps. "Tied to a chair... something over my eyes...

138

couldn't see..." Michelle was rapidly losing her composure and sinking once again into a state of delirium. She lapsed back into moaning. "...don't understand...why ...why?..."

Tracy realized that further conversation was useless, perhaps even dangerous. "Michelle, try to rest, try to get some sleep."

Surprisingly, Michelle obeyed. She leaned back against the upraised bed and closed her eyes. Warm sunshine from the window bathed her face. Tracy lowered the bed until it was level, and stayed at the bedside until Michelle's breathing became regular. As she was about to leave, her father entered the room.

"How is she?" Iverson asked.

"She's asleep. It's best not to disturb her now. She doesn't understand anything that's happened to her." Moving away from the bed and speaking quietly, she informed him of Michelle's utterances. "I can understand how he knew where we live," she said. "Michelle used her real name in her posting, and we're all in the phone book. But he was inside our garage. How could that be possible?"

Her father paused a moment. "The only thing I can think of is that he could have been waiting in the trees on the side of the driveway when Michelle drove up, then ducked quickly into the garage before the door came all the way down."

"But how would he know that neither you nor I would be home?"

Iverson shook his head. "He could not have. Perhaps he just took the chance. It does not sound logical, I know."

"It certainly doesn't. And he would have needed a car close by to take Michelle away. There's nowhere to park on the road, and he certainly wasn't in the driveway, or Michelle would have noticed."

"Well...he might have parked at that small turnoff at the

hiking trail. It is on our side of the road, and he could have dragged her through the trees. It is not that far, and Michelle probably would not have noticed a car parked there in the dark." His voice took on a grim tone. "I'll call the security company today and have them go over everything. We cannot afford to be this vulnerable."

Tracy made clear by her manner that she was not satisfied with any of her father's reasoning, but decided to say nothing further. For a few moments they both stared at Michelle's sleeping figure.

"Do you still think we should send her to the California sanitarium?" Iverson asked finally.

"Definitely. She's still very shook up, and mostly hysterical. And she needs to get away from here to a place where she'll feel safe."

Iverson nodded, and with a final glance at his sleeping daughter, he left.

Her father had scarcely left the room when Michelle began moaning again. "...someone else...not alone...someone else..."

"Michelle, what are you trying to say?"

"Someone else...was there."

"Someone else was where?"

"*There.*" Michelle's tone left little doubt where she meant.

"Someone beside the man who abducted you?" Michelle nodded. "But how could you tell? You were blindfolded."

For the first time Michelle looked directly at her sister, and her composure seemed almost normal. When she spoke it was with a tone of certainty.

"I knew someone else was there."

25

THE STARBOARD OUTRIGGER bent suddenly, the reel chattering as the line ran out. Mason grabbed the pole and adjusted the drag. General Talbot cut back on the throttle, slowing the *Lovely Lady* almost to a halt. It was all Mason could do to maneuver himself into the fighting chair, with the line zinging out rapidly. Seeing the situation, the general began backing the boat down on the unseen fish.

"It's diving," Mason shouted. The boat quickly overtook the line, which now pointed almost straight down from the stern, the pole bent sharply. Talbot put the engines in neutral.

"It's probably an *ahi*," he called out. "A billfish or a *mahi* would have jumped by now."

Mason checked the spool. "There's a lot of line out. I'm going to start reeling him in." Bracing his feet firmly against the deck, he began pumping the rod up and down, gradually taking up line. Suddenly the line sang again.

"He's making another run," Mason yelled, and the general put the boat in gear and once more began backing down on the racing fish. Mason continued to pump the rod, bringing in line even as the fish was taking it out. Soon, however, the fish began to tire from the uneven contest, and Mason was able to bring in more line than the fish could run with. When it sighted the boat, the fish made one last run, but its energy was spent. Minutes later, a struggling blue-green shape appeared below the boat, standing out above the deep blue depths.

"He's too big for the net," Mason said. "We're going to have to gaff him."

The general eased the gearshift into neutral, left the helm, and grabbed the gaff. As he reached Mason's side, a silvery torpedo appeared, and began to circle the struggling fish.

"Get him before that shark does," Mason warned, holding the rod high, line taut. The general lowered the pole into the water, positioned the big hook near the *ahi's* gills, and jerked upward, setting the gaff deep, just behind the head. Talbot pulled with all his strength, and the fish flapped aboard. Quickly, he struck it between the eyes with a miniature baseball bat, and the fish ceased to struggle. Mason then removed the hook, and they placed the fish in the large cooler of crushed ice.

"He's just about taking up all the space," Mason observed. "What do you think, forty pounds?"

"Closer to fifty," Talbot said. "We might as well head in. It's a two-hour run back to the Ala Wai."

Mason reeled in the other outrigger, secured both poles, and Talbot pushed the throttle forward. With a throaty rumble, the twin 75 diesels sent the Bertram on a course for Diamond Head.

Back at the slip, with the *Lovely Lady* hosed down, tied up, and connected to shore power, Talbot began fileting part of the big fish, while Mason made the dipping sauce and the martinis.

"You always get the hard part," Mason said, watching as the general carefully separated large sections of red meat from the bones.

"To each what he does best," Talbot replied. "Just make sure you don't screw up the martinis."

Mason grinned. The general was fanatic about how his martinis were made. He brought two empty glasses up from below. "Do you think I'm doing the right thing, refusing to help the Iversons?"

"Do *you*?" asked Talbot, never taking his eyes from his task.

"I don't see that I have much choice." Mason began rubbing the insides and rims of both glasses with a crushed garlic clove. "But you're the one who asked me to work on this. How well do you know the Iversons?"

"I've never met either daughter, and I don't really know Frederick Iverson very well. He sits on the symphony board with me, and he's a member of my lodge, which counts for something. We've met socially a few times." Talbot placed several large slabs of red meat in plastic bags and dropped them into the cooler. He flipped the fish over and began to work on the opposite side.

Mason had told Talbot that it was now Tracy who was determined to push the continued search for her sister's abductor, with her father appearing less enthusiastic.

"What do you make of the father's turnabout?" the general asked.

"I'm not sure it *is* a turnabout," Mason answered, tracing the rim of each glass lightly with a small slice of lime. "I think he's still trying to keep the whole thing under the rug. The longer it goes on, the more chance there is of exposure. But he's evidently going along with his daughter, reluctant as he may be."

"What do you think they intend to do if they find the person responsible?"

"I don't know what they *can* do. But then, I don't know what

Iverson's "resources" are. But I do know that they are both strong-willed, and angry, especially Tracy. They both want revenge."

Talbot remained absorbed with the fish as he spoke. "Vengeance is mine, sayeth the Lord."

Mason grunted. "The Lord, and Mickey Spillane." He went below and opened a can of powdered *wasabe.* He reconstituted a spoonful with a small amount of water and let the paste steep under cover of a glass jar. "How do you feel about vigilante justice?" he called up to Talbot.

The general was just about finished filleting the *ahi.* "If you had asked me that question ten years ago, I would have said it's a conflict in terms."

"Like military intelligence?" They both chuckled over the old, Vietnam era joke.

"Now, I'm not sure how I feel," Talbot continued. "There is so much violence these days, and the system seems overwhelmed…" Talbot wrapped all but one of the last fillets and slipped the *ahi* carcass overboard. A school of small fish followed its path downward, nibbling furiously. He selected a new knife, and began cutting the remaining fillet into small, thin squares. "How are those martinis coming?"

"On the way," Mason called back. He divided the *wasabe* paste between two small bowls, and mixed in different amounts of *shoyu,* a teaspoon for Talbot, a tablespoon for himself. He removed a half-dozen ice cubes from a small cooler, placed them in a shiny metal cocktail shaker, and carefully added three shots of gin, two shots of vodka, and one shot of vermouth. The general insisted the mixture be stirred for exactly thirty seconds, but Mason refused to time the procedure. When he judged they were cold enough, he poured the drinks into the garlic-lined glasses, and squeezed a twist of lime, rind only, over each, until he could see a small film of zest on the surface. He then brought the drinks and the sauce topside.

Seated in the *Lovely Lady's* cockpit, they raised their glasses.

"My favorite drink," Talbot said.

"And mine," Mason echoed. The whole thing was a ritual, but one they enjoyed. For both men, ritual had been an important part of their lives. They savored their drinks, taking in the ranks of boats and masts beneath the spires of Waikiki to the east, and the sunset-streaked sky to the west.

Talbot speared a slice of the raw fish and dipped it into the sauce. "Damn, that's good," he announced, his eyes watering.

Mason did the same, dipping it into his less mouth-blistering bowl. "What should I do about the new message?" It was the question they both knew he would eventually ask, and the reason for this meeting with Talbot.

"That's a tough call," the general said. "A damned if you do, and damned if you don't situation. If you let the Iversons know about it, you'll feel responsible for anything that might happen."

"And if I don't let them know about it...well, I don't feel good about that, either."

Talbot held up his empty glass. "Perhaps another one of these to cogitate over?"

Mason went below and made a new batch. Another thing the general believed fervently was that martinis must be made fresh each time. No leftovers, which would either be diluted by ice, or warmed by its absence. Mason brought the refilled glasses topside.

"I half expect Tracy to call me," Mason said, "even though we're not on very good terms. She's certainly going to want to know if there have been any more email replies to the 'Sara Grant' posting. It's the only possibility they have of finding *The*

Painmaster, unless Michelle is able to tell them anything. The problem is, even if I don't want to let them have the message, I won't be able to lie to her."

Talbot squinted at him across his glass. "Is there an emotional involvement, Mason? The only reason I ask, is that it might affect your decision."

Mason nodded, and he saw a tightening around the general's mouth. "You don't approve."

"I never do. Keep the hanky panky away from the flagpole."

"I don't run anything up the flagpole any more."

"Doesn't matter. Mixing business with monkey business will get you in trouble every time."

They watched in silence as the sun began to set. "Green flash," Talbot said, as the sun disappeared into the sea. Then he looked directly at Mason. "Serious?"

"Uh, what?" Mason wasn't following him.

"The girl, you dolt. Is it serious?"

"It could be."

Talbot thought that over. "You want my advice?"

Mason smiled. "That's why I'm here."

"All right. If she calls, you tell her about the message, but you say that before you give it to her you want to know exactly what they intend to do with it, what they have in mind."

"Suppose she tells me it's no longer any of my business?"

"Then stonewall her. She'll have to come around. It's the only lead they have."

"Okay, but suppose what she tells me is something I don't like, or is illegal as hell?"

"Then let her have the message and walk away from the whole thing."

"But won't I—"

"No, you won't be responsible, they will. Look, you both, along with Hatcher, composed the 'bait' message that prompted the response. You were working together when you posted it. Tracy has a right to see the answer. So if you can't live with her plans, like I said, let her have the message, and walk away. But walk away from the whole thing—and that includes her."

26

THERE WERE NO phone messages on his machine when Mason returned from the fishing trip with General Talbot. He had decided to accept the general's suggestion and let Tracy know about the message from *The Initiator* He dialed her number, and got her answering machine. He left a message saying that he had some important information for her, and asking her to call. He could have simply sent the message to her as an email attachment, but he did not. Analyzing why, he admitted to himself that he wanted to hear her voice again. He was too tired to turn on his computer, and decided to let whatever email he might have wait until morning. He no longer had any reason to have an interest in it.

The day had turned rainy and windy, but he was determined to jog anyway. He soon regretted his decision. The trades had shifted to northwesterlies, and a stiff wind blew in from the sea, bringing rain and salt spray directly into his face. Even the dogs failed to appear. About half way into his usual course, he cut it short and turned around. With the wind at his back, the return was not quite as miserable.

Showered and shaved, a cup of espresso at his side, the sunset breaking through the rain off his lanai, he changed his mind, and decided to read his email. There were only three messages, two of them personal, but he was surprised to see that the last was from "Laura."

Hi,

Well, you are probably surprised to hear from me again, and I did not expect to write to you again either. But the other day I was looking over some of my old stuff, and I found something from a lady [at least I think she's a lady] who claimed that she was mistreated by someone she met on darkchateau.com I've attached a copy so you can read it for yourself. I had forgotten about it, but then I got to thinking about the situation with your friend, and I remembered and thought, well, maybe there could be a connection. So, I wrote her a short note explaining things, and sent her a copy of Station Number One. Boy, what a reaction! She came back at me right away, swearing it was the same guy and begging me not to do anything that would put him on to her again [even though it's perfectly clear there is no way I could]. Anyway I thought you would like to know, and maybe try to contact her. I don't know if she will even talk to you, but it may be worth a try.

Good luck,

Barry, aka Laura.

Reading the message, Mason felt a surge of excitement, followed almost at once by a sense of letdown. Now that he had taken himself off the case, here was the first clue which might help find *The_Painmaster*. The irony of it did not escape him. He turned to the attachment.

URL: http://www.darkchateau.com/bb

FROM: bobbieking@aloha.net

I want to warn all readers of this bulletin board of the horrible, humiliating, and life threatening experience I had recently because I was stupid enough to become involved here.

I have never been turned on by the idea of receiving pain, but after browsing here for several weeks I began to wonder if I was missing something. I responded to a posting here, and started exchanging email with a man who sounded very nice and understanding. He assured me I could learn how to get pleasure from pain, and offered to be my guide and mentor. He offered to send me something that he was sure would "turn me on." Instead of arousing me, what he sent almost frightened me to death. It described terrible tortures that he was inflicting on a woman, and he kept using the second person "you" so that it seemed as though I was the person being tortured. When I stopped shaking, I wrote back and told him that what he had sent was terrifying, not stimulating, and I wanted nothing to do with it or him.

About a week later, leaving the library, I was grabbed from behind, just as I was getting into my car, and a cloth soaked in ether or some similar kind of drug was forced over my face. When I regained my senses, I found myself in the back of a van, with my hands and feet taped. I was blindfolded, and a rag was stuck in my mouth as a gag. It was him. He brought me to a house somewhere and kept me there the whole night. I will never talk or write about what happened to me that night, but it was the most horrible experience of my life.

I never went to the police or told anyone about my ordeal. I felt
too frightened, humiliated, and debased. I just wanted to die.
For those of you who may be toying with the idea of trying these
things, believe me, there was nothing erotic or sensual about what
happened to me. For those who really enjoy doing these things to
others, I can only believe that you are very sick people who need
help.

Mason stared at the screen. Now that he no longer had any interest in finding *The Initiator,* everything seemed to be breaking. If he were going to follow General Talbot's advice, he should probably pass on this new information as well. Whoever Bobbieking was, she might possess some information of value.

Mason's PhoneSearch showed over 2,000 matches for Bobbie King, far too many to explore. Besides, the name could easily be an email nickname, which would get him nowhere. But, whoever she was, she was the strongest lead to *The Painmaster* so far, and she could be contacted via email. He was unable to suppress a feeling of excitement, now that their efforts had borne fruit, and now, more than ever, he wanted to continue the search. Sadly, he knew that he could not. The price was too high.

27

TRACY HELPED HER sister pack the small valise. She was taking Michelle home, where she would spend the night before the trip to the private sanitarium in California. A nurse was en route from the sanitarium to Hawaii, and would arrive that evening. They would fly out the following afternoon, and Tracy would accompany them, staying long enough to see her sister settled.

Tracy wished that Michelle's mood would improve. Ever since she revealed to Tracy that she suspected someone else had been present during her ordeal, she had lapsed into a withdrawn state. Attempts by Tracy to get her to elaborate, or explain why she suspected a second presence only produced silence and a shaking of her head. Perhaps she realized that there was no basis for such a suspicion, and no longer wanted to talk about it, which was fine with Tracy. If only she could do something to improve her sister's spirit.

Michelle was obviously reluctant to leave the hospital, and, as they waited for the limousine, her agitation increased. It was all Tracy could do to get Michelle to leave the limousine, and enter the door of their home. Once inside, however, she seemed to relax. Frederick Iverson was not home, it was the maid's day off, and the house was quiet. After drinking a cup of cocoa that Tracy prepared for her, Michelle went to her room to lie down. Tracy then went to her own room, to pack for the trip. She checked on Michelle twice, the second time she found her sleeping peacefully. Returning to her own room, Tracy felt an overwhelming desire to lie down also. The whole incident with her sister had been a severe strain, and she had not had much sleep. Laying her head back on the pillow, she decided to take a short nap.

When she opened her eyes, almost three hours had passed. As she rose, she saw that the sky was darkening, and far below her window, city lights were beginning to appear. There were no lights on in the kitchen or the living room, which meant her father had not yet returned, and Michelle must be still in her room. But when she checked her bedroom, Michelle was not there. Proceeding down the hall, and passing her father's bedroom, she found the door open. Although there were no lights in the room, she could hear the sound of the shower running in his bath. She thought it strange that he had returned without turning on any lights, and even more strange that his door was open. Living in a house with two young women, her father was meticulous about maintaining his personal privacy.

Curious, she entered the empty room and walked slowly toward the bath. Reluctant to proceed at first, she finally glanced into the room. Behind the frosted glass enclosure, the shower ran steadily into the large tub. If someone was in the shower, she would have been able to see an outlined form through the frosted glass. She saw nothing. Puzzled, she crossed the room to shut off the water, opening the enclosure to reach the shower knobs.

Michelle lay full length in the bottom of the tub, a beautiful, white porcelain doll. The bleeding had stopped, but red smears were still visible on the sides of the tub. Even through the horror of the moment, small details of the scene burned into Tracy's consciousness—the gleam of the straight-edge razor lying open on Michelle's abdomen, the lifeless, gray-white pallor of her body contrasting so starkly with the scarlet splotches, and the thin wisps of red which still dyed the water as it made its way to the swirling drain.

28

MASON RUSHED TO the Iverson house as soon as Tracy called him. He arrived just as a police detective was interviewing her. The ambulance had already left with Michelle's body, and Frederick Iverson was in another room, being consoled by some friends. The detective was polite and solicitous. He had stopped his questioning when Mason arrived, introduced himself to Mason, and waited quietly until Tracy was ready to resume.

"We're almost through here, Ms. Iverson. I just have a couple of more things. It appears that your sister went to your father's bathroom because she knew he had a straight razor, is that right?"

"Yes, we were both aware that he had one."

"He must be one of the last people in the country to use one," the detective noted.

"He doesn't use it all the time, never when he's in a hurry, only when he wants a really close shave. And he's not careless with it. It must have been in the rear of his medicine cabinet, because Michelle evidently knocked over a bottle of his after-shave while reaching for it."

"So she finds the razor. Why do you think she...uh, used it there, in your father's bathtub, instead of, well, going back to her own room?"

"I've thought about that," Tracy said. "I think she may have done it in the bathtub because it would be...less messy." Tracy swallowed, but continued. "Maybe she didn't want to leave blood all over everything."

The detective nodded. "Also, warm running water would inhibit clotting, keep the blood flowing. Do you think your sister would have thought of that?"

"I don't know, it's possible."

"But why would she use your father's tub instead of her own?"

"There is no tub in Michelle's bathroom, just a shower. Her bedroom was originally designed to be used as a maid's room, but we've never had a live-in maid."

The detective now seemed satisfied, and with an expression of condolence, he left. It was several moments before Tracy spoke.

"She looked just like a doll, Mason, a lovely, life-size doll. But so pale..." Her voice was husky and barely audible.

"It might be better not to talk about it any more right now." Mason said.

She fell silent, and Mason could think of nothing to say. Then, she looked at him, her expression hardening, her eyes icy. "He's not going to get away with this, Mason. He killed her just as sure as if he used the razor himself. I'm going to find him if it's the last thing I do. You can count on it."

29

OF THE MANY people at the funeral, Mason knew only the Iversons, Hatcher, and General Talbot. Framed by the magnificent *Koolau Pali*, with its green, scalloped cliffs, Hawaii Memorial's rolling landscape resembled a golf course more than a cemetery. It permitted no upright gravestones, and even with the present tragedy occupying most of his mind, Mason could not help comparing it with the crowded, granite tombstones that competed for every inch of space in the Queens, New York cemetery where his mother had been buried.

Mason had not seen either of the Iversons since Tracy had called him about Michelle's death two days ago. He had offered his condolences to the father at that time, but the man had been in such a state of shock that he barely acknowledged him. Now, standing together at the graveside, Tracy seemed poised and in control, but Mason was struck by her father's appearance. Frederick Iverson seemed at a complete loss. Gone was the undercurrent of anger that had been present at previous meetings. In contrast to his daughter's composure, he appeared stunned and unfocused. Mason suspected that the father's prior reluctance to risk his business for his daughter's safety now haunted him.

In the preceding two days, Mason had been torn by conflicting thoughts and emotions, which continued right up to the funeral.

"Has this changed your plans?" Talbot asked, sensing his thoughts.

There was a long pause before Mason replied. Finally he spoke. "I'm thinking that maybe this guy has to be stopped."

Talbot made a slight, noncommittal nod, but did not reply.

When the services ended, Frederick Iverson, his head bowed, moved slowly toward the limousine which had brought him and his surviving daughter to the service. Tracy remained behind, staring at her sister's grave. Mason walked over to her side.

"There have been some developments you should know about. I'll tell you about them as soon as you've had some time."

"Tomorrow," she said, looking up slowly. "Come to our place tomorrow, about one o'clock." She saw the surprised look on his face. "I'm not going to sit around in a black dress, Mason. I want to get the creep responsible for this."

There was a fierceness about the statement that chilled him. He wondered if he had made the right decision. But he went ahead. "I've changed my mind," he told her. "I want to help."

She gave him a weak, weary smile. "Thanks. You won't be sorry, Mason. You can count on it."

"That's not why I'm doing it."

"I know that, but you can count on it anyway."

30

MASON STOOD SILENTLY staring out the large picture window of the Iverson home as Tracy and Hatcher read the printouts of his email. He had called Tracy and asked to bring Hatcher along. Frederick Iverson had declined to join them, and Tracy explained that he was still in shock over Michelle's death. A heavy mist swirled up the hillside, obscuring the city, and creating the effect of a house suspended in the sky. Tracy finished reading first. She looked up at Mason, her eyes very wide.

"My God, he sounds like he's describing what he did to Michelle!" Mason didn't say anything. He watched her expression of shock harden to rage. "What do we do now?" she asked him, her voice hoarse with anger.

"Well, first, we need to get back to him. It's been almost a week since he answered us. That's probably too long. We're going to have to come up with a good explanation for the delay if we want to preserve our credibility."

After a brief silence, Hatcher spoke. "In the two cases we know about, Michelle and *bobbieking*, *The Painmaster* proposed a meeting. We have to make our answer attractive enough so that he does the same thing again."

"And then what?" Mason asked.

"Then you turn it over to me."

They looked up to see Frederick Iverson standing in the doorway, a grim set to his jaw. Hatcher and Mason exchanged glances, but they said nothing. Iverson came toward them, and reached for the printouts that Tracy had placed on the coffee table. Her hand reached for them at the same time.

"Dad..." Father and daughter locked glances, and a silent message passed between them. Iverson withdrew his hand, leaving the printouts unread.

"I will leave the details of all of this to the three of you," he said, and then turned his attention to Mason. "But I want it clearly understood that once you find him, you turn the information over to me and tell no one else. At that point you can consider your work completed." He turned his gaze toward Hatcher, making it clear his words included him. It was the old Iverson, back in control, angry and determined. Whatever distress the death of his daughter had caused had been pushed aside, and he seemed once more focused on revenge. Neither Mason nor Hatcher said anything, bringing an uncomfortable silence to the room. Finally, with a nod toward his daughter, Iverson turned and left. The silence continued until Mason finally spoke, changing the subject.

"We should write *bobbieking*, too. Even though she was blindfolded, she might be able to describe something about him, or provide something else that's useful."

"I think I should be the one to do that," Tracy said. "She sounded very frightened. I think if I tell her the truth—that this man is responsible for my sister's death—we'll have a better chance of getting her help."

Hatcher and Mason agreed. "First things first, though," Hatcher said. "What are we going to say to *The Initiator*?"

It took them an hour, but when they were finished, they had a message they were satisfied with.

Master

Please forgive me for not responding sooner. My mother had an accident, requiring me to fly to her home and take care of her. When I returned, I found over a hundred pieces of email waiting. I started to read them in turn, but knew as soon as I reached yours that Destiny had brought us together. I can see that although you will cause me pain (as I want you to do), you are compassionate as well. I appreciate that although you are determined to cause me as much pain as possible, you are concerned not to leave permanent marks on my body or draw blood. I also know I can place myself completely in your hands, knowing that you will sense my limits of endurance, as you did when you overruled Marla's request to continue the torture. At the same time I know you will show me no undeserved mercy and will vent your needs on my body as you see fit. I welcome them. You are the one I have been seeking all my life. Please do not discard me. Your pain slave forever, Sara

"That should get to him," Hatcher said, after they posted the message. "It gets to me, and I'm not into S&M. At least I don't think I am."

Tracy then wrote the letter to *bobbieking*, and Mason and Hatcher approved it. They decided to meet again as soon as *The Initiator* responded, or Tracy had a reply from *bobbieking*.

Mason and Hatcher left the Iverson home and walked slowly toward their cars. They reached Mason's first, and after he unlocked his door, he turned to Hatcher.

"What do you think of all this, Ray? Do you think we're doing the right thing?"

"Only you can answer that, my friend."

"But how do you feel about your own involvement?"

"The way I look at it is that I'm helping out a friend. You asked me for assistance, and I'm providing it. I'm doing it for you, not the Iversons." Hatcher placed a hand on Mason's shoulder. "It's the coward's way out," he said, smiling wryly. "You've got the hard part."

Mason made no move to get into the car. "I wonder what Iverson is planning to do if we find this guy?"

"I don't know," Hatcher said, the smile suddenly leaving his face. "But I hope he's building something medieval in his basement."

31

SO, SHE HAD answered at last. Sandler had been baffled by her silence, considering how eager she had seemed. Then he assumed that she was, after all, just like all the others. His message had frightened her off. Now, here she was again, apparently eager to continue. But he could not shake a nagging suspicion. Was there another reason for her delayed response? What could it be? Perhaps he was suffering from a case of nerves. That was possible, since, in responding to "Sara," he had broken the new rules.

He turned his mind back to the message. He still sensed that something was not completely right. But he would answer, and move ahead. And he would begin his effort to find her.

32

THE SUN HAD just set when Mason heard the ship's bell at his door. It was Tracy.

"I was going crazy just sitting at home waiting," she told him. "I didn't think you'd mind."

"Mason smiled. "I'm glad to have the company." He led her out to the lanai, where the sunset had painted the sky and sea with the vivid colors only seen in the tropics. But Tracy failed to notice. She seemed restless and on edge. "Would you like a drink?" At first she declined, but then changed her mind and asked for a gin and tonic. When he brought it, she drank almost half of it at once.

"I guess it's just getting to me. I need to get my mind off things." She stared at him with a strange intensity which he had never seen before, and could not interpret.

Learning that she had not eaten since noon, he got her to agree to a light supper. Mason removed a package of vegetable chili from the freezer, and they ate it on the lanai. Mason was proud of his chili, which had won a prize in an Army cook-off in Germany. That had been something of a coup, especially for a chili without meat, but Tracy ate mechanically, her restlessness increasing. Abruptly, she put down her fork, and rose from the table. Crossing over to where he sat, she took his arm and, without speaking, led him to the bedroom.

It was not lovemaking. It was not even sex by any definition in Mason's experience. She tore at his clothes, pushed him down on the bed and straddled him. Eyes tightly closed, her body worked above him furiously, her mind in some far off place that Mason could not begin to penetrate. As her gasps and moans intensified, a wild hunger drove her to a frenzy of lust that she couldn't seem to satisfy. It was as though she were possessed by some carnal demon that had taken total control of her body and spirit. When he reached upward to caress her breasts, she shrieked at the intense sensitivity caused by his touch. Finally, with a furious pumping that ended with a moan that was more like a scream, she fell to his side. She lay there, panting with exhaustion, her body soaked in perspiration, her eyes still closed. Mason watched her quietly as her breathing slowly returned to normal, waiting for her to open her eyes. It was some time before he realized she had fallen asleep.

33

Mason woke to sunshine streaming into the bedroom. Tracy was not beside him. He found her on the lanai, already at the laptop. He knew from her expression that she had something, and her preoccupation prevented him from mentioning anything about the previous night.

"We have an answer from bobbieking." She moved aside so that he could see the screen.

Dear Tracy,

I was devastated to hear about your sister. It has been something I have lived in fear of happening, and was the reason I posted my message. I am so very sorry that it did no good, at least where your sister was concerned. I know that I must tell you everything I can about this evil person, but I cannot bring myself to meet with anyone, or give my address to anyone who I come in contact with on this bulletin board. Please understand that I am still very much afraid. I may be paranoid, but you could be someone like him, trying to trick me. Please forgive me, but that's how my fear makes me think. I will answer any questions I can that might help you. Just so long as it's via email and not in person.

Roberta King

"What do you think?" Tracy asked as Mason finished reading.

"Well, at least she'll talk to us, even if it isn't in person. I'll call Ray, and the three of us can brainstorm what we need to ask her."

"I wish we'd hear from *him*," she said. The sky had turned gray and a squall was moving in from the sea. She wrapped Mason's robe tightly around her, picked up the laptop, and moved inside.

Mason followed. "That was quite an evening last night."

She gave him a brief glance, then quickly looked away. He sensed she didn't want to discuss it.

"Do you think we lost him?" she asked, as they settled in the living room.

"I don't think so." He, also, was willing to drop the matter. Some things were better left alone. "He was interested enough in the first place to make that long reply. And we certainly did enough of a *mea culpa* in our response. I can't believe he would give it all up just because our message was delayed."

Mason placed the call to Hatcher, who had his last class at noon, and agreed to come up right after lunch. Mason suggested a swim, but Tracy declined, nor was she in the mood for another walk along the beach.

"We can take a short hike up in the hills," he offered, pointing to the high ground beginning a few hundred yards behind his house. "I can show you the spot where an Army radar team picked up the Japanese attack coming in on Pearl Harbor on December 7th, 1941."

Tracy frowned. "I never heard that. Why was it such a surprise, if they found them on radar?"

"The Officer of the Day told them to forget about it. He thought it was a flight of our own bombers that were expected in from the West Coast."

But she shook her head. "Why don't you go for your jog? I'll sit here and wait for him."

"It could be a long wait."

"I'll just have to be patient." Seeing his expression, she sighed. "You're right, I'm as impatient as hell about this. But I just can't concentrate on anything else right now except him answering."

When the squall passed, Mason went for his jog. He added an extra two miles, not turning around until Banzai Pipeline. By the time he got back, even the pit bulls were dragging. He cut short his swim, showered quickly, and found Tracy back on the lanai, her eyes glued to the laptop screen. As he approached, she said only two words.

"He's here."

Sara - Your excuse for not communicating with me is not acceptable. You should have informed me of your mother's illness and asked for my permission to go to her. Before I accept you as my pain slave, you must be punished for your insolence.

When you come to me this time, you find that Marla is once again present, along with two couples, who regard you with interest. I tell you that Marla will administer your punishment, but that I will prepare you for her. I demand that you strip, and you do. When I examine your breasts, I find that your nipples are not pierced. I inform you that the punishment requires this, and that I shall pierce you. You see that I have two long needles with wooden handles. You wince as you watch me place the tip of one of the needles in the flame of an alcohol burner. You now realize what I intend to do, and you tell me that you are afraid that you will not be able to stand the pain without moving. You ask me to tie you down so that you cannot resist. I refuse. Part of your punishment will be that you must remain still, or cause damage to your breasts. When the needle glows red, I dip it in an antiseptic oil and slowly push it sideways through your left nipple. White hot agony runs through your body, and your mind seems ready to explode from the effort of restraining your movement and your screams. When it completely pierces the nipple, I withdraw it slowly, twirling it as it goes. I then insert a small steel ring in the pierced channel. I repeat the process with the right breast, and when I am finished you are close to fainting, your body shining with bright perspiration. Two small rings now dangle from your nipples. You are ready for Marla.

She stands before you and fastens a leash to each ring, and then orders you to kneel. She ties your hands behind your back, and strews a large bag of sharp pebbles along a path in front of you. She then pulls sharply on both leashes, which tear at your nipples, forcing you to move forward on your knees over the pebbles. Even through the pain, you are aware of your humiliation at being seen like this in front of the two couples, who laugh at your plight and urge Marla to pull harder. Desperately, you crawl forward, trying to relieve the unbearably painful tension on your breasts. Back and forth she leads you until your knees begin to leave a trail of blood on the pebbles. I order Marla to stop. As you know, I do not like the sight of blood, nor do I wish it to be spilled. You are my possession. I do not want you damaged. I am satisfied that your punishment is sufficient, and I feel that you are now ready to become my slave. Are you? If so, the time has come. Tell me your address and phone number.

"My God, he's doing it again. He's reliving what he did to Michelle!" The initial horror in Tracy's eyes slowly turned to hate. "We've got to get this creep," she said, clenching her fists.

Mason winced, uneasy with the menace in her voice. As he groped for something to say, Hatcher arrived.

"Got out a little early," he announced. He saw them both at the laptop. "Well, it looks like we've got something." They waited in silence while he read both messages.

"Let's tackle the easy one first," he suggested. "Let's review what Roberta King has already told us about him, and what else she might be able to tell us."

"She hasn't given us very much," Tracy said. "She was gassed and blindfolded, just like Michelle, so she probably never saw him either."

"Maybe she heard his voice," Mason offered.

"You can count on it," Tracy said. "As voluble as he is in print, and from what Roberta King said earlier, he *had* to talk to her."

"He may have removed the blindfold at some point," Hatcher offered. "After all, she says he took her to a cabin. Maybe she can describe it."

Mason shook his head. "I don't see how that's going to help us. It looks like she only saw it from the inside."

"We might ask her if she noted anything peculiar about him," Tracy said. "Anything unusual, any mannerisms."

Hatcher noted it down. "Anything else?"

When there was no response, he gave his notes to Tracy, suggesting that she start on the message to Roberta King. Tracy finished it quickly and they sent it on its way.

"Now we need to knock around our response." Hatcher said.

"Frankly, I'm at a loss what to do now," Mason said. "He wants an address and a phone number. How do we handle that?"

"We certainly can't give him mine," Tracy said. "He probably knows that it was Michelle's, too. But I don't understand why he wants them in the first place. He can arrange a meeting via email."

"He doesn't want to waste his time," Mason said. "He wants the information so that he can check on her, to make sure she's real—which she isn't."

"But which she can be," Hatcher said. Seeing their puzzled expressions, he went on. "Suppose Sara Miller is someone who lives with her brother on the north shore? It would help explain why she doesn't have her own address and phone number."

"Sara and her brother don't have the same last name," Mason said. "If he checks, he'll find that out."

"It's her name by a previous marriage," Tracy offered. "A bad marriage will add to her cachet. That's why she's hiding with her brother. She's been hurt."

Mason shook his head. "She *wants* to be hurt."

"But not in the same way," Hatcher countered. "Tracy's right. She has had disappointing relationships with men, until *The Initiator* comes along." He sat down at the keyboard and cleared the screen. "Let's work up our answer. I think we should make it a little better than just the information he wants. Make sure we keep him interested."

They needed only a few minutes to agree on the message.

Master

I am very sorry that I did not ask your permission before going to my mother. It was utterly thoughtless of me, and I deserve, accept, and eagerly await your punishment. I promise never to be so thoughtless again. More than ever, I feel that I belong to you, body and soul, and all I now want from life is to serve you. I am yours.

Now that we are about to meet, I must tell you that I live in my brother's house, and have no phone or address listed under my own name. I prefer it that way, as I will explain in person. My brother will present no obstacle to our relationship. Although we live in the same house, we have separate lives.

I await your instructions. I will come to the ends of the earth to be with you.

Sara

Mason's name, address and phone number were added at the end of the message.

"Tracy should stay here with you for the next few days," Hatcher said, "so that a woman is on the premises, in case he investigates."

"I don't like using Tracy this way," Mason said. "It puts her in danger."

"Mason, I have full confidence in you," Tracy said, with a hint of humor in her voice. "I'm sure you can protect me."

"I wish I was as sure as you are," Mason replied, but he let it go. "Okay, let's say he makes contact. What do we do then?"

Hatcher took a moment to reply. "It seems to me that Frederick Iverson has made that very clear."

After Hatcher left, Tracy returned to the lanai. Making two gin and tonics, Mason joined her. They were both content to stretch out in the lounge chairs and relax to the sound of the small waves breaking on the reef. It was Tracy who finally broke the silence.

"Mason, with all the activity we've been involved in, there's something I've overlooked telling you." She then mentioned

Michelle's feeling that there was someone else present with *The Painmaster* while she was his captive.

Mason thought that over. "Do you know what she based that feeling on? Did she hear anything?"

"I don't really know why she felt that way. She was having a bad time during our conversation, and I didn't want to press her. But she seemed so positive about it."

"Did you mention this to your father?"

She nodded. "He was surprised, but he didn't believe she had any way of knowing something like that."

"I think he's probably right."

Tracy sighed. "I guess so." She continued to stare out to sea. They sat silently, enjoying the cool of the morning and the light breeze rustling the palms and the milo.

"Mason, how well do you know Ray Hatcher?" She had turned from her contemplation of the ocean, and was facing him.

"Fairly well, why?"

"How well is fairly well?"

"We're not buddies, if that's what you mean, but we see each other fairly frequently. We scuba dive together once in a while, we're both members of the Trail and Mountain Club. Why? What's this about, Tracy?" Then it came to him. "You can't be thinking that Ray had anything to do with Michelle's abduction? Just because your sister said something when she might have been delirious?"

"I don't know what to think, Mason. But if there *is* someone else involved, he certainly is a good candidate." Mason tried to interrupt, but she pushed on. "I've been studying the messages we've sent *to The Initiator*. Mason, they sound like they could have written *by The Initiator* himself."

"Tracy, those messages were a team effort. We all had a hand in writing them."

"Not really. Think about it. Ray actually wrote both of them. All you and I did was make a suggestion or two. I've gone back over them, and I swear, Mason, the style is the same."

"I don't think that's so strange. He's trying to get the guy's attention, hook him. He's naturally going to use a style he thinks will do that."

"Well, if so, he's damn good at it. Another thing, you remember the first night at the Cannon Club, after he wrote the first message? You said that if you didn't know him you would think he wrote things like that all the time? Remember his answer? He said, 'What makes you think you know me, and who says I don't?'"

"You've got a good memory," Mason said, smiling. "But he was joking. Surely you can see that. God, if he were...involved in this, you don't think he'd deliberately say something like that, do you?"

"Yes, I do. That's exactly the way *The Painmaster* comes across to me. A creep with a huge ego, completely sure of himself, who would enjoy playing that kind of game, daring us to find him out."

Mason shook his head. "Tracy, you're wrong about this, you really are. Ray Hatcher is here because I asked him to be. He's helping us. He has no secret agenda."

Tracy sighed and rose from her chair, yawning. "You're probably right. I guess I'm just getting paranoid. And I'm really tired."

"That doesn't surprise me at all." She gave him that same fleeting glance that told him she was still not willing to discuss last night. "Why don't you take a nap and I'll make something for supper, and call you when it's ready?"

She yawned again. "Fine. Make something big. I have a feeling I'm going to be hungry when I wake up."

Mason placed four potatoes on to boil. He emptied two large jars of sauerkraut into a pot, mixed in a grated potato and several slices of lean bacon, poured in a bottle of Fire Rock Ale, covered the pot, and turned the stove burner to medium. Later, from the freezer he took two boneless smoked pork chops, and a supply of wursts: two bratwursts, two bockwursts, and a kielbasa. He pierced the wursts several times with a fork, placed them in a large frying pan, and covered them with about a third of a bottle of gewurztraminer. When the potatoes were almost ready, he placed the pork chops on top of the sauerkraut.

He divided the sauerkraut between two large plates, positioning one of the chops in the center of each, on the bed of kraut, mashed the potatoes with their skins on, and placed them on top of the chops, molding them in a cone shape, forming a peak. He then surrounded the "mountain" with the wursts, and called Tracy.

"*Bernerplatte*," he announced. "You won't find it any better in Switzerland."

"It almost looks too pretty to eat," she said, and immediately proceeded to demolish it. He had opened another bottle of gewurztraminer, and they took what remained of it out to the lanai. Tracy collapsed in a lounge chair. Just when Mason thought she had fallen asleep, she turned toward him.

"This is where we first made love. It was nice, wasn't it?"

"It was." He could not help comparing the previous experience with her actions last night, wondering which was the real Tracy Iverson.

"Mason? How much of an invitation do you need?"

Their lovemaking was sweet, tender, yet somehow demanding

and passionate. It was as though they were reliving that first night. Afterward, as they lay side by side, watching the moon rise, she finally broke the silence.

"Well, which do you prefer, the tender lover or the wanton slut?"

"It's hard to say. Last night was a wild ride, but if I had to choose, I guess I'd take the tender lover."

"Good, because I doubt if you'll ever see the wanton slut again."

Thinking about it, Mason was not sure if he was relieved or disappointed.

34

"I'M HUNGRY."

Mason groaned. He had not slept well until early morning, and Tracy's prodding shook him from his few hours of deep slumber.

She pushed until he stumbled out of bed. "While you're making us something fantastic, I'll check the email."

Feeling better after a quick shower, he started the batter for his banana rum pancakes.

"We have an answer from Roberta King," Tracy called from the lanai. He read the message leaning over her shoulder.

Hello Tracy,

I will try to answer the questions you asked, but I don't know if I will be much help. First, yes, I did hear his voice. I don't think he tried to disguise it in any way. His voice was soft and low. He never raised it once, but there was, well, sort of an intensity about it, even an urgency, although I am not sure I am getting this right. He was like a low pressure salesman. He kept trying to convince me that pain and pleasure were really the same thing, and that if I would just accept this, and give in to my true feelings, he could give me intense pleasure. He talked for a long time before he finally started doing things to me that I still can't talk or write about.

He removed the blindfold as soon as he brought me inside the cabin. I call it a cabin, because I could see it was one large room with windows (curtained) on all sides. But I really don't know what it looked like from the outside. I never saw it. He wore a mask, though, one of those stocking things you see criminals using in the movies. He had a medium build, was about five-ten, and I would guess he was between 30 and 45 years old. He seemed strong for his weight, but I can't tell you what that was, I can't tell people's weights well at all. He was dressed in a sport shirt and jeans. As far as mannerisms are concerned, I didn't notice anything special, like smoking or nail biting. Like I said before, he had an intense, earnest way about him, like he was trying to prove something, or to find something. I just don't know. I can't think of anything else in answer to your questions, but if I do, I will send it on. I hope this helps.

Sincerely, Roberta King

"Not much help, is it?" Tracy said.

"No, but then what could we expect? But notice that he removed Roberta's blindfold, and wore a mask. With Michelle, he kept her blindfolded the whole time. I wonder if that means anything."

"It does if Michelle was right about someone else being in the room besides him. A lot easier to blindfold her than have a bunch of people wear masks." Tracy shivered and hugged herself as if suddenly taken with a chill. "God, it gives me the creeps to think of her on exhibition like that. It reminds me of scenes from the Inquisition, with a bunch of priests hovering over some poor heretic being tortured."

"We have no proof that happened," Mason said.

"We have no proof that it didn't." She stood up and walked toward the window, and stood staring out to sea. "Damn!" she said finally, "I wish *he* would answer."

"He will."

Rather than simply sit and wait, Tracy agreed to a short walk on the beach. Since no windows in the house faced the road, neither one of them saw the green Ford Econoline van which slowed almost to a stop as it passed the house. The driver leaned over to read the information on the mail box, noting the address and the names "Grant" and "Miller." The van then gradually increased speed and drove off.

Once on the shoreline, Mason led Tracy in the opposite direction from his jogging course. He showed her the spot where a female monk seal had come ashore last year to give birth. An endangered species, the seals were rarely seen on the inhabited islands, and this female was far from its normal grounds at French Frigate Shoals, hundreds of miles to the northwest.

"I spotted them on my morning jog, and called the Fish and Wildlife people," he told her. "They came and cordoned off a 100-yard section beach around the seals, and I lent them a tent." He explained how a volunteer watch was set up to keep dangerous dogs and curious people at bay, and that he had taken several turns on the watch. The picture of Mason acting as baby sitter to the seals brought the first real smile to Tracy's face since the funeral. He told her that although TV reporters came out to photograph the seals, and the story appeared on the nightly news, the location was kept secret.

"What happened to them?" Tracy asked.

"About six weeks later, mamma seal lumbered across the beach with her offspring, and disappeared into the surf. Less than two dozen people had seen them."

Rounding Kahuku Point, they were immediately buffeted by blustery trades. Despite the wind, it was a bright, clear day, and Tracy seemed to enjoy being outside. They continued their walk for another half-hour before turning back. When they returned, Mason checked the email, Tracy watching over his shoulder. There was one message. It was from *The Initiator*.

Sara,

Meet me the day after tomorrow at 1 PM at the Makai Market, Ala Moana Shopping Center. You will be standing at the bar, in the center of the court. You will wear a red ribbon in your hair so that I may recognize you. Do not be late. Wait for me no matter how long it takes. I shall be there.

"The Makai Market." Mason shook his head. "That's just about the most crowded place he could pick, especially at that time of day."

"I'm sure that's the point," Tracy said. "He wants to look me over without being conspicuous. If he doesn't like what he sees, he can just leave."

"I'll call Ray," Mason said. "We need to come up with a plan."

"That won't be necessary, Mason."

Mason's eyes narrowed. "What do you mean?"

"We've found him," Tracy said. "This is the point where my father and I take over. He told you that when Michelle's abductor was found, your job was over, remember?"

"Tracy, just what in hell do you think you're going to do?"

"You don't need to be concerned with that."

"If you think I'm going to stand by and—"

"That's exactly what you're going to do, Mason. You don't want to be involved in what's going to happen. You made that clear."

"Tracy, I told you that I changed my mind. I said I was willing to help."

"And you *have* helped," she said, her voice softening. "But now this is something my father and I have to do alone. We can't involve anyone else in…well, we just can't involve anyone else."

Mason took a deep breath, but it did little good. His anxiety and frustration mounted. "Tracy, what are you going to do, hit him on the head and throw him in a sack? Kidnapping is a federal offense, for God's sake."

She refused to answer him.

"Won't you at least *tell* me what you're planning to do?" he pleaded.

She shook her head. "The less you know about it, the better for you."

After Tracy left, Mason called Ray Hatcher, bringing him up to date. "Can we get together, Ray?" Maybe we can work out a plan for tomorrow."

Hatcher explained that he would be tied up all of the next day with a presentation he had to give to a visiting HEW delegation from Washington. "It's critically important to the University's funding, Mason, and there's no one else who can do it for me, otherwise I'd be at your disposal."

Mason then called General Talbot.

"You never should have gotten involved," Talbot said, after Mason had filled him in.

"Hey, it was you who *got* me involved!"

"I mean involved with the daughter. It's only your personal involvement that's causing a problem. My original advice still holds—even more so now. The whole thing is out of control. Walk away from it and everyone connected with it. Everyone."

35

THE MAKAI MARKET was still crowded with lunching shoppers, and space at the circular central bar was tight. Tracy found herself wondering if *The Initiator* would be able to pick her out, even with the ribbon in her hair. She glanced at her watch. One fifteen. Where was he? Afraid to look around in case her nervousness showed and warned him off, she stared down at her glass of orange juice.

Across from the bar, on the *mauka* side of the market, Martin Sandler watched her, as he had for the last twenty minutes. She had arrived five minutes early, evidently alone, and appearing more nervous than he would have expected. He had already been there for half an hour. He had nursed his tea, carefully observing the crowd, watching especially for persons sitting alone and not eating, as he was doing.

In the come and go of shoppers, Sandler had singled out three men. One, balding, heavy set, and wearing a blue aloha shirt, had his face buried in a newspaper, a large glass of beer on the table. Another man, dressed in a yellow aloha shirt and shorts, had neither food nor drink in front of him, and kept checking his watch. A third had arrived about five minutes later. He wore a tan sport shirt and khaki slacks, and carried a paper plate from one of the market stands. Whatever it was, he was eating it very slowly. None of the men appeared unduly interested in their surroundings, and none of them glanced in Sara Miller's direction. But, then, he wouldn't expect them to. Sandler looked at his watch. Time.

It was one twenty-five when Tracy felt the tap on her shoulder. Turning, she saw a man about four inches taller than she was, green eyes and brown hair. He stared at her for only the briefest instant before speaking.

"Come with me," he said.

She obeyed, her heart beginning to pound heavily. Leaving the food court, he led the way toward the *makai* side of the shopping center. A moment later, the man in the tan shirt rose, abandoned his food, and exited the food court by the same route. Almost immediately, the balding, heavy set man rose also, and began following the one with the tan shirt.

Tracy's nervousness increased as the stranger led her toward the parking lot. She had not expected that he would drive her anywhere. She had thought they would sit down at a table and talk, get to know each other. What would she do if he wanted her to get in his car? Fortunately, he continued on through the parking lot, to Ala Moana Boulevard, where he stopped at a crosswalk, waiting for the light to change. She had not expected this cold silence either. He made no effort to speak, or even look at her.

After crossing the street, they entered Ala Moana Park, heading for the seashore. When they reached the edge of the beach, the man stopped and finally turned toward Tracy.

"I was told to give you this," he said, handing her a small, white envelope.

"What?" Without saying anything more, the man turned to leave. "Wait!" she cried, grabbing his arm.

"Hey!" The man whirled and tried to jerk his arm free, but Tracy held fast. He began beating at her arm with his free hand, and as they struggled, the man in the tan sport shirt ran up to them. Within seconds the heavy set man from the market also appeared, knocking the one in the tan shirt to the ground.

Mason recovered at once from the blow, jumped to his feet and lunged at the man who had knocked him down.

"Mason! Dudley! Stop it!" Tracy cried. "He's getting away!" The man who had led her to the park was now racing back toward Ala Moana. Muttering a curse, the man she had called Dudley charged after him, and after a moment, so did Mason. Dudley caught up with the runner as he tried to cross the traffic-choked boulevard. Yanking his right arm behind him and twisting upward, he turned him back toward where Tracy was standing.

"Hey…Ow!…What the hell do you think you're doing? OW!" Relentlessly, Dudley maneuvered the man back until he was once more facing Tracy, who had opened the envelope and was holding a small folded note.

"Who gave you this?" she shouted.

"I don't know," the man gasped, wincing with pain from the vice-like grip on his arm. "Some dude asked me if I wanted to make an easy twenty bucks. OWW! It's the truth, goddammit!"

"When…where did this happen?"

"Right here in the park, about an hour ago. I was just sittin' on a bench. He tells me all I have to do is take this lady with a red ribbon in her hair to the beach and give her this envelope. He even tells me exactly what to say. I never seen him before. That's all I know. I swear."

Dudley caught Mason's gaze. "Get his wallet," he said. "Look inside."

Mason did so, revealing three singles, a five, and a crisp $20 dollar bill. He returned the money and stuffed the wallet back in the man's pocket. "What did he look like?" he asked him.

"Ordinary lookin' guy. Medium build, about my height. Brown hair. That's all I remember."

A small crowd had begun to gather. "Police business!" Dudley announced in a loud voice. "Move along!" As the crowd began to melt away, he turned to Tracy. "What do you want to do, Miss Iverson?"

"Let him go," she said, her voice drained of all emotion. "He's probably telling the truth."

Dudley released his hold on the man's arm. "Okay, pal, on your way." Muttering under his breath, and massaging his arm, the man left. Without speaking, Tracy handed the note to Mason.

SARA

THIS WAS A NECESSARY PRECAUTION. IF ALL WENT WELL, I WILL CONTACT YOU AGAIN.

There was no signature. As Mason handed the note back to Tracy, he saw that there were tears in her eyes.

"Damn it! Damn it!" Her fist clenched around the note. "We've lost him."

From his table in the Makai Market, and the bench across the park where he now sat, Martin Sandler had seen it all. He nodded his head slowly. How interesting. How very interesting.

36

MASON INSISTED ON seeing Tracy home, and he now sat opposite her in the Iverson living room. Tracy, still devastated over the day's failure, sat listlessly on the couch.

"Who is Dudley?" Mason finally asked, hoping to get some understanding of what was going on.

"Dudley Carson is a private detective who sometimes works for my father."

"If you have a private detective working for you, why did you need me?"

"Dudley is someone my father uses to make background checks and things, but his talents are limited. He couldn't have done what you did."

"Why am I not flattered?" Mason didn't know whether to walk out or press for a further explanation. He decided on the latter. "And so you and your father—"

"My father had nothing to do with it."

That stopped Mason. "You mean you still haven't told him?"

"I still haven't told him," she confirmed. "He doesn't know anything about our efforts to trap Michelle's abductor. He thinks we're still just trying to find him on the Internet. Dudley was working privately for me."

"Don't you think it's time he knew?"

Tracy sighed. "Yes, it's more than time. And I don't look forward to telling him, now that so much has happened."

Mason crossed the room and knelt down in front of Tracy, taking both her hands in his. She gazed down at him, a faint hint of amusement in her eyes.

"Are you asking for my hand, Mason?"

"What I'm asking is that you give up this senseless vendetta, which is putting your life in danger."

"My life wasn't in danger."

"It wasn't? How do you figure that? You go out to meet the man who abducted your sister, someone we know is a dangerous sexual pervert, and your life wasn't in danger?"

"Dudley was capable of handling the situation, and so was I. He was armed, and I had a pistol in my purse, and I know how to use it if I have to."

"That's just great. What did you intend to do, shoot him?"

"We were going to turn him over to my father. He would have handled it from there."

"And what would he have done?"

Her silence was all the answer he needed. "Tracy, how can you possibly expect to get away with something like that?"

"I haven't thought about it. I don't know exactly what my father has planned."

"How convenient for you."

Her eyes blazed at him. "If you think I'm trying to get out of responsibility for anything that happens to him, you're wrong. I wanted him dead. I still want him dead. I can't think of anyone who deserves to die more than he does."

"And you have the right to be his executioner?"

Her mouth set in a grim line. "More than anyone. We may

never find him now, but that doesn't mean I'm going to stop trying. You can count on it."

Mason rose and sat beside her, continuing to hold one of her hands. "Tracy, this whole idea is not only criminal, it's insane. Give it up. Please."

For a moment she gazed at him, her eyes very wide. Then her eyes narrowed and she looked away.

"I can't."

37

AFTER MASON LEFT, Tracy finally told her father what they had been doing. Although she expected some anger at keeping him in the dark, she was unprepared for the violence of his reaction. She had hardly finished speaking before he rose from his desk and began pacing furiously back and forth across his study.

"My God, I cannot believe you have done something so reckless, so irresponsible," he raged.

"Dad, it's not that bad. We made sure I was protected—"

"You have no idea what you were dealing with. You stupid, stupid..." He stopped pacing, breathing heavily, staring at her.

Tracy stepped back. She had never seen him like this.

A brief, precarious moment passed, and then Iverson seemed to regain control of himself. "I'm sorry, I should not have spoken like that." His voice was quieter now, and most of the anger seemed dissipated, but there was resolve in his eyes and his expression.

"We are going to stop this, Tracy. Immediately. No more searching for this...this madman. No more internet messages, no more tricks. It is over."

"Dad—"

"I will not hear any more on the subject. We are finished with it. I want your promise that you will end all your activity immediately and tell your friends to do the same. We must get on with our lives."

Tracy lowered her head, but said nothing.

"Tracy? You know I have to go to San Francisco tomorrow, and I don't want to have to worry about this while I'm gone."

Finally, she raised her eyes and looked at him.

"I promise," she said.

38

MARTIN SANDLER COULD not get her out of his mind. Who was she? Why had she tried to trap him? He could not understand why a stranger would have such an interest in him. The answer had to be that she was no stranger. Someone he had met before? He reviewed past contacts, but came up with nothing. A friend or relative of someone? And how about the two men? Were they police? Somehow, he didn't think so, but he couldn't be sure. If they weren't police, who were they?

At first, he had thought it best to quietly walk away from the situation. After all, no one had seen him, he could not be traced, no one knew who he was. But the more he thought about it, the more disturbed he became. Whoever they were, and whatever their motives, these people were after him. He had no way of knowing what resources they had at their disposal. This was a small island. He would not be safe until he knew the answers to these questions. And there was one way to find out.

The woman would tell him.

39

THE NEXT MORNING the weather turned unseasonably rainy, and a gray overcast hung over the islands. It fitted Mason's mood. The house was chilly, and the bedding and upholstery damp and clammy. To dry things out, he built a fire in the free-standing fireplace in his living room. The heavy ironwood logs were soon crackling in the grate, but the warmth was slow to spread through the rest of the house. He sat on the couch facing the fire, staring morosely at the flames.

Now that Tracy had returned home, the house seemed empty. He had come across her apricot bikini in the dryer that morning. It had worsened the emptiness. He also found a pair of earrings she had left behind. He debated calling her, but decided against it. There was a movie he had been planning to see, and the rainy weather made it a good day for it. On the way, he would drop them by her house.

He lunched on a bowl of pea soup, from a batch he had made earlier and frozen in meal-size containers. He sliced a fat German knockwurst into the soup just before it came to a boil, and ate it with a heavy slice of his own Russian black bread. It was a favorite snack on a damp, rainy day, but he ate mechanically, without pleasure. He waited for the fire to die down to embers, and then drove his car out of the garage. He paid no attention to the dusty, green Ford van parked down the highway in the opposite direction from which he turned.

In the green van, Sandler debated whether to follow Mason, but decided it was too risky. He knew nothing about surveillance techniques, and would probably either lose the car or alert its driver. Perhaps the woman was in the house, and the man had just gone out for a short errand. He decided that, for the time being, he would remain where he was.

Tracy had slept poorly, and stared out at the gray, rainy day that hid Honolulu from view. Her father had left for the airport half an hour ago, after once more securing her promise to end the search, and call off Mason and Hatcher. She had been delaying phoning Mason ever since, but finally decided to make the call. When she connected to his answering machine, she decided that, rather than leave a message, she would drive up to see him. It was something that needed to be handled in person anyway. As she backed out of the garage, she wondered how he would react to her telling him that the search for *The Painmaster* was over. She knew that it could only improve their relationship, which was a good thing.

After an hour of waiting, Sandler decided to risk a closer inspection of the house. As he left the van, he picked up a small day pack from the passenger seat and took it with him. It might be needed. He crossed the highway and made his way to the shoreline. It was difficult to tell anything about the house from its road side, but it opened itself to the ocean. He strolled by slowly, taking quick glances through the high glass windows and sliders. There was no one in the parts of the house he was able to see. He quietly made his way onto the lanai and found the sliding door unlocked. Quickly conceiving a plan to ask to use the phone for a minor emergency if anyone was home, he called out several times. Receiving no answer, he cautiously entered the house, wiping the door handle he had used to enter.

Being certain not to touch anything, he made his way through the rooms. He found no sign that a woman lived there. There were three bedrooms, but only the master had clothes in the closet, all male. There were no cosmetics or women's toiletries in either of the bathrooms. The two-car garage was empty. As he was digesting this information, he heard a car pull into the driveway. Quickly, he moved to the entry hall, where a glass panel beside the front door allowed him to see the driveway and at the same time make a hasty retreat to the lanai. He saw a woman get out of a Mercedes sedan and start toward the house. It was the same woman who had been at the Makai Marketplace. He backed up into the hall bathroom, where he opened his backpack. He smiled. This was his lucky day.

Receiving no answer after ringing the ship's bell at the door, Tracy used her key to let herself in. She was hoping Mason was jogging on the beach, but was disappointed when she found that his car was not in the garage. Gazing out to sea, she saw rain clouds lying heavily on the water, obscuring the horizon. As she was deciding whether to wait for Mason to return, an arm suddenly grabbed her from the rear, pinning both her arms to her side. At the same time, a hand forced a cold, reeking wet cloth over her face. She gagged at the sickening smell and her stomach churned. Dropping her purse, she fought desperately to break loose, but a buzzing was already sounding in her head, and soon she found herself in the center of a whirlpool, being sucked down into blackness.

40

WHEN MASON ARRIVED at the Iverson home, he was disappointed that Tracy wasn't there. He had wanted very much to see her again. He left the bikini and the earrings with the day maid. When he pulled away, seeing the movie no longer appealed to him. The promise of seeing Tracy had been his real motivation for driving into town. He considered calling Hatcher, but realized he wouldn't be good company for anyone right now. The weather was worsening, and the thought of his fireplace glowing against a background of the stormy sea, a good bottle of zinfandel at his side, made up his mind. He turned the car around and headed home.

It was raining hard as Mason rounded the curve just before his house, and he paid no attention to the green van that passed him, going in the opposite direction. As soon as he entered the house he saw Tracy's purse and its spilled contents. He called out, but received no reply. Then he noticed the lanai door was open. Rushing out, he almost stumbled across an overturned end table, its lamp smashed on the hard floor. At the right side of the lanai, he saw that the *naupaka* bushes had been broken, obviously by someone pushing through them. Mason could see a clear trail disturbing the sand and the carpet of milo leaves, suggesting that something, or someone had been dragged through from the lanai. Realizing that the trail had to be very recent, or it would have been erased by the rain, he followed the path as fast as he could, until it ended at the highway a short distance past his house. There was no sign of it continuing on the other side of the road.

Racing back to the house, he dialed 911 and reported a kidnapping. Breathing heavily, his pulse pounding, Mason tried to think. He had to decide if it was wise to tell the police everything, and if not, how much to reveal. While waiting for them to arrive, he called the Iverson house. The maid informed him that Frederick Iverson was on a business trip to the West Coast, but she had no further information. He then called Iverson's office, but received a voice mail message stating that the office was closed, and that Iverson would return on the 23rd, two days away. It went on to say that if the call was a matter of importance that could not wait, his daughter Tracy would know where to contact him. Damn!

It took Mason only a minute after hanging up to go to his computer, where he typed a hurried message to Roberta King. Telling her what happened, he appealed to her to contact him immediately, adding,

You are the only person who can help me now. I need to talk to you. There may be something you can tell me in person that has been overlooked, if we can talk. I will agree to any safeguards you want, and go anywhere to meet you, but please contact me. A woman may die if you don't.

He ended by giving his address and phone number, telling her she could call collect. Then he called General Talbot.

"It's never a good idea to withhold information from the police," the general advised. "Yet, you may be putting Frederick

Iverson in difficulty if you tell them everything. If you only had a way to contact him. You say his office is closed?"

"According to Tracy, he only has one employee, Barbara something...a sort of Girl Friday. Tracy said it's not unusual for him to take her along on business trips."

"Unfortunate timing."

"Damn it, I can't believe he doesn't have a cell phone. How can he conduct business?"

"The older generation conducts business differently. Most of his customers probably don't have cell phones, and if you've noticed, I don't either."

Mason thought about what he would tell the police. "I'm going to tell them everything," he announced to Talbot. "The more I withhold, the less they have to go on to try to find Tracy." He began pacing the floor again. "Can you think of anything I can do," he asked, desperate for a role and chafing at his helplessness.

"Call me after you talk to the police. In the meantime, I'll see what I can do."

He had hardly hung up the phone when his ship's bell rang. He let in two men, one a uniformed policeman, the other in civilian clothes, who introduced himself as Detective Sergeant Albert Silva of the Honolulu Police Department. Mason explained that he was afraid that Tracy had been abducted, pointed to the purse on the floor, which he had not touched, and then led him to lanai, with its overturned table, and the trail through the woods, which had now washed out considerably in the sandy part, but was still clearly visible through the ironwood needles.

"So you think she was here waiting for you, and someone took her away by force. Any idea how he got in?"

"The lanai door was probably open. I don't always lock it."

Mason saw Silva grimace. "You live way out here on the beach and you don't lock your doors?"

"Only the lanai door, I lock the front." Mason realized how lame that sounded. "I've never had any trouble," he added.

"Until now," Silva said. He motioned to the uniformed officer, who moved toward the lanai and began dusting the door for fingerprints. Silva then took out a notebook, and indicated to Mason that they should sit down. "You got any idea who might want to do something like this?"

Mason started at the beginning, relating everything except the incident at the Makai Marketplace, and any events suggesting it. He was afraid Tracy had crossed the line of legality here, and felt that his own involvement was also questionable. He also left out any reference to Roberta King. Silva began taking notes, but soon after Mason started speaking, he put down his pen and, except for an occasional jotting, just listened. When Mason finished, Silva spent a few moments staring at him, before he spoke.

"You and your friends have been up to some pretty weird stuff," he said finally. "Didn't it occur to you that something like this could happen?"

"I guess we thought we could handle it." It was all Mason could think of to say.

"Uh huh. You know for a fact that the sister was a suicide?"

"I don't have any reason to doubt it."

Silva nodded. "It'll be a matter of record. I'll check on it. You say the father won't be back until the day after tomorrow?" Seeing Mason's nod, Silva continued, "I need to talk to..." he consulted his notebook..."Thatcher, Medeiros, and Haupt."

"Did I mention Haupt was confined to a wheelchair?"

"You mentioned you saw him sitting in one."

Mason got him the required information. "Now, if you could

print out those messages you talked about," Silva added, "I'll send someone around to pick them up. Anything else you think I need to know?"

"Nothing I can think of right now," Mason answered. Silva rose and walked toward the door. "Sergeant, excuse me if I sound out of line, but can you tell me...what you can do to find her. God knows what she might be going through right now."

Silva turned in the doorway. "We're going to give it top priority. Kidnapping is a federal offense, and we'll notify the FBI. They'll come in on it right away. If we'd known about the first sister's abduction, we might have some leads on this guy by now."

Mason could do nothing but nod in agreement.

As the police officers were driving away, the phone rang, and Mason seized it.

"This is Roberta King."

Mason breathed a sigh of thanks. "Ms. King, thank you very much for calling. Can we get together?"

"Yes, if you come where I tell you."

"Just tell me where, and I'll be there." She gave him the name of a small coffee shop in Pearl City. "I'm on my way," he said.

41

"I STILL DON'T know how he found me." Roberta King grasped her coffee cup with both hands. So far she had not raised it to her lips. The page boy cut of her black hair accentuated dark eyes set in an attractive, ivory-hued face. Despite her western name, Roberta King's Asian background was obvious.

"Were you on the Dark Chateau's membership list?" Mason asked.

"I was then, I'm not now."

"That's how he found you."

Roberta King reminded him that he agreed not to ask specific questions about what had happened to her during that night, if she told him her story. She had come with a squat, burly man she introduced as her brother, who sat at the table with her, glaring suspiciously at Mason. He was obviously along to provide protection as well as moral support. It was now just past 7 P.M., four hours since Mason had found Tracy missing.

"I was so naive," Roberta King began, "and so excited by the possibilities of the computer. I wanted to communicate with everyone, and wanted everyone to be able to communicate with me. I learned the hard way how stupid that was."

"Will you tell me what you can about that night?" Mason

asked gently. He could see her eyes beginning to glisten with the start of tears.

She wiped her eyes and then crushed the tissue, which she continued to hold as she spoke.

"It happened at the Aiea Heights Library, just as I was getting into my car. I had stayed too late, later than usual. It was after dark. He came up behind me and forced this awful smelling sponge or something over my face. It was so sudden, and the first breath I took made me so dizzy, that I'm afraid I didn't resist at all. I just sort of sagged over, and everything went black." Her hands began twisting the tissue as she recalled the scene. The brother's countenance darkened and his eyes narrowed.

"I don't think I was unconscious very long," she continued. "It was the motion that woke me. I could tell I was on the floor of a truck or van of some kind. My hands and feet were tied, there was a gag in my mouth, and I was blindfolded."

"Did he ever remove the blindfold while you were in the vehicle?" Mason asked.

"No, like I said in my email, he didn't take it off until after we were inside the cabin. He sat me down in a chair, tied me to it, and then took it off."

"And he had the stocking mask on at that time?"

She nodded. I never saw him without it."

"Can you remember anything about the inside of the cabin at all?"

"No. I was really much too frightened to pay attention to anything. I don't think there was much furniture. There was a couch, and a table, and the chair I was in, which was sort of in the center of the room."

"Is there any way you could tell where he had taken you, what part of town you were in?"

She shook her head. "As I wrote you, there were closed curtains on all the windows, and I was blindfolded coming in and going out."

Mason leaned forward. "Miss King, this is very important. Try to remember everything you can about the ride inside the van. Could you tell what the road was like, how many turns you made, how long it took, anything unusual about it?"

Roberta King thought for a moment. "Well, when I first became conscious of where I was, it seemed we were riding on a very smooth road, without any stops or turns, maybe like the freeway. Then we started going uphill, and around a lot of curves. I could tell because I kept sliding back and being pulled from side to side in the van. And I remember he stopped several times and got out. I could hear the van door open and close. It was only for a minute or so, then he got back in, and we started moving again."

"Can you think of any reason for those stops? How about opening a gate?"

She thought about that and then nodded. "Yes, that could be it. In fact, now I remember that I heard what sounded like a gate opening—and closing." Suddenly she became animated. "And there's something else. Every time he stopped, he stopped twice. He would get out, get back in the car and move just a short distance, and get out again."

"Like he was opening a gate and then closing it again behind him?"

"Yes."

"How many times did this happen."

"Two, at least, but it could have been three." She seemed frustrated by her inability to recall precisely. "I think two."

"How long would you say the whole trip took?"

"It's really hard to say. I was so scared, I wasn't thinking about anything like that. Maybe forty-five minutes, maybe an hour, it could even have been longer, because I don't how long I was unconscious. I just don't know."

"And coming back?"

It was a long moment before she answered, and she began rubbing her hands together as she spoke. "I can't remember much about that. I was really in shock. I thought he was taking me some place to kill me. I wasn't thinking clearly. But I do remember the downhill feeling and the turns, so I guess it was the same road." She paused briefly, before continuing. "If I had to say, I think it was about an hour from the cabin to where he let me go, but I just can't be sure."

She was obviously uncomfortable now, and her brother's scowl deepened. But Mason decided to try to push on.

"Where did he take you?"

"To Kahe Beach Park, where the electric power plant is. He led me out of the van, sat me down on a bench, and told me not to take the blindfold off for five minutes. Afterward, when I was sure he was gone, I called my brother from the pay phone, and he came and got me."

Mason could think of nothing more to ask, and that frustrated him. This would be his only chance to talk to this woman, and he had gotten very little information. Meanwhile, Tracy was missing and God knows what was happening to her. Perhaps the police would be more successful with their questions.

"Ms. King, would you be willing to tell this to the police?"

Roberta King started violently. "No! No!" Her voice became high-pitched. "I already told you I can't do that! They would ask too many questions. I can't go through that. I can't!"

"Okay, that's it!" The brother pushed his chair back and rose from the table. "No police, no more questions. And you, guy, you say nothin' to nobody about this, got it?" Accepting Mason's half shrug as agreement, he turned to his sister. "C'mon, sis, we're outta here." With a final angry glare at Mason, he led his sister out of the coffee shop.

42

MASON AND TALBOT poured over maps at the general's house in Waialae Iki. It was 10 P.M., eight hours after Tracy's abduction. Road maps and several sheets of USGS topo maps were spread out on the kitchen table.

"Roberta King said she remembers a straight, smooth ride, followed by a series of uphill curves," Talbot mused. "That means if she was picked up in Aiea Heights, she was still unconscious during the winding drive down to the freeway. He could have taken her either east or west on H1, and possibly north on H2."

"How about over the Pali?"

Talbot shook his head. "I think we can leave out the windward side. There are no roads going very far up into the hills for as long as she describes. Now, here are the places going east that might fit the description of her uphill ride." His finger pointed to places on one of the maps as he named them. "Pacific Heights Road, Tantalus and Round Top Drives, St. Louis Heights, and Wilhelmina Rise. All of them are too populated for anything like King experienced except the Tantalus-Round Top area. That could be a possibility. A lot of isolated homes up there, and plenty of space."

"How about the gate business, though."

Talbot scratched his chin. "I had forgotten that. There are no gates across either road, of course. He could have stopped to open one gate leaving the road, but two...?"

"She said there could have been three."

"Well, I think that lets Tantalus and Round Top out." The general studied the map again, his finger tracing westward this time. "Where did you say he released her?"

"Kahe Beach Park, on the leeward side. It's right in front of the Hawaiian Electric plant. It's the same place where Michelle was found."

"It fits." Talbot jammed his finger decisively at the map.

Mason bent over to look closely. "Makakilo? That's a housing development. It's just as crowded as the others we already eliminated."

"Not Makakilo—above it." Talbot traced the line of a road extending up into the hills from the north end of the development and winding up into the Waianae Mountains. "It's called Palehua. I was up there a few years ago with a Boy Scout troop that was staying in a camp run by one of the churches. There are some homes up there, mostly pretty rustic, on lots of acreage." He pointed once more to the north end of the housing development. "There is a gate across the road right here. You need a combination to get through. And there are other gates."

"How many?"

"I'm not sure. One more, at least, depending where you're going."

"And Kahe Beach Park is only about ten miles away." Mason brought his fist down on the table. "It's got to be the place."

"Unless our friend was being cagey and took her on a roundabout to throw her off."

"I don't think so. After all, she was unconscious and blindfolded driving in, and scared as hell driving out. No, I've got a feeling this is it." Suddenly Mason's euphoria collapsed. "But what can we do about it? We certainly can't go pounding on doors all over the place. Even the police can't do that."

Talbot reached for the telephone and pressed the speaker button. "Let's see what we can find out about Palehua. Ed Nishimura is the principal broker of Kahuna Realty. They specialize in farm land and large properties."

They heard the phone ringing, and then Ed Nishimura's voice sounded in the room. Talbot explained the situation quickly. "What can you tell us about Palehua that may help?" he then asked.

"Gee, Roger, that's going to be one tough place to find anyone. There's about two dozen properties, all spread out, some of them behind locked cattle gates. And the road up there is gated. Only residents have the combination."

"How many gates are there?" Talbot asked.

"Depends on where you're going. The first gate will get you to the lower properties and Camp Timberline. There's one more gate on the main road, but there are also some gates on private roads leading off the main one."

"Does your company have the combination to the gates on the main road?"

"Yeah, we got them, but they change every so often. I'd have to check to see that they are up to date."

"Would you happen to know which properties are secluded, or far away from neighbors?"

"That's the problem, they're just about all like that. Most of them, you can't see one place from another. The further up the mountain you go, the more isolated they are."

Talbot decided to take a different approach. "How can we find out who lives up there?"

Mason frowned. "What good will that do?" He kept his voice low enough so it would not carry to the speaker. The general held up his hand.

"I've got the tax map key in my data base," Nishimura said. "That will tell us who owns the property, but not necessarily who lives there. A lot of the stuff up there is on leasehold land, and the skinny is that the leases are not gonna be renewed. So a lot of the houses are just deteriorating. Owners have rented them out for whatever they can get. The ones higher up have no city water or sewage. They are on catchment, with cesspools. Not legal anymore."

"Can you make me a printout? I can come over and pick it up."

"No need, I'll just email it to you. Give me about half an hour to get it together and you'll have it. I'll send the gate combos too. Just make sure you destroy them when you're finished."

"I'm never going to be completely computer literate," Talbot said after hanging up. "I still think in hard copy."

"But what good is that going to do?" Mason said again. "We don't have a name."

"We'll have to wait for the list," Talbot said. "Maybe it will tell us something. I've contacted an acquaintance who is a friend of Frederick Iverson's. He told me he always stays at the St. Francis when he's in San Francisco. I got through to his room, but there was no answer. I left an urgent message for him to call me immediately. I doubt if he can shed any light on things, but he needs to know that his daughter is missing." Talbot glanced at his watch. It's past midnight on the West Coast. He should be returning to his room soon."

Mason began pacing the room, and then suddenly headed for the door. "I'm going up there."

Talbot raised his eyebrows. "In the middle of the night, with nothing at all to go on?"

"I can't just stay here and wait," he said. "It's driving me crazy thinking what may be happening to her. Maybe just nosing around I can find out something. You can get me on my cell if you get something useful from Nishimura or Iverson."

"Do you have the pistol?"

Mason nodded.

"Just don't do anything foolish," Talbot cautioned.

"I'm going to have to do something," Mason said. "Even if it's foolish."

Tracy had been bound to the chair for what seemed like hours. She had regained consciousness just as her abductor opened the back door of the van. As he dragged her toward the door, she vomited. She would have choked on it if he hadn't yanked the gag out of her mouth. The acrid, sour odor of stomach acid mixing with the sickly sweet smell of chloroform made her vomit again.

The man swore and reached for a rag, trying to clean up some of the mess. He then picked her up and carried her from the van. She was only dimly aware of him tying her to the chair, a stocking mask over his face. He went back out the door then, leaving her alone. From a time she heard sounds coming from the van, and assumed he was cleaning it. Then there was only silence.

She drifted in and out, until one time when she opened her eyes, she saw him looking at her, his eyes staring through two holes in the mask. Despite her fear, her mind focused on the fact that he had also been masked during Roberta King's abduction, but Michelle had been blindfolded. Her thoughts were interrupted by his voice, which surprised her by its calm, almost gentle tone.

"Who are you?"

She tried to think. Did he really not know? Or was he testing her, to see if she would lie to him? She remembered that she had her purse when he attacked her. She must have dropped it, and if he had it now, he had all her identification. But suppose he hadn't bothered about it?

"Do you know me from someplace?" he asked.

The uncertainty in his voice made her think that perhaps he really did not know who she was. What should she tell him?

"Why did you try to trap me?"

She still didn't know what to tell him.

"I have ways to make you talk—lots of ways. Would you like me to use them?"

She shook her head. "I didn't."

"You didn't what?"

"Try to trap you."

"Then who were those two men?"

She took a deep breath. "My brother and his friend. My brother found out I was going to meet you. He refused to let me do it unless they watched over the meeting to make sure everything was all right."

"They were friends? That's why one of them knocked the other one down? You're lying." He turned and walked to a counter at the far end of the room. He picked something up and came back to stand in front of her again. He showed her a small metal object resembling a vise, with a screw at one end.

"Do you know what this is?"

She said nothing.

"It's a thumb screw. An authentic one, from the Middle Ages. For such a small object it's capable of causing incredible pain."

He placed it on the arm of her chair and guided her thumb

into a metal track, then fastened a leather strap over the thumb, holding it in place. Her heart began to pound against her ribs. She didn't know what to say now. She stared, mesmerized, as he began to turn the screw.

43

MASON SHINED HIS flashlight past the rickety wooden gate, toward the house about 100 yards away. There were no lights. The driveway was overgrown, and the property weed-choked. The rusty lock on the gate looked like it hadn't been opened in months. He got back in his car without checking it further.

It was the sixth house he had checked, and the third that appeared deserted. When he had seen lights, cars, or other signs of life, he had surreptitiously approached the house, feeling like a thief, but concern for Tracy driving him on. Twice he had aroused dogs, once barely making it back over the gate before the animal reached him.

He was finding that very few names, and in some cases not even a street address, was posted at property entrances. At times, a dirt road leading off the pavement led to a distant dwelling, other times it would peter out into a track or a trail across pasture land. It was all frustratingly time consuming, and he seemed to be getting nowhere. He found himself fighting back a growing sense of desperation and panic.

44

SANDLER TURNED THE screw slowly and saw her wince as it made contact. He had replaced the gag in her mouth. He was sure that there was no one who could hear her scream, but he didn't want to hear it, either. There was no pleasure in this for him. He hoped she would not try to resist. He needed to know what was going on, that was his only concern. He knew she would tell him eventually. It would be foolish for her to suffer needlessly.

He heard her moan behind the gag. He stopped for an instant, to see if she was ready to speak. When he saw no sign, he started turning again. Her moans increased, and he could see her biting down on the gag. He stopped again, waiting. But her eyes were closed, not communicating with him. How stupid this was! Why did she choose to suffer? What was the point? She was bound to tell him. He turned the screw again and her whole body began to writhe against her bonds. Why was she resisting so stubbornly? Was something wrong here? He tightened the screw once more. This time her moans rose to a pitch that would have been screams except for the obstruction in her mouth.

"Are you ready to tell me?"

She nodded frantically, her chest heaving. He backed off the screw, and removed the gag. She gasped for air, tears streaming down her cheeks. He waited until her panting subsided and her tears stopped.

"Who are you?" he asked.

"My name is Tracy Iverson," she said, staring straight at him.

It took a moment to register. "Michelle? You're related to Michelle?"

"I'm her sister."

"Jesus Christ!"

45

IT WAS PAST four A.M. and Mason's desperation increased. He inched his way through a gap in a wooden gate and walked slowly toward the house. There was a light on the porch, and a car was parked in the driveway. A dog began to bark furiously and he stopped. Fortunately, it must have been tied up, as it did not approach him, but it would not stop barking. A light went on in the house, and Mason stepped behind a tree. The front door opened and he could see a figure silhouetted against the light.

The roar of a shotgun blast was followed instantly by the sound of pellets raking the tree. Mason fell to the ground and drew his pistol. But the door closed as quickly as it had opened, and the light went out. The dog stopped barking. Mason lay where he was, listening. He heard nothing more. Finally, he concluded that he had encountered a trigger-happy idiot rather than Tracy's abductor, and he returned to his car. As he reached it, his cell phone rang. It was Talbot.

"Listen carefully. The anonymous internet server in Finland has come through."

Mason felt his heart rate surge. "What—"

"There isn't time to go into it now. One of my classmates at the Command and General Staff College was a Finnish Army major.

He's a general now. He was able to apply the necessary pressure. Both the *The Painmaster* and *The Initiator* messages were sent by a Martin Sandler, who is listed in the printout Nishimura sent me as the owner of 84-165 Palehua Road."

As stunned as he was by this sudden information, Mason knew that Talbot was right. There was no time for further talk. His heart began pounding even harder.

"Martin Sandler," he repeated, writing down the name.

"I've notified the police and they're on the way. Where are you now?"

Mason read the number on the gate he had just exited. "I'm at 66-120. It's further up the mountain. I'm going up."

"Don't you want to wait for the police?"

"I can't. They're at least an hour away. God knows what could happen in that time."

"I understand. But Mason—be careful."

Mason was already in the car, phone tossed on the passenger seat, tires screeching.

46

TRACY HAD EXPECTED her abductor to be surprised by her identity, and she actually enjoyed his astonishment. For what seemed an eternity, he simply stared at her, his eyes wide circles in the mask. Then he rose and began pacing the room. Suddenly he turned toward her, his eyes blazing.

"What the hell are you doing here?" he shouted.

"You brought me here, you creep!" she screamed back at him. She felt anger and fear at the same time, the fear prompted by what appeared to be his suddenly irrational attitude.

That seemed to calm his somewhat. "I brought you here to find out what you want with me."

"You killed my sister." She spoke the words calmly, but with such certainty that he was temporarily silenced.

"She killed herself, he said finally."

"How do you know about that?"

"I can read. It was in the papers."

"She killed herself because of what you did to her. You're as responsible as if you murdered her."

He turned and walked slowly to the other side of the room. "I wouldn't be so sure of that," he said.

Her eyes narrowed. "What do you mean?"

"Who were those two men?" he asked, ignoring her question. She made no attempt to answer him. "We can go back to the thumb screw, if you prefer."

"One of the men works for my father—"

"Your father put you up to this?"

"My father knew nothing about it. It was my idea."

"And the other one?"

"The other is....a friend."

"And what were they planning to do?"

"The friend was not supposed to be there. He knew about our meeting, and came on his own, without my knowledge. He was trying to protect me. The other man had a gun. He was going to..." She was about to say "take you to my father," but that made no sense now, since her father had been unaware of her plan, and made her abandon it when he discovered it.

"He was going to do what?" She could not answer him, she was at a loss what to say. "You're lying," he said. "But it doesn't matter. I can fill in the rest. The problem now is what to do with you."

47

HIS TIRES CHURNED shoulder gravel as Mason tried to get a better view of the few houses along road. He was in the 80-series of house numbers, but he didn't know where. The last number he had seen was 81-257, but he had gone by several properties in a row which showed no numbers. The road climbed steeply now, there were more curves, and houses were farther apart. His frustration mounted as he passed two more with no numbers. Suddenly he passed a number, but too quickly to read it. Gears grinding, he backed up. His flashlight picked up the number—84-171. He had gone too far.

He spun the car around. He knew, that although house addresses ran consecutively, they did not necessarily use every number in the sequence. The next property could be the one he was looking for. As he approached the last gate he had passed, he slowed and turned off his lights. In the moonlight, he could see the silhouette of a house about 150 feet in from the fence. There was no number on the gate or anywhere on the fence. The gate was locked, but he climbed over it easily. As he approached the house, he could see no sign of occupancy, no lights, no car in the driveway, and, thankfully, no dogs.

Quietly, he peered in one of the windows. He could see

nothing. He walked to the end of the house, looked in another window, with the same result. As he turned to leave, he saw the moon reflecting from a metal surface at the back of the house. He realized it was a vehicle. When he reached it, he found it was a windowless van. The van fit. He turned the flashlight toward the back of the property, and saw a second, smaller house, more like a cabin. It sat about 100 feet behind the main one. He could see that curtains were drawn over its windows, but a rim of light showed at the bottom.

48

"HAVE YOU HEARD of the Marquis de Sade?"

Sandler had moved Tracy from the chair in the center of the room to a couch along one wall. Her hands remained untied since the use of the thumbscrew, but her feet were still bound. Sandler sat on the same couch, turned in her direction. Except for her bonds, it could have been a normal conversational setting.

"Of course," she answered. "He was that creep who liked to torture women."

Sandler smiled. "Simplistic and inaccurate. He was a writer and a philosopher, a great one."

"He was nothing but an insane sexual pervert."

He smiled again, but not quite as broadly. He could tell by the tone of her voice that she was feeling more confident now, more willing to talk to him. But her education left much to be desired. He rose and walked over to a shelf along one wall, returning with a small book. "Listen to this," he said, as he opened it and read.

"What is an atheist? He is a man who destroys myths which are harmful to his species, in order to lead men back to nature, experience, and reason. He is a thinker who, having contemplated matter and its energy, its properties and behavior, does not need to invent fictitious powers, imaginary deities, and the like, in order to explain the phenomena of the universe and the operations of nature."

He closed the book. "Does that sound like the work of a madman?"

"How about *The Philosophy of the Boudoir?* she shot back. "Tell me that collection of scatological filth isn't the work of a depraved lunatic."

There was no smile this time. Her view was biased and inaccurate, and it angered him. Nevertheless, her acquaintance with de Sade's works was surprising. He would try another approach.

"What do you know about the connection between pleasure and pain?"

"That there is none."

"Oh, but there is. Many people acknowledge it."

"Sick people."

"Like your sister?"

"...Like my sister." He saw her harden at the mention of her sister. She looked at him, her stare icy.

"No matter what you think, there are many women who appreciate the aphrodisiac qualities of pain, who yearn for it."

"Why don't you associate with them, then, instead of torturing others who want nothing to do with you."

The injustice of her assertion brought an anger to match her own. He sprang to his feet. "You stupid fool! What do you think I'm trying to do? Did I seek out your sister? She was the one who sought *me*, pretending to be something she wasn't. What right did she have to do that? What right did *you* have?"

She didn't answer him, her eyes staring sullenly at the floor. He allowed himself time to calm down. "Why did your sister post her message? Why did she respond to me?"

She seemed to be groping for an answer. "I really don't know. She didn't confide in me."

"Was your sister a masochist?" He saw her wince at the word.

"I…she may have been. But that doesn't justify what you did to her."

He sat down beside her again. "I was trying to put her in contact with her inner feelings, get her to acknowledge them."

"And did you succeed?"

"No. It became too painful, for both of us."

"I bet."

She was beginning to exasperate him. "Look, I admit I took her beyond where she wanted to go, but that is necessary in some cases. There's a threshold of pain that needs to be crossed before true feelings are liberated and enlightenment is reached. But I'm not evil. I never intended your sister's death. When I saw it wasn't working, I released her."

"Released her so damaged physically and mentally that she killed herself."

"That's a lie! Something else must have made her do that." He saw the surprise cross her features.

"What are you talking about? How could there possibly be anything else?"

He would not continue the conversation in this direction. "Your sister is responsible for her own death. She never should have contacted me. I don't want unwilling partners. I don't need them." His voice became suddenly soft, almost hushed. "I want… someone like—"

"You killed her and you're too cowardly to accept responsibility for it." In her anger, Tracy failed to pick up on the change in his manner. "I don't believe anyone would willingly submit to the things you want to do."

He smiled tolerantly. "You're wrong," he said, speaking as though from a dream. "I had such a woman once. She was wonderful. She would let me do anything, absolutely anything."

"What happened to her?"

He frowned, as he pondered her question and tried to remember. It had been so long ago. "She…she went away."

"I don't believe she ever existed. She's just a figment of your imagination."

"No, you're wrong." He closed his eyes and an image of *her* appeared. It had been *her* idea, something new, something different. At first he was reluctant. It was dangerous. But it was also exciting, and so he finally agreed. Somewhere he had lost control, and before he realized there was blood everywhere—too much blood—*her* blood. He pressed his hands against his eyes, trying to block out the scene. Tracy watched him warily.

Abruptly, he opened his eyes and cocked his ear toward the door. A few seconds later, he rose and walked to the table against the wall and picked up a large knife. Tracy's eyes widened. "What are you going to do?"

He returned to the couch, and stood behind it, the knife poised at her throat.

"Don't make a sound," he said. "It appears that we are about to have company."

49

AS MASON EASED around the van, he drew his pistol, and his flashlight bumped the car, the metallic clank shattering the stillness. He froze, waiting for some reaction. When there was none, he continued to approach the house. There were no cracks in the curtains to see through. He listened at the door, but heard nothing. Then he saw a faded number on the door, indicating this had probably been the original house on the property, and that the other had been built in front of it later. He finally made out the number, "84-165." He was in the right place. He leaned back, and with all the force he could muster, he kicked the door, handle high. The door crashed open.

He blinked rapidly, his eyes unaccustomed to the sudden light. At first, all he saw was Tracy, sitting on the couch, staring at him.

"Drop the gun." He saw the knife at her throat now, and the figure crouched behind the couch.

"Drop it," the voice repeated. The knife moved, just enough to send a gleam of light reflecting off the blade. Mason dropped the pistol.

"Now kick it over here, and lie down flat on the floor."

"The police are on their way here right now," Mason said.

"Thank you for the warning." The voice sounded surprisingly calm, but even through the mask, Sandler seemed to be weighing the information. "Now do as I said, and get down on the floor."

As Mason sank slowly to his knees, Tracy suddenly grabbed Sandler's arm with both hands, jerked it away from her neck, and threw herself off the couch in Mason's direction. Her hobbled ankles tripped her and she fell to the floor, but the couch was now a barrier between her and Sandler. Mason lunged forward, but Sandler reacted instantly, racing out a door to his rear.

Mason bent over Tracy.

"I'm all right," she shouted. "Get him!"

As Mason rushed from the house, the van crashed through the closed gate, its tires spewing gravel. Mason ran to his car, reaching it just as the van started down the hill. He was following it in a matter of seconds, trailing it by several hundred yards. Suddenly the van swerved, and made a screeching U-turn, bouncing off the road and the shoulder, churning dirt as it plowed up the soft earth of the pasture. Back on the pavement, it careened wildly, then headed directly for Mason.

Mason jerked the steering wheel frantically to the right and his car went off the road, sideswiping a wooden fence before he was able to get it turned around. As he did so, he saw what had caused Sandler to reverse direction—a line of flashing blue lights, snaking up the hill. For an anxious moment Mason was afraid that Sandler was heading back for Tracy, but the van sped past the house and continued up the mountain.

Dawn was beginning to break as Mason tried to picture what lie ahead. He had never been up here, but from Talbot's maps he knew the road ended at an abandoned military site, and that a trail ran from there along the summit ridge of the Waianae Mountains. But where it went, and how far, he had no idea.

His short wheel base SUV was gaining on the van, the sharp, narrow turns slowing the larger vehicle down as the road narrowed to little more than one lane. A concrete building loomed ahead, and the road ended. The van braked and Sandler jumped out and ran around the right end of the building. Mason skidded to a stop, and as he flung open the door, he realized that in his haste to pursue Sandler, he had forgotten his pistol back at the cabin. Racing after him, Mason could only hope Sandler had done the same with the knife.

Rounding the corner of the building, Mason could just make out Sandler disappearing into the trees. He passed a sign reading

"PALEHUA TRAIL - CAUTION: DANGEROUS DROPOFFS"

He kept going. He caught occasional glimpses of Sandler, now about a hundred yards ahead. The trees were spaced too far apart for an ambush, so Mason continued running, even when he lost sight of Sandler. Soon the trees gave way to a narrow, open ridge, suddenly revealing the leeward coast and the ocean far below. The trail ahead contoured the ridge, just below the Waianae summit. Sandler was visible now, making his way along the trail. In the distance, on a promontory, Mason saw an abandoned World War II coast artillery bunker. Sandler was heading toward it. There was no other choice, the ridge dropped off precipitously on one side of the trail, and was too steep to scale on the other. Mason followed.

The trail disappeared temporarily around a large rock, barring any further view. The narrow path hugged the rock, leaving little room to walk and none for a misstep. Cautiously, Mason began making his way around.

The first thing he saw was the knife, appearing out of nowhere, lunging for his midsection. Reacting instinctively, as he had been taught in countless close-combat drills, Mason jammed both arms downward, grabbing the wrist holding the knife with both hands, his arms stiff at the elbows. The knife stopped only an inch from his gut. The follow-through was to take a step to the side, turn his back on the assailant, and, with both hands still firmly grasping the man's wrist, twist the knife-arm over his shoulder, breaking the arm. There was no possibility of that here. The rock rose like a wall directly off the left side of the trail, and a step to the right would launch him in space.

A sudden blow to the head jarred Mason's senses, followed by another. Unlike Mason, Sandler still had one arm free, and he was using it. Mason did the only thing he could. Still holding the knife at bay, he kicked at Sandler's shin. Because of his stance, it was a weak kick, but the pain caused Sandler to temporarily shift his balance. In that instant, Mason jerked Sandler's knife arm down and to the right, smashing his hand into the rock face. The knife fell from Sandler's grasp, and as he struggled to maintain his footing, Mason kicked the knife, which dropped off the trail. With part of his brain, Mason traced its long, clattering fall. Both men were now only inches from the edge of the cliff. Mason released his hold on Sandler's arm, preparing to back away and regain his footing. Before he could do so, Sandler pushed him hard. Mason struggled to regain his balance, but with a sickening wrench in his stomach, he felt himself going over the edge.

The first part of the cliff was angled at about sixty degrees, so that he slid, rather than fell. Frantically grabbing at tufts of grass and small shrubs—none of which held—he felt himself slipping faster toward the final brink, a sheer drop of almost 2,000 feet. His feet bumped over something which then jabbed him painfully in the groin as his body passed over it. A stunted ohia tree scratched his face as he slid by, and he made a desperate grab for it. It held.

Looking down, he could see that his feet were already over the edge of the precipice.

For a long moment he could do nothing but hold on, his face pressed to the earth, gasping for breath. When he looked up, he saw Sandler staring down, a rock about the size of a baseball in his hand. Mason flinched, hunching his shoulder to protect his head. The rock struck his ear, giving his skull a glancing blow. The pain was intense and points of light danced in front of his eyes, but he retained his grip. When he looked up again, Sandler was standing on the edge of the trail, evidently contemplating coming after him. Apparently, there were no more rocks. Sandler took a tentative step, and a stream of loose pebbles began sliding under his foot, almost causing him to slip. He pulled back, stared a bit longer, and then started running along the trail toward the bunker.

Slowly and painfully, Mason began a tortuous crawl back up the crumbling slope. Grasping the clumps of grass and small, stunted bushes, he made his way, every inch of his body pressed tightly against the steep, unstable surface. Twice he slipped and began a terrifying slide backward, but he was able to stop himself. Finally, he hauled his body over the edge and back on the narrow path, where he lay for several moments, shaking and panting hard. Finally, he rose and rounded the large rock, where once more the trail came into view. He saw Sandler reach the bunker, now about two hundred yards away.

Still breathing hard, Mason paused, pondering his next step. He considered waiting for the police. But the police did not really know where they were. There was no assurance they would drive to the end of the road looking for them. He decided to go forward. At least Sandler no longer had the knife, placing them on equal terms.

After rounding the rock, the trail rose to the summit of the ridge, where it made its way along a narrow edge, with drop-offs on both sides. His knees still shaking, Mason slowly made his way to the concrete bunker. Upon first inspection it appeared to be fairly small, with a single gun port pointing out to sea. A rusted steel door, hung by one remaining hinge, gaped open at an angle, revealing an interior room littered with empty beer cans, rotting vegetation, and assorted trash. As he entered the bunker, the smell of damp concrete assailed his nostrils. A circular mount in the center of the room revealed where a coastal artillery gun had once pointed toward the ocean, protecting the island from an invasion that had never come. There was no sign of Sandler.

Mason noticed an opening in the floor, where a metal ladder led to a lower level. Descending cautiously, he found himself in another room, which must have been the magazine, which had stored the shells for the artillery piece above. The only light came from small slits in the concrete walls, near the ceiling. He found still another trap door, with another ladder leading downward. This time he could see down two levels. As he was about to descend he heard a sound from below. Waiting, he saw Sandler come into view at the lowest level, and start up the ladder.

When he was halfway up the first ladder, Sandler looked up and saw Mason. For a moment their eyes locked, and then Sandler started back down. Mason went after him. When he reached the first level, Mason stopped, listening for any sound below, then slowly started down the ladder. He heard a sudden scream from below, followed by what sounded like a heavy object falling outside the bunker. Wary of a trick, he did not respond, but continued his careful descent.

Reaching the bottom level, he found another gun port. Satisfied that the room was empty, he went to the port and looked out. Pebbles and dirt were still sliding down a sheer drop to the valley far below, but he could see nothing else. Three steel rungs bolted to the outside wall of the bunker led down to a few jagged pieces of concrete, which at one time may have been a platform. The remnants of a steel cable, swaying slowly in the wind, indicated that the bunker had once been supplied by a small cable car. There was nothing there now but yawning space.

Mason looked around the room. There were no more hatches or trap doors, and no other way out except back up the ladder. Sandler must have found himself trapped, and tried to come back out—until he saw Mason. Had he tried to climb down the outside rungs, hoping there was something below, and then fallen to his death? Or had he jumped? Mason looked out of the gun port once more. There was no way to reach either side of the ridge by descending the three rungs. Far below, the cliff wall ended in a series of deep gulches. There was no doubt about it, he realized. Nothing could survive that fall.

50

BACK AT SANDLER'S house, several police cars lined the road. Police appeared to be searching the main house, and Mason found Tracy in the cabin. She had just completed telling Detective Sergeant Silva what had happened. Silva turned to Mason, and he related what had occurred on the trail. The detective radioed for a police helicopter, asking Mason to accompany him to point out the spot where Sandler had fallen. He then produced Mason's pistol.

"This is registered, right?"

Mason nodded.

"How about a permit to carry?"

"I don't have one."

"I'll have to hold it then," Silva said. "You'll have to answer for that later." He then left them, going over to the main house until the helicopter arrived.

Mason went to Tracy, hugged her, and then held her at arm's length.

"That was one hell of a chance you took, grabbing that knife from your throat like that."

"Not really. I remembered how much he hated the sight of blood. He mentioned it in two messages, and there was a scene here, which I don't completely understand, but which reinforced it." She related Sandler's strange behavior near the end of the confrontation. "I just figured he wouldn't want to get my blood all over him."

"And if you were wrong?"

She smiled at him. "I wasn't."

When the helicopter arrived, Mason and Silva boarded, and in less than a minute they arrived over the bunker. Mason pointed, and the chopper began a slow descent of the cliff wall. As it dropped below the bunker, Mason could clearly pick out the three ladder rungs, the remains of the ruined platform, and the steel cable hanging in space, undisturbed by the chopper's turbulence. At the base of the cliff were two distinct gulches, each one steep-sided, vegetation-choked, and impossible to see into. The helicopter hovered briefly over each of them. Silva turned to Mason, speaking through the intercom.

"Which one do you think he landed in?"

Mason shrugged. "From the bunker, it looked like he could have gone into either of them."

Silva signaled the pilot and the helicopter climbed up and away from the cliff and returned to Sandler's property. Tracy stood outside, watching the chopper come in. After dropping Mason and Silva, it took off again.

"We'll start searching right away," Silva said, "but I don't know how far we can get into those gulches." The police had finished in the main house, and Silva headed for his car. "You two plan to stick around town for a while. I'll need to talk to you again."

They both nodded, and Silva drove off. Mason turned to Tracy.

"Ready to get out of here?"

She nodded. "More than ready."

When they reached his car, Mason spent several minutes prying the front fender away from the right front wheel, and then began the long descent. Tracy leaned back against the head rest and closed her eyes.

"God, I'm glad that's over."

As he was ready to drive off, Mason's cell phone rang. It was Talbot, informing him that he had finally contacted Frederick Iverson, who was on his way back to Honolulu. Mason clicked off with a brief acknowledgement, and relayed the information to Tracy. Now that the excitement was over, Mason should have been at ease. But he wasn't. Something was wrong. For the first time in their long relationship, General Talbot had lied to him.

51

AN ALL-DAY search by the police and fire departments failed to find Sandler's body. Helicopters were of no use, so teams with dogs were sent in to fight their way through the thickly overgrown gulches.

"We're not gonna beat the bushes looking for him anymore," Silva told Mason on the phone at the end of the day. "His body is probably up there somewhere, but there are places up there even the dogs can't get to. When he starts to stink, maybe some hunter will find it. Either that, or the pigs will get it."

That night, Frederick Iverson invited Mason to his home to discuss contributing additional funds to the Kathryn and Merrie Grant Foundation. He wanted to establish several scholarships in memory of Michelle Iverson. The size of the bequests surprised Mason. He had assumed Iverson was well off, but was unprepared for the five million dollar donation. He was equally unprepared for the change in the man himself. No longer the imperious financial manager, exuding confidence, he appeared battered and subdued, presenting anything but the demeanor necessary to his profession. His eyes were vacant, and he seemed to have trouble focusing them. Mason could see that Tracy was also aware of the change in her father, and was visibly distressed. After a meal at

236

which no one ate very much, Iverson excused himself, saying he had an after-dinner appointment at a client's house. Mason and Tracy moved to the deck with coffee.

Since that day at Palehua, Tracy had also been a different person. The nervous intensity and the hardness that had characterized almost all her actions had dissipated, allowing a relaxed charm to shine through. Mason now found her more attractive than ever. For the first time, he saw Tracy as a truly beautiful woman. But his thoughts of her were disturbed by other considerations.

"I would sure feel better about things if they found Sandler's body," he told Tracy, as he gazed at the view overlooking the lights of Honolulu.

"But you said yourself no one could survive that fall," she reminded him.

"I know."

"But something about it still bothers you."

He smiled. "There you go, reading my mind again."

"It's not a difficult feat, Mason."

He didn't mention the other thing bothering him, General Talbot's lie. So far he had not confronted his old friend, preferring to try to reason the matter out himself. His effort so far succeeded only in taking him in a direction he didn't want to go.

"I just have this feeling that something's not right." He stood up and walked to the deck railing, staring down into the darkness at the gulch below. The trades were blowing, and the swaying trees returned his mind's eye to the bunker where Sandler had fallen. He saw again the steel cable, swaying slowly in the wind. Suddenly it came to him.

"Damn!" He turned back to Tracy. "I've got to call Silva right away." He started toward the telephone.

"I don't think so," a male voice announced quietly. Mason turned and saw Sandler standing in the doorway to the deck, a pistol in his hand. "Go over there and sit back down with your girl friend," he ordered. Mason did as he was told. Sandler stepped out onto the deck, keeping the pistol trained on them both.

"So you're not surprised," he said, smiling at Mason. "How did you figure it out?"

"The cable," Mason said. "It was moving when I looked out the gun port. I assumed it was the wind. But it didn't move when the chopper generated an even stronger wind. It was moving when I saw it because you had just released it after climbing onto the part of the broken platform that extended under the bunker. That didn't look possible, but you live up there, you had checked it out. I suppose that when I left, you climbed back out, and waited in the bunker until things quieted down. You dropped a rock, or maybe a piece of the platform, to make me think you had fallen."

"Very good. If you had realized that at the time, things might have worked out differently."

Mason stared at him. "I'm very much aware of that."

"What do you want here?" Tracy asked. Mason noticed that the hardness had returned to her voice.

Sandler smiled again. "Release," he said. "Release from your persecution of me." He stepped further into the room and addressed Tracy. "Where is your father?"

"On the mainland, on a business trip," she replied without hesitation. If Sandler had been watching the house for a length of time he would catch the lie, but he seemed to accept it.

"You two have just about destroyed my life here," he said. "I should kill you both for that, but as I told you before, I am not a murderer. However, if you don't do exactly as I say, I will take the greatest pleasure in changing that, I promise you. Fortunately, I have assets to keep me going for a short time. But to start over somewhere, I need more, a lot more. And your father is a rich man."

"My father will give you nothing," Tracy flared.

"Oh, but he will. You see, that's the only way he'll get you back. I have a nice little place even more isolated than the previous one. And to induce your father to do business quickly, you and I will play some very interesting games while we wait. Who knows, you may even come to enjoy them."

"You're bleeding," Mason said.

For a moment Sandler did not seem to understand. Then he looked down at his left hand, where a thin line of blood ran over his fingers. A drop dripped every few seconds from his middle finger. As he looked at it, Mason saw Sandler go pale.

"It was that damned window," Sandler said, barely above a whisper. "It seems I'm not very adept at break-ins." His hand shook as he reached for a napkin from the coffee table. "You two get down flat on the floor, with your hands behind your heads." When they had done so, Sandler sat down in an arm chair about fifteen feet away.

"Now I am going to put the gun down on the arm of the chair while I bandage my hand. It would be very foolish of you to think you could do anything before I could pick it up again." Biting his lip, he then began to wind the napkin tightly around his hand.

Lying on the floor, Mason's face was in contact with the edge of a light, shag throw-rug. Raising his head slightly, he could see the other end of the rug, about ten feet away, just short of the chair Sandler was using. He could see Sandler watching them. He had positioned his injured hand so that even while he wrapped it they were in his line of vision. Mason observed that Sandler's complexion was ashen.

Using his right hand and his teeth, Sandler tied a knot in the napkin, his hand trembling visibly. He retrieved the pistol and stood up. One foot stood on the throw rug.

"All right, you can get up now. One at a time, ladies first." Tracy rose and he motioned her to return to the couch. As he did so, his other foot moved closer to the rug, but still not on it. "Now you," he said to Mason, taking a step toward him. The step placed his second foot on the rug.

Mason raised himself to his knees, his arms on the floor in the pushup position, both hands at the edge of the rug. He glanced at Sandler. Even from this distance he could see the sweat gleaming on his forehead. Although still pointing the gun at him, Sandler seemed distracted, and he was breathing heavily.

As Mason stood up, he grasped the rug and jerked with all his power. Sandler toppled backward, falling awkwardly into the chair. Mason was on top of him in an instant, shoving his right elbow into Sandler's throat and slamming his gun arm across the arm of the chair. The pistol clattered to the floor. Within seconds Tracy had it in her hands, pointed at Sandler. Mason stepped back.

Sandler gazed at them both impassively, shrugged, and sat back in the chair, placing his injured hand in his lap.

"So now you call the police, I presume," he said. "Go ahead. We both have interesting stories to tell. But I think they will be more interested in mine. The younger sister begging for my services, the older sister insane with jealousy because I was showing preference to the younger. The boy friend, trying to kill me for alienation of affection. I wonder who they'll believe?"

He was surprised that his words drew no response from Tracy. He had expected an explosion, or at least an indignant denial.

"Then there are those bulletin board messages," he continued.

"They tend to favor the defense, don't you think?" Still no reaction, just the pistol leveled straight at his chest. He was wondering what to say next, when she finally spoke.

"You don't get it, do you?"

Sandler stared at her with a questioning frown.

"There aren't going to be any police."

"Tracy—"

"Stay out of this, Mason," she snapped. "This would be a good time for you to leave."

Mason remained where he was.

Tracy turned her attention back to Sandler. "Do you really think we'd be stupid enough to let you go to trial?"

For a moment, Sandler seemed unsure of the situation. He looked from Tracy to Mason, and then back to Tracy. Then he spoke.

"Do you really expect me to believe that you're going to shoot me in cold blood?"

"You can count on it."

"And how would you explain that to the police?"

"You let me worry about that."

"Tracy, for God's sake—"

"I told you to keep out of this, Mason." Tracy's voice had risen several octaves, and now betrayed a hint of panic, which reflected in her eyes. Mason saw that Sandler had detected it. His eyes turned toward Mason, and their message was clear. There would be no shooting. He then turned and smiled at Tracy.

"I'm tired of playing games, and I'm afraid I need treatment for this hand. If you won't call the police, I will. Let's see how your father will like the whole story being made public" He rose from the chair and started toward the phone.

The sharp crack of the pistol in the closed room battered

Mason's eardrums. The bullet caught Sandler squarely in the middle of the chest, propelling him backward as his legs collapsed beneath him. The final expression in his eyes, before they closed forever, was of shocked disbelief.

Mason turned to Tracy, who was staring at Sandler's body. It was only then that he realized she had not fired the weapon in her hand.

Frederick Iverson stood in the doorway, slowly lowering a pistol to his side.

"I…I couldn't let you be the one," he said, his voice barely above a whisper. "All of this was my fault. I couldn't let you take it on your conscience."

Mason knelt down and checked Sandler's pulse. His shirt front was covered in blood, but the bleeding was a heavy leak, rather than a flow. Mason looked at Iverson as he rose. "No need for an ambulance, but you'd better call the police." His gaze shifted to Tracy. "Unless you have other plans."

She shook her head wordlessly, dropping Sandler's pistol to the floor. Her father walked to her side and embraced her as she leaned into him. Mason could see she was crying. Iverson seemed even worse off, his composure and confidence, already shaken by his daughter's death, were now completely shattered.

"Mr. Grant, don't you think you should leave?" Iverson's voice was little more than a whisper. "There is no need for you to be involved in this."

"I'm afraid I *am* involved. If I left now, it might come out later that I was here. That would create a big problem."

"How could it come out?"

"Trust me, those things have a way of happening."

Iverson did not argue further. "Would *you* call the police then? I am not up to it, I'm afraid."

For a long moment, Mason just stood and stared at them. Then, slowly, he picked up Sandler's pistol and wiped it clean of Tracy's fingerprints. He stepped over to the body and pressed the pistol into Sandler's lifeless hand, bending the index finger through the trigger guard and against the trigger. He placed the pistol on an end table on the other side of the room. He turned to the Iverson's, who had been watching him wide-eyed. He and his daughter both appeared close to a state of shock.

"Okay," Mason said, "now here's how we'll handle it."

52

DETECTIVE SERGEANT SILVA surveyed the scene briefly.

"Okay, what happened?"

Mason spoke before Iverson or Tracy had a chance. "He broke in here as Miss Iverson and I were talking. He apparently wanted to kill us both. Mr. Iverson returned from an appointment, saw him pointing the gun at us and shot him."

Silva took that in without comment. He turned to Iverson and Tracy. "That about how it happened?"

They both nodded, as if in a daze.

Mason lowered his voice. "They're both pretty shook up, sergeant."

Silva turned his attention to Sandler's body again, and then back to Mason. "You mind stepping over here a minute?" He guided Mason to the other side of the room, out of earshot of the Iversons. "You expect me to believe that the old man just happened to have a pistol with him when he came home? What does he do, carry one around on his hip? There's blood on that chair and on your shoe. How'd it get there?"

It took Mason only a brief moment to decide to answer the second question and ignore the first. "He cut his hand breaking into the house. When he first came out here, he sat there to wrap it up. He was bleeding at the time."

"Uh huh."

"And then he got up and started coming toward us, pointing the gun."

"Uh huh."

"That's when Mr. Iverson shot him. I guess…well, maybe he saw what was happening and had time to get the pistol from his office or somewhere—"

Silva held up his hand. "Please."

"Anyway," Mason continued, trying not to appear flustered, "as soon as he fell, I ran over to get the gun away from him, in case…in case he could still use it. I guess I stepped in the blood. I put the gun over there on the table. You'll probably find my fingerprints on it, too."

"Uh huh. I tell you what. I want all three of you to give me a written statement right now. I want you to separate yourselves in different parts of the lanai, and I'm going to put a patrolman with you to see that you don't talk to each other or collaborate in any way until after the statements are handed over to him."

Mason's heart sank. It was a clever technique. It would be a miracle if the three statements told the same story in every detail, and Silva would pounce on the inconsistencies.

The crime scene personnel began entering the room and Silva spoke again. "And don't anyone leave town without clearing it with me. No business trips," he said, turning to Frederick Iverson. He then looked directly at Mason. "There's a lot more here than meets the eye."

53

THE FROST ON the martini glasses had melted, sending small rivulets of water down their sides.

"It shows we're not drinking them fast enough," Talbot said, as he rose and headed back to the drink trolley near the sliding doors. His lanai faced the ocean, and on clear days, such as this one, the islands of Molokai and Lanai were clearly visible.

"I don't think the police are accepting the self-defense version of Sandler's death," Mason said. "I've had a call from Sergeant Silva. He wants me to come in. I'm sure he's doing the same thing with Tracy and her father. I'm going to have to talk to Frederick Iverson."

Talbot turned, and walked toward the table, carrying the shaker of newly mixed drinks. "But that's not why you're here."

It was a moment before Mason spoke. "It was the Finnish connection," Mason said.

"I thought it would be."

"Finnish officers were not invited to attend the Command and General Staff College when I attended, and they couldn't have been when you did, either. Finland was too close to the Soviet Union, both geographically and politically."

The general poured the fresh drinks, filling the glasses to the rim. "I didn't like deceiving you, but given the situation at the time, you had more than enough on your mind. It was a piece of information you didn't need to process just then."

Mason raised his glass and stared across the top of it, directly into the eyes of his old friend. "There was only one other way you could have gotten that information about Sandler."

For a long moment the two men stared at each other. It was Talbot who spoke first.

"And now?"

"And now," Mason replied, still meeting his gaze, "the chickens have come home to roost."

54

AFTER LEAVING TALBOT, Mason drove slowly down the curving road which led from the general's house to Kalanianaole Highway. Exiting the guarded entrance to the community, instead of turning immediately onto the highway, he crossed over to Kawaikui Beach Park, and pulled into the small lot. He sat silently with his thoughts as the sky darkened over Maunalua Bay. Finally, he dialed the Iverson residence on his cell phone. Tracy answered on the first ring. He asked her if her father was home, and said he wanted to stop by and speak to him, if he was not busy.

"Just a minute, Mason," she said, "I'll get him." Rather than Iverson, it was Tracy who came back on the line. "It's fine, he'll be home all evening. You can come by any time."

It was still a few moments before he put the car in gear and drove out of the park. Tracy met him at the door, and it hurt him to see her evident pleasure at his visit.

"I'd like to see your father alone," he informed her, "if that's okay."

"Sure. He's in the study." She asked for no explanation, and he was grateful for that.

Frederick Iverson was behind his desk when Mason entered the study. He rose, and offered Mason a drink, which he refused.

Iverson had improved since Mason had seen him last. Some of his confidence had returned, and he seemed to have come to terms with what had happened. He motioned Mason to a chair, and sat down across from him, waiting for him to speak.

"Detective Silva has asked me to come to see him at the police station . I assume you've gotten the same message?"

Iverson nodded. "He wants me to 'drop by' on Tuesday. I suppose you are here to discuss the matter." He paused a moment before continuing. "How do you suggest we handle it?"

"We could start by telling the truth. It usually comes out anyway."

"The truth? That I shot him because I was afraid my daughter was about to do so?"

"That's not why you shot him. But let's go back earlier and start with Michelle's death."

Iverson leaned back in his chair and took a deep breath but said nothing, waiting for Mason to continue.

"To use Detective Silva's expression, Michelle's death involves a lot more than meets the eye," Mason said.

"Are you suggesting that Michelle's death was not a suicide, brought on by her ordeal?"

"Oh, I think she killed herself, and that her experience had a lot to do with it. But that's not what drove her over the edge." Iverson made no attempt to interrupt, and Mason continued. "You remember that Michelle told Tracy that she felt there was someone else present beside Sandler?"

"Michelle told us she was blindfolded. At best, it could only be a suspicion. She couldn't see anything."

"She couldn't see, but she could hear. If there was someone else in the room, he could have made a movement that she heard. But, perhaps even more important in this case, she could *smell*.

Maybe she noticed just a hint of a scent that seemed familiar to her. Tracy mentioned that when she entered your bathroom looking for Michelle, she found a bottle of after shave, apparently broken by Michelle as she reached for the razor. But suppose Michelle had not come there looking for the razor? Suppose she was trying to confirm or deny something she had detected in that room, and she found it in the after shave? And it was only then that she reached for the razor, when the thought that her own father could be part of this obscene thing that had been done to her became too much to bear."

He could see Iverson go pale. "How dare you! How DARE you!"

"There are other indications. Your refusal to go to the police, and hiring me instead. I should have seen it for what it was. I was an amateur, someone who could be depended upon to stumble around without getting anywhere."

"Which is exactly what you have done. You have come to an erroneous conclusion based on fallacious assumptions."

"You were even willing to pay off Kevin Medieros to keep him from complicating things."

Iverson gave Mason an icy stare. "I think you had better leave."

"And it would have all been covered over if it hadn't been for Tracy. Her decision to continue to pursue Sandler after Michelle's death without letting you know almost caused a disaster. I can imagine how Sandler reacted to that. He must have wondered if you were involved. When you ordered Tracy to stop the search, you thought that would end the matter. But you didn't know that Sandler had seen her and followed her to my house. When Sandler abducted Tracy, you had no choice. You didn't want to lose her, too. It was you who told General Talbot how to find her."

The frost slowly dissolved from Iverson's eyes as he continued to stare at Mason. "Did Talbot tell you that?"

"No. He didn't have to. There was no other way he could have gotten that information, and you were the only person he talked to after I left him that night. That's how I know you and Sandler were working together. General Talbot told me a phony story about breaking through the anonymous server in Finland, but it was just a temporary cover. I guess he was allowing you time to work things out in your own way."

"Yes, I'm sure he was." Iverson rose and walked slowly to a cabinet beside his desk. His shoulders sagged and his whole body seemed diminished. His hands shook as he poured himself a drink. Mason would have gladly accepted one now, but none was offered. Instead of returning to the chair, Iverson sat back down behind his desk. Although he kept his eyes on Mason, his gaze had a faraway look.

"How *did* you and Sandler get together?" Mason asked.

Iverson shook his head. "Does it matter?"

"Was it the Dark Chateau web site?"

Iverson sighed and nodded. "I had been watching it for some time, posted a few things, but nothing really transpired. I met Sandler in the chat room. We found that we had the same... interests. Privately, he let me know that he had abducted someone once, but that it had not gone well. When I saw Michelle's message posted on the site, it brought back...well, you know the rest. I knew Tracy would be concerned about Michelle's disappearance. It had to look like I was trying to find her. That is where you came in."

"It was all over for you once you told General Talbot how to find Tracy, but you shot Sandler anyway," Mason continued, "to keep him quiet."

"I shot him so that Tracy would not. You know that, so does she."

"Tracy would not have shot him. She was wavering all over the place. I saw it, Sandler saw it, and from where you were standing, you must have seen it also. Sandler was the only person who could implicate you in Michelle's abduction, other than General Talbot. And he was letting you work it out your own way. With Sandler gone, you thought you could do just that. Except that I knew also, and you didn't know that."

"No, I did not know that." Iverson reached in his desk draw. When he withdrew his hand, it contained a pistol, and he pointed it directly at Mason. "But now that I do…"

Mason was totally unprepared for the situation. The police had taken the pistol that had killed Sandler, and Mason had not even considered that Iverson might have a second one. But, more than that, from Iverson's standpoint killing Mason made no sense.

"You can't be serious," Mason said. "You might think you can get away with killing Sandler. There's no way you can get away with killing me."

"You misunderstand my purpose, Mr. Grant. I have no intention of getting away with it. My only concern is that this sordid story goes no further."

"And you think that if you kill me, General Talbot will remain silent?"

"Under the circumstances, I think he will. A despondent father, grieving over the death of his daughter, a young man attempting to prevent him from taking his own life, they struggle, the pistol goes off, the young man is killed needlessly, because he does not change the outcome."

Mason realized then that Iverson had intended to take his own life ever since his conversation with Talbot. That is what "working it out in his own way" meant. He had been putting his affairs in order. Mason cursed himself. He should have seen it. Now it was too late. Iverson would never allow the story of the abduction to become known to Tracy, or anyone else. Life held nothing for him now, and in death, at least his reputation would be protected.

Slowly, but firmly, Iverson pulled back on the slide of the pistol, and then let it snap forward, sending a round into the chamber and cocking the hammer. Mason swallowed hard.

"Dad!"

Iverson looked up, and Mason turned. Tracy stood in the doorway, an expression of horror in her eyes. "My God, Dad, don't do it! Please!"

Mason turned back to Iverson just in time to see an image of pure agony distort his features. The he rose from his desk, standing unsteadily, one hand supporting himself on the desktop, the other still pointing the pistol at Mason.

"Please stay where you are, both of you. Do not follow me."

As Iverson left the study, an icy chill that previous situation failed to create now ran down Mason's spine. He knew what was about to happen, yet he sat paralyzed, until he heard the sound of the single shot.

55

"SUICIDE SEEMS TO run in this family." Detective Sergeant Silva had completed his preliminary examination of Frederick Iverson's death scene, and forensic specialists were now combing it more carefully. "If it was suicide," he added, staring pointedly at Mason.

"I can vouch for that, sergeant."

"Like you vouched for Sandler's shooting being a case of self-defense?"

Mason decided his best course of action was to ignore the remark. The subject would come up later in the week anyway, and he was considering legal representation. "He had a reason to kill himself."

Silva sat down and removed a small notebook and pen from his shirt pocket. "I'm listening."

Mason told him everything he knew about Iverson's involvement with Michelle's abduction. When he finished, Silva looked up from his notebook, his features expressionless.

"That all?"

"You don't seem surprised."

"I'm never surprised."

"Even that a father would do such a thing to his daughter?"

Silva snorted. "Don't you read the papers? Fathers are doing that kind of crap to their daughters all the time—beating them, sexually abusing them, raping them, forcing them into prostitution—and that's before we even get to mutilation and murder. Work with me for a while, it'll turn your stomach. Besides, it was his stepdaughter. That makes a difference."

"So you suspected him right from the beginning?"

"I suspect everybody right from the beginning. I would have suspected my mother, except she's visiting my son on the West Coast. But Iverson was a likely candidate."

"May I ask why?"

"For one thing, he hired you."

"You mean instead of someone competent?"

Silva smiled. "Let's say instead of someone professional. And his wanting to keep the police out of it was a red flag. No good father would put his business before his daughter in a situation like that, no matter how much damage it would cause."

Mason, already acutely aware of his gullibility in allowing Iverson to maneuver him as easily as he had, remained silent.

"I'm going to have to talk to Tracy Iverson," Silva announced. "You said she's in her bedroom?"

"Sergeant, she's just witnessed that mess in there. It's the second time in a couple of weeks that she's seen the violent death of a member of her family. Besides, her doctor gave her a heavy sedative, and she's probably asleep by now."

Without further argument, Silva agreed to postpone his interview with Tracy. There was only one more point of business that Mason could think of.

"What day do you want me to come down to the station?"

The forensic team had finished its work and coroner

personnel were coming out of the bedroom bearing Frederick Iverson's body. Silva looked from Mason to the stretcher.

"I'll be in touch," he said. He folded his notebook and headed toward the home's entrance, Mason accompanying him.

"By the way," Silva said, turning to Mason as he reached the door, "we're through with the dead girl's computer and stuff. Considering the situation here, do *you* want to pick it up?"

"Uh, sure, I'll come by." Michelle's computer occupied a low rung on Mason's scale of priorities just now. He would pick it up when he went for his interview with Silva.

"We didn't need the password you gave us," Silva added. "The program wasn't password protected. Our boys got right in."

Mason frowned. "Are you sure? Tracy tried for several days and couldn't open the files until she figured out the password."

Silva shrugged. "Like I said, when we tried, we got right in, no password required."

Mason's confusion increased. "Well...I guess that once Tracy discovered it, she must have figured there was no need for a password any longer. It was just in the way, so she removed it."

"Not that one."

"Why not?"

"It wouldn't have worked."

56

IT WAS A perfect day, warm and sunny, the trades blowing briskly across the harbor. Mason met Tracy at Gordon Biersch, in the Aloha Tower Market Place. As they sat down at one of the outdoor tables, a large cruise ship began to slowly leave the dock, two tugboats fussily pushing it from its berth. Mason ordered two tall glasses of *mairzen,* brewed on the premises. Although Frederick Iverson's funeral had been only two days ago, Tracy seemed relaxed and composed. Once more, Mason was struck by how beautiful she was.

After a few pleasantries, Tracy mentioned she thought that Detective Sergeant Silva appeared to be dropping further inquiry into the case. "I guess it's not worth it," she said. "With my father dead, it would be pointless to pursue it."

"He could have chosen to pursue us—me, for false statements about a homicide," Mason said. "He's not stupid. He knows."

"It would be hard to prove though, wouldn't it?"

Mason shrugged. He was not interested in this conversation. He needed to discuss something else, and he was having trouble deciding where to begin.

Tracy came to his aid, flashing him a radiant smile.

"What's on your mind, Mason?"

He smiled. "You're good at reading my mind, why don't you tell me?"

She shook her head. "I'm not good at it today. But I can tell that something's bothering you. What is it?"

"Sleeping Beauty."

"Sleeping Beauty?" She appeared perplexed. "You mean the books Michelle had?"

He shook his head. "The password."

He saw her forehead crinkle in a puzzled frown. "What about it?"

"It didn't work."

"It didn't work? I don't know what you mean."

"I believe you."

"Mason, this isn't making much sense."

"I believe you don't know what I'm talking about."

"Well, will you please enlighten me, then?"

He gazed at his beer. Beads of moisture had formed on the outside of the glass, almost obscuring the bubbles rising to the top on the inside. He did not reach for it. "The police didn't need a password to access Michelle's email program. It wasn't password protected."

He was watching her closely, but saw nothing in her eyes but relief as her smile returned. "Is that all that's bothering you? They didn't need the password because I deleted it. There was no need for it any more. It would only have slowed us down."

It was the obvious answer and the one he had prayed she would not give. An ache began in his chest which sank swiftly to his stomach. Although he tried to remain impassive, Tracy could see his distress.

"Mason, what is it? What's wrong?"

He glanced at his beer again, but knew he could not touch it now. The cruise ship was sailing into the main part of the harbor under its own power now, the tugs in escort.

"When I got Michelle's computer back from the police," he began finally, "I tried to program sleepingbeauty as the password. It was rejected, and I got a message stating that a password could be any combination of letters and numbers, containing between six and twelve characters. Sleepingbeauty has fourteen. You didn't know about the restriction because you had no reason to try to enter a password into Michelle's program. Her program was not password protected, but you pretended it was. You lied to me, Tracy. Why?"

Mason could see the anxiety that clouded her features. She reached across the table and laid her hand on top of his. "Oh, Mason, Mason, can't you see why I did it?"

He wanted to see. He wanted desperately to believe anything she told him now.

"I wanted to work with you so badly," she continued. "I wanted so much to help find Michelle...I needed time to convince you. I couldn't let you have access to her program until you agreed to let me do that. It was the only lever I had." She placed her other hand across the table now, on top of the first one, and looked directly into his eyes. "I'm sorry I deceived you, Mason, but please don't let a simple thing like this come between us."

Mason met her gaze. She had never seemed more beautiful. What did he see in those captivating emerald green eyes? Concern? Sincerity? Or something else? He wanted to believe her, take her in his arms and dispel the nightmare that was threatening to engulf them both. Accept what she is saying, a voice inside him shouted. End this! Tell her you believe her.

"I can't buy that," he said instead. "I could have believed you if you had told me this as soon as I mentioned that the police had not found a password. There was no need to lie at that point, but you did. You said that you had erased the password. Why did you lie, Tracy?"

"Mason..." Her eyes never left his, and he could see the appeal in them as she struggled to find words. "Mason, please don't let a stupid misunderstanding like this come between us."

God, what if he *was* wrong? What if she had a perfectly logical explanation for her action? Despite his uncertainty, something pushed him forward.

"It wasn't that you *wanted* to work with me, it was that you *had* to. You had to be with me every step of the way, to insure that everything went according to plan."

"Plan? What plan? Mason, You're making no sense at all." He could see a trace of anger replacing the concern in her eyes.

"You had to keep me busy," he persisted. "You had to keep me going up blind alleys to allow your father to enjoy Michelle's suffering."

"Mason, do you know what you're saying?"

He took a deep breath. "You were in it with him, weren't you?"

As his statement sunk in, Tracy withdrew her hands from his and slowly sank back in her chair. She seemed truly shocked, as if having difficulty believing what she had heard. Even though he continued to watch Tracy, Mason suddenly became acutely aware of everything around him. He saw the bubbles slowing down in his beer, the heat waves shimmering off the pier, and the cruise ship leaving the harbor and turning toward the seaward side of Sand Island. It was a long moment before Tracy spoke.

"No, Mason, I was *not* in it with him."

Her words were so forceful, so positive, and her gaze so direct, that he knew she was telling the truth. A cold chill crept down his spine as he realized the enormity of his error. An icy stare replaced the concern in her eyes. "You have no idea how far from the truth you are."

Panic seized him, as his mind struggled frantically for some way to make amends. Try as he might, he could only think of one thing to say.

"What is the truth, then?" His words came out as little more than a hoarse whisper.

"Do you really want to know?" She seemed to be studying him, deciding something in her mind.

"Tracy, I *have* to know."

The change that came over her began with her eyes, which seemed to turn dull. Her expression lost all anxiety, and assumed a neutral, flat quality. He sensed a withdrawal, a separation that was more than physical. She had made her decision. When she spoke, it was almost as if a stranger were talking, a voice he had never heard before.

"You were right, Mason, everything *did* have to go according to plan, and it did. Perfectly."

"But you just said—"

"I said that I was not acting together with my father, and I wasn't." It was apparent that she was waiting for him to prompt her to continue.

"Will you tell me about it?"

Again, she seemed to consider his request. "Why?" she asked finally.

"Just because I'd like to know, maybe to understand."

"Fine," she agreed, apparently once more coming to a decision, "where would you me like to start?"

"How about with when you first found Michelle's posting."

"Michelle didn't post that message. I did."

"You...?"

She seemed to enjoy his surprise. "Michelle couldn't have found her way to the *darkchateau* site if her life depended on it. The Sleeping Beauty books weren't hers, either. They were mine. Michelle didn't have an S & M bone in her body."

Mason tried to sort out what he was hearing. "If you posted that message, then you would have also read the replies and posted the answers."

"Of course."

"But how could you do all that using Michelle's computer, without her knowing about it?"

"It wasn't her computer. It was mine." Again, she smiled at his surprise. "Michelle was totally computer illiterate. The only reason she bought one was because everyone else had one. But she couldn't type, so she gave up on learning word processing. She just hunt-and-pecked her email. She knew absolutely nothing about getting onto the Internet and had no interest in it. For a while she played computer games, but she soon got bored with that. So her computer just sat in her room gathering dust. When mine gave up, she suggested I take hers."

"So you did all that stuff on the *darkchateau* site, pretending to be Michelle?" Mason was having difficulty absorbing what he heard. "But why, Tracy, why?"

"I saw a chance to see that both of them got what they deserved."

"Both of them?"

"Michelle and my father." She sighed and turned to stare out across the harbor. "It's a long story, Mason. Are you sure you want to hear it?"

Mason had an eerie feeling that he was not here at all, that he was having a nightmare that would have to play itself out before he could wake up and he and Tracy could go on with their lives. She was waiting for his answer. He had no choice. He would play his part. He shrugged his shoulders. "I have nothing else to do today."

For the third time during their meeting, Tracy seemed to deliberate with herself before continuing.

"I was always jealous of Michelle. I was my father's natural daughter, but it was Michelle that he always favored. I hated her because my father showed her so much more attention than he did me, and I began to hate him for the same reason."

She paused and glanced at her beer, now warm and going flat. "I don't want that. Mason, will you order me something else, something cold?"

He had to clear his throat before he could answer her. "What would you like?"

"How about your favorite drink?"

Her attempt at humor brought a wave of sadness that caused a tightness in his throat. He motioned to the waitress, who removed the untouched beers and brought two margaritas. They took the first sips in silence.

"I knew very early that my father was a closet sadist," Tracy began anew. "Before I even started school, I sometimes found magazines beside his bed. He probably thought I was too young to notice them. They were pulp magazines, the kind that have been out of circulation for years, even back then. They all had lurid covers. Women being whipped, stretched on racks, or strapped to wheels that rotated over a blazing fire, all kinds of stuff like that. Although, at that age I couldn't fully understand what was going on, those scenes aroused me, and made me light-headed. My mother used to read to me at bedtime, and I knew even in my child's brain that the written characters on the pages in my father's magazines would tell me more about the covers I was looking at. That probably gave me an incentive to learn to read at an early age."

She gave him a slight smile, which he found himself unable to return.

"Anyway, I knew what was going on when he watched Michelle being spanked, and it almost made me sick with jealousy and frustration. After a while, he began instigating things himself. He would come home from work and ask my stepmother if Michelle had been a good girl, or whether she had done anything to deserve a spanking. My stepmother must have been the same way, because, they made a game of it. Poor Michelle, I should have felt sorry for her, but it only made me hate her more. If my father had any awareness at all, he would have seen that he was doing it to the wrong daughter. But he ignored me. It was always Michelle that he wanted."

"Did it ever occur to you that the reason he didn't choose you was that you *were* his natural daughter, and he didn't have those kinds of feelings toward you?"

"It eventually did, when I was much older. But by then it was too late. I already hated them both. Besides, that didn't seem to stop my stepmother from whipping *her* natural daughter. Anyway, it all stopped when my stepmother died. It was time anyway. By then Michelle was getting too old to be spanked.

"One night, about a year ago, my father was working on his computer when he got a phone call that caused him a lot of agitation. He left the house quickly, telling me there was a serious financial problem that had come up with one of his clients, and he had to meet with him immediately. Later, as I passed his study, I noticed light coming from his computer screen, and realized that he had left so quickly he had forgotten to turn off his computer.

I thought I would do it for him. I glanced at the screen, to make sure I wouldn't turn off the computer in the middle of work that he hadn't saved, and saw that he was logged on to the *darkchateau* site and had just started a response to a posting from someone who called himself *The Painmaster*. It began by saying that he, also, was looking for a woman who would satisfy his sadistic fantasies, but it stopped in mid-sentence. The phone call obviously interrupted him. I thought it was pitiful, but that was before I knew just how many people there were like that out there. I left his computer just as I found it, and went back to my own room and logged on to *darkchateau*.

"So you knew about *The Painmaster* all along. But why didn't we find that posting when we were searching?"

"We didn't go back that far, Mason. I made sure of that. Anyway, it was while I was getting acquainted with *darkchateau* that I began to toy with an idea. What if I posted provocative messages on *darkchateau* supposedly from Michelle? Postings that my father was bound to see. At first, the plan was just to tantalize him, to see what he would do. By then I knew that he was in contact with *The Painmaster*. I was reading his email."

"You turned on his computer? Didn't you worry about him finding you in front of it?"

"My father was a man of established habits. He went to work and returned at regular times. You could set your watch by it. Besides, I didn't do it every day, I didn't have to. I'd just look at his "Messages Sent" and "Messages Deleted" boxes and get both sides of the conversation. Everything was there. He only emptied them about once a month. And I know what your next question is going to be. No, his programs were not password protected, except for his business related stuff. It never occurred to him that either Michelle or I would violate his privacy, any more than he would violate ours.

"To make a long story short, my father took the bait. He began to speculate with Sandler about somehow responding to Michelle, but, of course, it would have to be through Sandler. When I saw how their plan finally evolved, I was thrilled. It was more than I could have hoped for."

"You hated her that much?" Mason was having a difficult time equating the woman sitting in front of him with the Tracy he had come to know.

"I hated them both that much. I knew that my father would have to come up with a scheme covering his reaction to Michelle's disappearance, but I knew he couldn't go to the police. Calling you in was perfect."

"So it was for nothing, the things we did together. The postings, the searches, the trip to Redmond..."

"I had to keep you busy, Mason, while daddy was busy with Michelle. I didn't want to interrupt his fun."

After absorbing one shock after another from Tracy's narrative, Mason had reached a point where he was able to listen to Tracy with a certain amount of detachment. His senses had been battered so much by her revelations that they had grown numb. He found that he was able to speak calmly, in a conversational tone.

"Why didn't you just keep the 'password' lost? That would have kept me in the dark about everything."

"Because I had no idea what you would do, or what you might find out. You were a loose cannon, Mason. I had to control your actions, and that was the best way to do it."

"But then after Michelle returned, and especially after she killed herself, why did you keep it going? Why didn't you just end it?"

"Because the plan was only half completed. There was still my father." She seemed to enjoy his obvious distress. "I didn't expect my plan to have quite the outcome it did. I certainly didn't anticipate Michelle's suicide, or even want it. I didn't want my father's death either. What I *did* want was to sow suspicion between him and Sandler, which I thought would have a good chance of bringing everything out in the open, ruining him."

"He ruined himself," Mason said quietly, "and he did it to save you. When he told General Talbot how to find you, he knew there was only one conclusion Talbot could draw. But he did it anyway."

She gave a short, unpleasant laugh. "And am I supposed to be grateful? He should have thought a little about me years ago, but he didn't. He was too infatuated with Michelle."

"I think you're wrong. If he didn't care about you, he wouldn't have done what he did."

She sighed and sank back in her chair. For the first time he detected a sign of sadness in her expression, but it vanished quickly. "Whatever he might have felt for me, it was too late. Anyway, everything worked out."

"It might not have, though. After Sandler abducted you, suppose I hadn't found you when I did?"

"That was certainly unexpected," she admitted. "At first I didn't know how to deal with it. I couldn't let him know that I knew what had been going on. I had to play the frightened, kidnapped daughter. Poor Sandler, on an eternal quest seeking the perfect object of his desire, not realizing he had finally found one. But I *am* grateful that you found me when you did, Mason. But if you didn't, he would have let me go eventually, like he did with Michelle. And, in the meantime, it might have been fun." She grinned at him, again enjoying his discomfort. "But it worked out better with your intervention. It forced my father to play his hand."

"And how about when Sandler came for you the second time, when he wanted money from your father? Do you think that would have been fun too?"

"My father would have paid him the money, and he would have released me." She stopped for a moment, her expression thoughtful. "I could tell that, from the day of Michelle's suicide, my father was thinking about ending his life. The way he was going around, arranging his affairs, the money he gave you for Michelle's memorial fund. He made up his mind when he had to reveal himself to Talbot."

"To save you."

"Yes."

"What I don't understand is why your father didn't end everything after Michelle's death. He must have realized the risk of us continuing to look for Sandler."

"Oh, I'm sure he wanted to, but he had no choice except to go on with his act, especially with Michelle's death to be avenged. And with me pushing him the way I was, it would have looked suspicious to stop the search, when there was now more reason than ever to continue it."

She paused to take a sip from her drink, and Mason marveled at her composure. The entire story had been told with no more emotion than if she had been relating her day's normal activities.

"Tell me something," he said finally, "when you picked up Sandler's gun, and he started for the phone, would you have shot him if your father hadn't arrived?"

"I had a bad moment there," she admitted. "I knew I had to act the part I'd been playing, but I certainly couldn't shoot him. I didn't want to go to prison. How was I to know that you would come to the rescue again, arranging everything to look like self-defense? I owe you a lot, Mason." She reached over and once more placed her hand on his. Her touch felt cold. Mason slowly pulled his hand away. Behind her, the cruise ship disappeared behind Sand Island.

"So it was all a charade," Mason said, more to himself than to Tracy. "A play worthy of Shakespeare and an actress worthy of an academy award. You earned an Oscar hands down—the bit with John Bridges, pretending you suspected Hatcher, the scene at the Makai Market. What would you have done with Sandler if you and Dudley had caught him?"

"I would have turned him over to my father and stayed for the show. Can you imagine the predicament that would have put him in?"

Mason sighed and reached for his margarita. He felt emotionally drained, exhausted, dead. He was a boat that had slipped its mooring, drifting without power or direction. He saw Tracy staring at him over her glass.

"This doesn't have to be goodbye, Mason."

He shut his eyes momentarily, as if closing them would make his words easier to say. "I'm afraid it does."

"Look at me, Mason. You love me, don't you?"

He opened his eyes. "I did."

"You still do and you know it. Why can't this be a new beginning for us? Forget about everything that's happened. It's over. It has nothing to do with us."

Mason wanted to speak but his throat was too dry. Tracy leaned forward.

"There will be a whole new dimension to our lovemaking," she promised. "You'll find it fantastically exciting and incredibly erotic. We'll walk the shadow world together, Mason, you and I."

Her voice was like a siren song, luring him toward an abyss. The frightening thing was, that deep within, a part of him was listening. But he shook his head.

"Would you like to whip me, Mason? Would you like to see me writhing and moaning at your feet, welts rising everywhere on my body? Would you like to hear me begging you for mercy, knowing that you had the power to stop or continue, to do anything you wanted with me?"

He struggled to speak, but his throat and mouth were so dry no sound would come. He could only shake his head again.

"No?" She rose slowly from the table. "I don't believe you." She picked up her purse, and pulled its strap over her shoulder. "If I call you some day and ask you to come to me, will you refuse? Will you really turn me down, Mason?"

Her smile, seductive and confident, almost overwhelmed him, but now he knew the evil that lay behind it. He finally found his voice.

"You can count on it," he said.

PREVIEW

THE DARK SIDE OF GLORY

By

RICHARD MCMAHON

271

PROLOGUE

Setagaya-ku, Tokyo, Japan, February 9th, 1953.

THE BODY LAY NAKED on its side in the middle of the room, the knees drawn slightly toward the chest. She was young and still very beautiful, even in death. Her arms, tied together at the wrists, were extended above her head. Her legs were also tied together at the ankles. A white silk scarf was tied across her mouth, apparently to act as a gag. Her long black hair spilled over her shoulders and onto the tatami-mat floor. There was a head wound to the rear of her left ear, apparently caused either by a blunt instrument or a fall. Other than that, she was unmarked in any way.

Inspector Shimizu gazed impassively at the body as the medical examiner crouched over the nude form. Whatever he was thinking, nothing could be construed from his expression.

"She has been dead for some time," said the examiner. "At least 12 hours. I cannot be more precise until I have examined the body more fully."

Shimizu turned his attention to the woman's clothing, folded neatly on top of a tiny bureau standing against the wall. There was no sign that it had been removed hastily or roughly. He picked up the top garment, a pink blouse. His body stiffened as he saw the cloth object that lay beneath it.

"We must leave here at once," he said.

The medical examiner stopped what he was doing and turned to stare at him, incomprehension in his eyes.

"We must leave," Shimizu repeated. "We have no authority here."

CHAPTER 1

THE FUNERAL
SIXTEEN YEARS LATER

*National Memorial Cemetery of the Pacific, Honolulu, Hawaii,
June 6, 1969.*

I SOMETIMES THINK that had I known what lay ahead, I would not have agreed to write the life story of General Philip Sheridan Coursen. But, then, when I'm being honest with myself, I admit I probably would have done so in spite of everything. Somewhere deep inside most of us lies a taste for mystery and violence. "Sex and violence," my writing professor used to say, "is the secret of a commercially successful novel." And through the lifeless eyes of General Coursen I was destined to encounter plenty of both.

AWARDED THE 2014 GOLD MEDAL FOR HISTORICAL
FICTION BY THE MILITARY WRITERS SOCIETY OF
AMERICA

In this mystery/suspense novel set during the Korean War, Matthew Clark, the biographer of a respected and highly decorated Army general, learns that there is a hidden side to his life, involving a brutal, covered-up murder, a secret mistress, and an abandoned illegitimate daughter. As he delves deeper, Matthew discovers an intriguing mystery and a tragic love, in a world of surprises where nothing is at it seems.

Tracing the general's earlier career during the occupation of Japan and through the early days of the Korean War, Matthew follows the lives of four principle characters: Philip Coursen, who appears to be the perfect Army officer, but with a disturbing dark side, Miriam Coursen, equally perfect Army wife, who may hide a secret agenda, Calvin Carter, an idealistic young West Pointer, beset with guilt as a result of his clandestine affair with another officer's wife, and Samantha Winstead, the beautiful, vivacious cause of Calvin Carter's discomfort. The biography takes a personal turn for Matthew, as he finds himself drawn into the story when he falls in love with the young woman who claims to be Coursen's daughter.

PRAISE FOR *THE DARK SIDE OF GLORY*

The Dark Side of Glory by Richard McMahon ranks right beside David Baldacci's bestselling novels when it comes to plot twists and turns and jaw-dropping surprises. Just when you think you've figured out what happens next, McMahon throws a ten-pound sledgehammer through your preconceptions. It's an edge-of-your-seat thriller by a top-flight talent. Truly, The Dark Side of Glory is a stunning triumph!

> **—Dwight Jon Zimmerman, award-winning military historian and #1 New York Times bestselling author. President, Military Writers Society of America.**

In this page-turning suspense novel, Richard McMahon expertly switches between two settings and time periods, the earlier being the Korean War, and the current a who-done-it mystery. McMahon's novel is ranked up there with some of the most renowned mystery writers of our time. You will stay up late reading it all the way to the very end, when the final secret is revealed.

> **—Michael Christy, Editor, *Dispatches,* official member publication, Together We Served.**

Fans of "M.A.S.H." (and who isn't?) will enjoy this tale of sexual and military intrigue during the Korean War. Winner of a gold medal for historical fiction by the Military Writers Society of America, the narrative jumps about in time from a young woman's murder in 1950s Tokyo to a burial in Punchbowl in 1969. The Honolulu author's suspenseful plot is nicely carried by sparse, clean prose.

> **—Honolulu Star-Advertiser.**

AMAZON FIVE-STAR REVIEW EXCERPTS

It has been a long time since I have been totally immersed in a book. This was just such a book. I could not put it down. The romance, the intrigue, all were page turners.—**Mary Lou Lee.**

This is a great book. Do not start reading with a hot cup of coffee, because next time you take a sip it will be cold. It is extremely well written and will hold your attention from front page to last. It has a surprise ending, one you will not expect.—**Jay Feldman.**

I loved this book! The twists and turns keep you guessing as you experience this wonderful love story filled with military action, mystery and intrigue.—**caligirl.**

Richard McMahon's The Dark Side of Glory is a classic, probably the best insight into the pre-Korean War US Army, and the war itself, ever written. The book is, at the same time a subtle and multifaceted mystery that captivates and seduces the reader until the last page.—**William F.**

McMahon deftly captures all audiences by producing a manuscript worthy of a factual military history, while sating a romantic's appetite, and tipping the scale toward a true mystery who-done-it. It kept me up past my bedtime, and entertained me throughout my day until the last sentence was read—**Ms. Ann Thrope.**

Great book, I could not put it down, and what an ending!—**Helga G. Minderjahn.**

It was a pleasure to read & I hated to see it end. It had the true ring of authenticity and it gave me an insight into Army life I didn't have.—**Jim Haas.**

I don't often write reviews, but this book deserves one. It's terrific; one of those that you are sorry to see end. The plot is more than engaging and the characters eminently believable. Additionally, it's realistic. I served in the military for 30+ years and the author captures the culture entirely. I also served several times in Japan and again he does that justice. I probably read at least a book a week and likely more. So far this is the best novel I've read in a year—**Neil, San Diego.**

You cannot put this book down, as you want to know what's happening next, and you are still surprised at the end. Highly recommended!—**Nadia LeBon.**

Richard McMahon does a fantastic job writing truly believable and mesmerizing fiction. I sat in a chair, in my jammies, from morning to night reading till the surprising end. This book is that kind of read. You won't be able to put it down and you will continue to think about it for a long time after you do.—**Amazon Customer.**

This book is a fun and interesting story. It has all the elements of a great read: mystery, romance, betrayal, action and more. Overall a great story written by a great story teller.—**lilseal18**

First I don't normally read "war stories" unless I'm researching my father's time as a POW in WWII. That being said I'm really glad that I read this one. I quickly became invested in the characters, I mourned when a character was lost to the brutalities of war and cheered when they survived. The book has it all love, hate, revenge and everything in between. The intrigues will surprise you and keep you reading til the end. Out of the ashes of the broken lives of the characters rises a rebirth called love. This book could easily be turned into a mini-series reminiscent of "Winds of War"—**trekker**

Excellent writing. I enjoyed the story line and especially the fact that I did not guess the outcome.—**Sandy Speed**

This work has an unusual and interesting plot. It was an "I can't lay this down until I find out what happens next" type of work. Very good writing style—**bigbaddoc**

AVAILABLE NOW IN EBOOK AND PRINT EDITIONS
FROM AMAZON, BARNES & NOBLE, AND
OTHER BOOK SELLERS..

CPSIA information can be obtained at www.ICGtesting.com
Printed in the USA
LVOW07s2009101215

466280LV00009B/1065/P

9 780996 156875